WITH TOOTH AND NAIL

Thrilling action and suspense

The Max Donovan Adventures #2

RIALL NOLAN

THE BOOK FOLKS

Published by The Book Folks

London, 2023

© Riall Nolan

ISBN 978-1-80462-102-8

www.thebookfolks.com

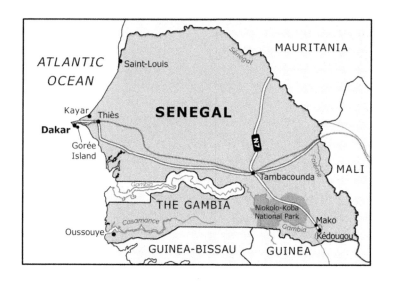

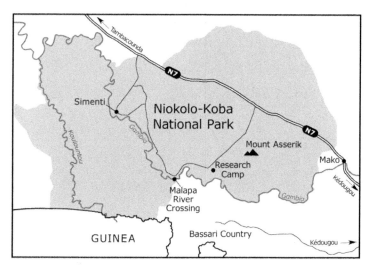

This is for all the boys and girls of the Société,
wherever they may be.

PROLOGUE

At the edge of my vision, I saw something move. I glanced up and saw a bright green snake coiled around one of the rafters. As I sat frozen to the spot, it dropped on the table between us.

There was a crash, and plates flew in all directions. I looked down to see Lindy's bushknife deeply embedded in the tabletop, and on either side of the broad blade, half a snake. I hadn't even had time to let go of my beer.

"Cripes," I said after a moment.

"Practice makes perfect," she said, pulling the blade out of the wood. "The snakes come in looking for frogs. The frogs come in to get the mosquitoes. The mosquitoes come in to get us. So this is just completing the cycle."

I stared at the two halves of the snake. "That's a green mamba, isn't it?" The tail was still twitching.

"Yes, it is." She stood up. "And if you'll get rid of it, sweetie, I'll get us both another beer."

CHAPTER ONE

The sun was hot, the sand under me coarse and gritty. I lay perfectly still, flat on my stomach, trying to keep from being spotted. From behind my reflecting sunglasses, I stared at the woman in front of me.

She had walked into my life less than five minutes ago, striding up the deserted beach with long legs and a firm step, dressed in a loose blue chemise and carrying a cloth beach bag. As she walked, she gazed out to sea, stopping from time to time to examine a shell or a piece of driftwood at her feet. I lay ten meters back from the water's edge, half-hidden behind the low ruins of a sand castle. She hadn't noticed me yet, and I was carefully doing nothing to change that situation.

I guessed her to be in her early thirties. She had narrow hips above long, shapely legs, and the broad shoulders of a swimmer. Her skin was the color of amber honey, set off by straight blonde hair which fell below her shoulders. Although she was tall, I calculated that I would probably have to bend just a bit to kiss her.

I didn't think I'd be getting the chance, but it doesn't hurt to rehearse, in my experience.

She had stopped at the water's edge, her beach bag at her feet, and now she was taking off her clothes. She was doing it the way the French girls learn at convent school – getting your underwear off underneath your dress, without showing anything.

I turned over on my back and gazed up at the sky, not wanting to play the role of voyeur. Nobody liked being spied on, especially not when they're getting undressed. So I closed my eyes and thought instead of the two weeks of total relaxation in Dakar which stretched out before me like a magic carpet. As far as I was concerned, I'd earned every minute of it.

My mind wandered back to the events that had brought me here. I'd been minding my own business down in Baja, celebrating being alive after a fairly hair-raising caper in New Guinea involving stolen birds, sharks, drug-crazed tribesmen, and a renegade missionary.

And then the call came.

It had turned into a tough two-month assignment in the Malaysian jungles outside of Kuantan that had left me financially solvent but physically and spiritually impoverished. I'd made it back to Kuala Lumpur in one piece, but with an empty head, a bruised body, and a very weary soul. I told them to put the check in the mail, and then I took off, looking for a place to sit and lick my wounds.

The Malaysia job had been a hush-hush assignment to track down a wealthy Chinese businessman who'd disappeared together with his million-dollar yacht from the Straits one fine weekend. I'd found him in a pirate's camp outside a small village halfway up a jungle estuary, and my error of judgement had been simple but fundamental. I'd assumed that international law would tie up any loose ends, but an incompetent government strike force had moved in first, and when the smoke had cleared over the wrecked kampong there were four dead bodies on the ground.

Three of them were pirates. One was the Chinese businessman, victim of a stray round.

I'd seen enough of death and the Malaysian jungles to last me a while, but I wasn't about to trade them for mayhem on America's freeways. Or for the Americans, for that matter. The last time I'd been Stateside, the women there seemed to have decided that they'd all look terrific with rouged cheeks. I thought it made most of them look like marathon runners.

In any case, my extremely pleasant interlude in Baja California with one Samantha Young had come to a mutually agreed end, with no hard feelings whatsoever on either side. But Sam's day job as a homicide detective in San Francisco was, as we both knew, never going to fit in with the kind of life I seemed destined to lead. We'd said sweet and tearful goodbyes on that beach in Baja, and I headed back across the Pacific once again.

But when the Malaysian job was finally done, I made my way to the West African coast, hoping to recharge my batteries and shed the accumulated skin of civilization and its discontents, rather like a snake in the spring. I could have gotten the Chinese businessman out alive, I told myself for the thousandth time. If I'd stayed on my own, done it my way, it would have worked.

Sure, said my inner conscience. But maybe not. Maybe you'd be sharkbait right now. Forget it, you did your best.

Maybe I did. But it wasn't good enough, was it?

My conscience was silent.

I rolled over and sighed. No, it hadn't been good enough. But there would be other chances to do it better, of that I was certain. In my business, there were no end of chances, no end of good deeds that needed doing. I'd find one eventually, and then I'd redeem myself, but it could wait. And in the meantime, a few weeks of quiet time in Senegal would do me good.

I opened my eyes and peered at my watch. Four hours to lunch and the first beer of the day. I ran my tongue around the inside of my mouth. Half an hour more in the sun, I decided, and then a run along the beach. To the lighthouse and back.

I looked back across the sand toward the water. The woman I'd seen a few minutes ago was still there, now wearing a tiny yellow bathing suit. I decided that it was probably all right to stare a bit now, and so I did.

She stood with her back to me, looking out at the water. The breeze turned her hair into a golden halo in the sunlight. She is absolutely lovely, I decided. Is she French? Is she married? Is she even real?

Then she picked up her bag, adjusted her sunglasses, and walked out of my life, disappearing into the seclusion of the rocks which ringed the tiny cove to my right.

I let out a long breath. Easy come, easy go.

I sighed and turned my head back toward the water's edge. The Pointe des Almadies, westernmost tip of the African continent, extended into the ocean to my right. Three hundred yards offshore, the surf crashed slowly off the reef. And beyond that, the brilliant blue-green Atlantic stretched away over the curve of the world.

Towards noon, swimmers would start arriving, but for now, the beach was virtually deserted. My closest companions were three hundred meters away, where a Senegalese woman sat by the water's edge cleaning fish while her children wandered up and down pushing wire-wheel toys through the sand.

I rolled over on my back and closed my eyes, feeling the early-morning sun on my face. Ah, the tropics are hell.

A scream erupted from the rocks beside me.

I sat up. The scream came again, full-blown and shrill with fear. I struggled to my feet just as the blonde emerged from the rocks, running like a racehorse. She hit me square in the chest and both of us went down, me on the bottom.

I grasped her elbows and rolled her to the side. She was shaking, her eyes wild with fear and horror.

"*Calmez-vous, madame.*" I spoke in French. "What's the matter?"

"*Oh, monsieur–*" She took a big gulp of air, got to her knees, and stopped. "*Il y a–*" She stopped again, the muscles in her face working.

I got up and helped her to her feet. Then I let go of her and stepped back a pace. "*Quoi?* What is it? Can you tell me?"

She put her hand on her throat. Her large eyes were greenish-gold, and as I watched, tears began to spill from

5

them and run down her cheeks. "*Là-bas*," she said at last, her breath coming in hard little spurts. "*Dans les rochers. Il y a– il y–* oh, it's just horrible!" She burst into sobs.

I did a double take. "Wait – you speak English?"

She flashed her wide eyes. "Yes. Do you?"

I nodded. "I'm an American. Now tell me what's wrong."

She wiped her eyes and grimaced. "Over there," she said, pointing to the cove. "Behind the rocks. There's a– a–" She stopped, her voice strangled.

I glanced at the rocks. "What? A snake?"

She shook her head. "No, not a snake," she said. "A man. Someone just knifed him. I– I think he's dead."

* * *

She was right on all counts. There was a man in the rocks, he'd been knifed, and he was as dead as anyone would ever want to be. He lay sprawled on his back, eyes wide open to the hot sky, the sand around him dark with blood. Flies were already buzzing excitedly around the body, as I stared down at him.

"You saw this?"

She turned stricken eyes to me. "Just a few moments ago. I was coming through the rocks, looking for a place to spread my towel. I came through here" – she indicated a narrow passage between two boulders – "and I saw this one man stab the other. Oh, God, I feel sick." She buried her face in her hands and turned away.

"Where's the other guy now?"

"I don't know." Her voice was muffled. "He ran away when he caught sight of me. Up the slope there, toward the road."

I glanced behind me. A steep scarp, almost a cliff, led up from the rocks to the corniche road above. There was a figure moving up it, climbing fast, almost at the top.

"Stay here," I said, and took off running.

I had my sneakers on, and I made good speed over the sharp rocks as I charged up the slope. The man I was chasing was some two hundred yards ahead, but if I didn't slip, I'd catch him eventually. He had a knife, but I'd worry about that when the time came. First I had to catch him.

Gasping for breath, I cleared the top of the cliff and looked around. The man was nowhere to be seen. Then I heard an engine start up over to my left, and a second later, I saw my little rented Renault 4 coming down the corniche road, straight for me. The bastard was stealing my car.

"Hey! Hey, that's my car! Stop, you sonofabitch! *Arrêtez!*"

I was in the middle of the road now, waving my arms, but the car kept coming, picking up speed. A black man was behind the wheel, his lips drawn back in a snarl, exposing prominent front teeth. Then the window came down and I saw something else, too. The muzzle of a pistol, pointed directly at me.

I jumped to the side as the man fired twice, and then I was rolling over and over in the sand beside the road, hearing the roar of the motor recede as my car sped away into the distance.

I picked myself up and brushed off as much of the sand as I could reach, watching my Renault dwindle to a speck. "Well, I'll be a sonofabitch," I said softly.

Then I turned and began to trudge back to where I'd left the woman and the dead man.

* * *

The dead man wore an over-the-belt shirt, cotton trousers, and black plastic sandals. He was a Senegalese, judging from the silver bracelet on his wrist and the leather gris-gris pouches on a rawhide string around his neck. Although I knew that most Senegalese were Muslims, I also knew that almost all of them wore gris-gris amulets for protection and good luck. Here as elsewhere, the distinction between magic and religion was largely academic.

He'd either bought his gris-gris at a garage sale, or else the warranty had run out. He'd been knifed, sliced across the belly like a marlin, by someone whose blade had been very sharp. He'd been young and fit, but now he was little more than a dried husk, curiously shrunken, one of his hands clutching at the wide slash in his belly that had let his life bleed away into the uncaring sand.

He was wearing a shoulder holster, and it was empty. "Figures," I grunted.

"What figures?" She stood close beside me, staring at the body. She smelled of sea salt and coconut oil.

"His gun's gone." I pointed up the cliff. "I got shot at up there. Twice. And he stole my car, too."

"Stole your car? How'd he do that? Did you leave the keys inside?"

I glared at her. "I'm not that dumb," I said. "He must have hot-wired it."

"Don't be so touchy," she said. "Look, I found this on the sand." She handed me a plastic ID wallet.

I flipped it open and glanced inside, giving a low whistle of surprise. "This guy's a cop. An officer in the Gendarmerie Nationale."

Her eyes met mine. "What should we do now?"

I stood staring at the dead body for a moment. So much for my quiet day at the beach. The sound of the surf seemed suddenly far away, the sunlight not quite so bright now. Overhead, gulls wheeled and cried plaintively.

"I think we'd better get in touch with his office," I said finally, "and tell them he won't be coming in."

CHAPTER TWO

The Police Centrale on the Rue Dr. Thèze was an old colonial building in a state of gentle decline. A red, yellow and green Senegalese flag drooped listlessly down from the pole jutting out from the second floor. We'd flagged a taxi on the beach road and come straight in.

"Listen," the blonde said to me as we trudged up the broad steps. "I don't even know you. I don't know what the hell's happening here. Can't we just–"

"The less you say here, the better," I said quietly. "Just answer their questions and let's get out of here. Don't volunteer information, just speak when spoken to. And speak French, not English."

I knew that we had to report the murder, so the visit to the Centrale was a formality, a going-through-the-motions exercise, but I didn't want to get tangled up in anything. A man was dead, but nothing would bring him back to life. And although my car was gone, the insurance company would take care of that if necessary. I had a mild interest in finding the guy who'd stolen it, but since he was also likely to be the murderer, I figured I'd let the cops deal with that, and stay as far away from them as I could.

If you spend time in developing countries – and that's where I spend most of mine – you learn to be careful around cops. The ground rules are a little different out here, and cross-cultural misunderstandings can lead to anything from a night in the local lock-up to a blindfold and a last cigarette. French-speaking Africa uses the Code Napoléon as the basis for the legal system. Under the code, you're presumed guilty until proven innocent, so the less said at this stage, I figured, the better.

That went for the blonde as well. She didn't know me, I didn't know her. I could be Vlad the Impaler for all the cops knew, and she could be Ma Baker's granddaughter. And whatever her story turned out to be, I had some reasons of my own for not wanting the Senegalese police to do too much poking around in my past. So the trick was to play it straight, tell our story, and get the hell out of there.

I fixed a smile on my face, raised my chin, and walked into the office.

Half a dozen policemen in wrinkled uniforms lay dozing on benches inside the squad room. The two officers who were awake were playing checkers, slapping the dames down hard and chuckling at each other. In response to my query, one of them jerked a thumb toward the back.

In the next room, I could see a skinny corporal drawing a monthly *emploi du temps* with a ruler and a set of colored ballpoint pens, working with all the speed and intensity of a medieval monk on an illuminated manuscript. The man at the desk next to him was busy on the telephone, discussing the price of fresh fish.

The first words out of my mouth got everyone's undivided attention.

We spent the next half an hour giving a *procès-verbal* to the corporal, who fought it out word for word with a typewriter that should have been in a museum, using two fingers and pausing frequently to unstick the keys. We took turns talking while he typed. Every now and then he would shake his head and cluck his tongue sadly.

As our story unfolded, we began to collect a small crowd. They stood quietly and listened as we recounted the details of what we had found. Overhead, fans coated with thick black dust turned slowly, wafting cooking smells in from the street.

We finished the deposition at about nine o'clock and waited while the corporal read it through.

"Can we go now?" I said.

He shook his head. "Not yet," he said. "The commissaire needs to see this."

I sighed and followed him out the door.

The commissaire's office was down the hall, a large room with a high ceiling. Rows of bookcases sagged under the weight of dusty files, and most of the floor was obscured with stacks of official-looking papers. On the wall, the president of the republic peered down at us, sashed, beribboned and gilt-framed, looking a little like a highly intelligent stork.

Behind the wide desk in the center of the room sat a small man with steel-rimmed glasses and a bald head like a polished horse chestnut. He was staring intently at the horoscope section of the morning edition of the *Soleil*, spread out in front of him over a mound of lesser paperwork.

He ignored us, continuing to read. I stood very still, my shirt sticking to my back in the damp heat, listening to the buzzing of a fly somewhere behind me and to the right. Overhead, an ancient fan with filthy blades slowly stirred the humid air.

Finally he looked up, folded the paper carefully, and set it to one side. He picked up our *procès-verbal* and read it slowly, puffing his breath in and out like a slow bellows. When he was through, he took out a large handkerchief and wiped his glossy forehead and the bulb of his nose. With his greying sideburns and basset-hound eyes, he looked like Uncle Remus, but I doubted that he'd gotten to be top cop in a city this size by telling animal stories to the kiddies.

He cleared his throat, a sound like gravel coming down the chute of a cement mixer. "I am Dabo," he said. "Commissaire de Police for the Region of Cap-Vert." His eyes swiveled across us like cannon traversing. "*Vos passeports, s'il vous plaît.*" It wasn't a request – it was an order.

The first few seconds, in my experience, are crucial. If you're going to make a good impression, this is the time to do it. I whipped my passport from my pocket and laid it on the desk with a little flourish. "Hi, my name is Max Donovan," I said. "I—"

"Be quiet." Dabo stared at my passport for several minutes. Then he picked it up and examined it, fanning the pages, turning it this way and that, viewing it from different angles as if it might contain some secret which could be suddenly uncovered by an adroit glance.

Finally he closed the passport carefully and tapped it on the desk. "You have a tourist visa," he said accusingly. "Anyone can get one of those at the airport. What are you doing in Senegal, Monsieur Donovan?"

I gave him my aw-shucks smile. "I'm on vacation, Mr. Dabo. A couple of weeks of rest and recreation, before I go back to work."

"What do you do for a living?"

I was ready for this one. "I'm a businessman, sir," I replied with what I hoped looked like absolute sincerity.

Dabo grunted. He picked up the woman's passport, giving it the same careful scrutiny. "Miss Lindsay Elizabeth Greenwood," he intoned.

"Lindy."

His eyes came up. "*Quoi?*"

"Lindy," she repeated. "That's what I like people to call me."

Her French was very good, with hardly a trace of accent. Unlike English, which actually sounds better when spoken by foreigners these days, French requires the proper accent to avoid sounding like a series of nasal grunts. Try saying '*un bon vin blanc*' into a tape recorder sometime and you'll see what I mean.

Dabo was turning pages. "You have a residence visa, Miss Greenwood," he said at last. "One may assume, therefore, that you are not on vacation?"

She nodded. "I work here. In the game park in Niokolo-Koba, out in the eastern province."

Dabo's eyebrows went up. "In the game park? And what do you do there, take pictures of the tourists?"

She gave him a small smile. "No, I'm a researcher. An animal psychologist. I'm doing a project for the Yerkes Center in Atlanta, in the United States." She paused. "I run a school for chimpanzees."

Dabo looked at her as if she had suddenly grown a second head. He put her passport down. Then he stood up and walked around the desk, staring at her. I didn't blame him; I was staring at her, too.

"A school?" Dabo intoned, echoing the question in my own mind. "A school for – chimpanzees? Is that what you said?"

"Well, I know it sounds strange," she said with an embarrassed shrug. "But it's not. I'm working with a dozen chimps that were reared in captivity. It's an experiment, you see, to find out if they can be rehabilitated."

"Rehabilitated?" Dabo mouthed the word with difficulty, as if he were using his facial muscles for the first time.

"Yes," she said. "To see if they can live in the wild again. I teach them how to find food, how to build nests, that sort of thing."

"I see," Dabo said finally. "And is there a great deal of money in such activity, Miss Greenwood?"

"Money? Oh, no. It's a research project, funded by a grant. The payoff's in knowledge."

"Knowledge of what, exactly?"

"Well, we want to find out if it's possible to reintroduce the chimps into their original environment. If it works, we'll discover a lot about how non-human primates learn things – how smart they are, and how they pass on what they learn. And we'll be able to put a lot more chimpanzees back into nature where they belong."

Dabo had come all the way back around the desk, staring at Lindy Greenwood the whole time. Now he sat down, closed his eyes, and massaged the bridge of his nose with tired fingers.

"Miss Greenwood, I am a Mandingue. I was born in a small village in the Casamance, and from the time I was old enough to walk, I was sent to guard my father's groundnut fields from the monkeys. Monkeys do a great deal of damage to crops."

I thought it was time I said something. "Technically," I said, "chimpanzees aren't monkeys."

Dabo opened his eyes and fixed me with a look that could vulcanize rubber. "If I wish to hear from you, Monsieur Donovan, I will let you know. As far as I am concerned, they are *all* monkeys."

"Yes, sir." I clasped my hands behind my back and stood at parade rest. As the Arabs say, if at noon the king says it is night, then behold the stars.

Dabo turned back to Lindy Greenwood. "As a Westerner used to buying your dinner wrapped in plastic at the supermarket," he continued, "perhaps you have no direct experience – as I have – of watching your family's food supply being devoured by the *monkeys*." He bit the word off viciously. "Why on earth anyone would seek to introduce yet more of these disgusting creatures into our poor country is quite beyond my comprehension." He paused. "In fact, if it were up to me, I would send them all to France or somewhere equally deserving."

He picked up the *procès-verbal*, handling it with reverence. "But all of this is beside the point. This, ah, incident on the beach is a most regrettable affair," he said, staring at the typed statement. "We have very few murders in this country, as a rule." He looked at Lindy Greenwood. "I am deeply sorry that you had to be the one to discover the body."

"Who was he?" she asked.

A voice spoke from the doorway behind us. "His name was N'Diaye, madame; Malick N'Diaye. And he was my partner."

We turned to see a tall man in the blue uniform of the Gendarmerie Nationale standing in the open doorway, his face tense and strained.

With a shock, I realized that I knew him. It was my old friend Bari N'Dour, and the last time I'd seen him, he'd been wearing Senegalese Army camouflage fatigues and captain's bars.

He was staring at Dabo, his lips compressed in anger. He strode into the room, dominating it. "Why in hell," he said, his fury coming out in even, measured tones, "was I not informed of this before now? I got a call from the hospital, not from you. Malick is dead, for God's sake."

Dabo stood his ground. "I will discuss the details with you later, Brigadier N'Dour," he said calmly. "If that seems appropriate. Meanwhile, let me remind you that this case is under my jurisdiction, not yours, and that the rules of procedure are in full force."

N'Dour glared at him, his handsome face clouded with anger. "To hell with that," he said. "I want to know why this happened."

They stood facing each other for a moment.

"You have no authority here, Brigadier," Dabo said at last. "I will thank you to leave my office now." He swept his arm toward us. "I am busy, as you can plainly see, with Monsieur Donovan and Mademoiselle Greenwood."

"Donovan?" The gendarme turned, seeing us for the first time. His eyes widened as he recognized me. I stepped forward and raised my hand, about to speak, but something in his glance stopped me. He gave a slight sideways shake of the head and the merest flicker of his eyeballs. 'Later,' his glance said. 'Not now. Not here.'

I stepped back, making my face a neutral mask. If Bari N'Dour was telling me to shut up, then that's what I'd better do. His advice had kept me out of trouble before, and I had no reason to doubt it now.

N'Dour drew himself erect and nodded curtly. "*A vos ordres, mon commissaire*," he murmured. He stepped back a pace, put on his gold-braided cap, and saluted smartly. Glancing at me one last time, he turned on his heel and went out the door.

Dabo watched him go with evident satisfaction. He turned back to us. "Brigadier N'Dour is understandably upset, but procedure must be followed, *n'est-ce pas?*" He handed the typed sheets across the desk. "Now, if you will please each sign one of these, our business here is concluded."

We picked up the statements and read them through. Then we scrawled our names at the bottom and handed them back to Dabo.

"What happens now?" Lindy asked.

Dabo's eyes went up again. "What do you mean?"

"Well, will you be needing either of us again?"

He shook his head. "I doubt it very much." He picked up our passports and handed them to us with a flourish and a small smile. "But if we do, we will get in touch, you can be sure." He walked us to the door. "Again, my apologies for this tragic affair. And now, good day."

We were out on the street almost before we knew it. The sun was bright and the sky was blue, but somehow it seemed as if the day had already ended. Lindy Greenwood and I looked at each other.

"Do you believe that?" she said.

"Believe what?"

"That incredible blow-off, that's what." Her eyes were wide with indignation. "Christ, he–" She stopped. "What's your name again? I'm terrible with names."

"Donovan. Max Donovan."

"Oh, right. Well, look, Mr. Donovan–"

"Call me Max."

"Max, then. I mean, do you believe this? We found this guy dead on the beach barely an hour ago, and that clown upstairs just acted like he couldn't wait to get us out of there. He barely glanced at our written statements. I had the feeling that he just wanted to get us out of there and forget the whole thing." Her eyes held mine. "Didn't you?"

I nodded. "You're right."

"And did you notice the way he cut off the other guy? The one who walked in at the end? Why do you think he did that?"

I looked up to see Bari N'Dour striding down the steps toward us. "I don't know," I said. "But I'll bet he can tell us himself."

N'Dour's smile was broad as he hugged me. "*Nom de Dieu*, it's been years. You look good, Max. What are you doing back in Senegal? Africa still in your blood?"

I grinned. "Like a disease." I stepped back. "This is, ah, Lindy Greenwood," I said, indicating the blonde beside me.

"*Enchanté*," said Bari.

"What the hell was going on upstairs just now, Bari?" I said. "You looked like you were about to poke the commissaire in the nose."

N'Dour's eyes darkened. "Did you tell him you knew me?"

"No, but–"

"Good. Dabo's an idiot." He took my arm. "Come on, we've got things to discuss. I'm on my way up to the hospital; we can talk in the car." To Lindy Greenwood he said, "You come, too."

Without waiting for a reply, he turned and walked off down the street toward an official blue 2CV camionette.

Lindy looked at me. "You know this guy?"

"It's a long story," I said. "Let's go. He's already half a block ahead of us."

CHAPTER THREE

Dakar's traffic is a real-life video game. Bari N'Dour played it smoothly and aggressively as he maneuvered his 2CV around the Place de l'Indépéndance, racing neck and neck with a heavily laden peanut truck. He slid the car to a halt in front of the traffic lights, edging out the truck by centimeters.

A blind paraplegic beggar on an oversized skateboard shot out from the curb and rolled to a halt beside us. "Alms for the love of God," the beggar croaked, snaking a wizened hand in the window and banging with his fist on the steering wheel.

Bari passed him a coin. "*Yalla na yalla mai la djamm,*" rasped the beggar, giving us the standard blessing and pushing off quickly to confront the next vehicle in line.

The light changed and we roared off, leaving the beggar planted in front of the peanut truck, shouting at the driver, who leaned on his horn and raced his engine alarmingly.

Lindy leaned forward from the back seat. "Okay, tell me," she said. "How come you two know each other?"

Bari smiled at her, showing large, even teeth. "Well, Max and I did a little work together some years ago."

"What kind of work?"

"Flying cargo down into the Casamance region – the southern province," I said quickly.

Bari laughed then. "Cargo and other things."

Lindy looked at me enquiringly, but I stayed quiet. I was thinking back to the hot sweaty time in the Lower Casamance, back in the days when Bari N'Dour was a newly commissioned captain in the Senegalese Army. I was thinking about how a job that had begun as a straightforward weekly cargo shuttle to the bush airstrip outside of Oussouye quickly turned into clandestine resupply for the PAIGC rebels across the border, inside Portuguese Guinea. I could never pass up excitement, especially when it was attached to the possibility of making an extra buck or two.

And so I'd agreed – for a modest honorarium – to fly the supplies in at night, landing blind on short-run peanut fields, guided down by Bari and his troops. We stockpiled food, ammunition and medicines for the guerrillas, flew out their wounded, and helped the others find safety in the small forest villages along the border.

Bari's unit, technically neutral and strictly non-combatant, had finally gotten caught behind Portuguese lines one day. I'd picked up the message on the radio and gone in to find them, but a broken fuel pump had stranded all of us on the ground in enemy territory.

From then on, we were fresh meat. By day, General Spínola's men searched for us on the ground, and by night, the gunship helicopters circled low overhead, their searchlights probing the bush.

I remembered how I'd pulled Bari from the burning hut when the Portuguese planes had napalmed our hiding place; how we kept each other alive for three days and nights in the snake-infested rice paddies before we made it back across the border.

It wasn't the sort of thing you could explain to someone. As they say, you had to be there. So I just looked at Lindy Greenwood and smiled, saying nothing.

We pulled up at the entrance to the Hôpital Principal, parked, and pushed through a door marked '*Soins Intensifs – Entrée Interdite.*' Bari led us down the narrow corridor, maneuvering around the beds and equipment which littered the area. There was a pervasive odor in the building, a smell characteristic of hospitals, composed of decay, iodized alcohol, and feces.

A barefoot orderly chewing a lemon stick pushed past us with a chipped enamel bedpan containing bloody dressings and what looked like loose bits of skin. Before he went out the door, he paused briefly by an open window and spit through it. From somewhere down the hall, a patient was screaming.

Malick N'Diaye lay on a gurney at the end of the corridor, covered with a grey sheet. A European doctor stood beside the gurney, writing something on a clipboard.

He caught sight of us and turned, taking off his mask and gloves. He was a young Frenchman, obviously a military doctor, and his face was pinched with exhaustion and concern.

"Brigadier N'Dour? I'm Dr. Renaudeau." He nodded to Lindy and me, brushing idly at a fly that buzzed around his head, drawn by the smell of blood. "Let's go in here, shall we?" He opened the door to a tiny lounge.

"How did he die?" said Bari when we were inside.

Renaudeau grimaced. He opened his tunic and took out a packet of Gauloises. "Smoke?"

We all shook our heads. I fished out my ancient Zippo and lit his for him. I'd given up smoking years ago, but I still carried the Zippo. It comes in handy for setting things on fire.

"*Merci.*" Renaudeau drew the smoke down deep, grimacing, letting it out in a nervous rush. After a moment, he spoke again. "How did he die? He was knifed, of course; sliced almost in two. From behind, I would guess, by someone who knew what he was doing." He paused. "I grew up in Marseilles, and this kind of thing was not uncommon in the hospital I trained in. It is uncommon in Senegal, fortunately." He fixed solemn eyes on Bari. "Your partner was killed by an expert, *monsieur*. He probably died immediately, if that's any comfort to you. There's nothing else I can tell you, really. We'll do an autopsy, of course, but I don't really expect any surprises."

He pulled a small envelope from the pocket of his scrubs and gave it to Bari. "This is what we found in his pockets. Do you have any idea who did this?"

Bari shook his head. "Not yet," he said quietly. "But I will."

We went back out into the corridor to where the dead man lay on the gurney. Bari lifted up the end of the sheet, and stared for a moment at Malick N'Diaye's face. Then he sighed. "Thank you," he murmured to Dr. Renaudeau. He turned to us. "Let's go."

* * *

We were standing in the parking lot of the hospital, squinting in the glare of the sun. Bari was sorting through the contents of the envelope Renaudeau had given him. "ID card, four or five thousand francs, and this." He held up a receipt and peered at it. "Dragon d'Or," he read. "*Cuisine Nord-Vietnamienne*. What the hell?"

I looked at the receipt. "Looks like it's a bill for lunch or something," I said. "What's so unusual about that?"

Bari looked at me. "Malick hated Asian food, Max; Vietnamese, Chinese, anything like that. He never went near those places." He stared at the receipt for a moment longer. "Maybe Dabo's men can figure it out. Assuming," he added, "that any of them can read."

"Listen," I said, "will you explain something to me? What's going on with you and this Dabo guy? How come you're so pissed off at him?"

"I told you, he's an idiot. And unfortunately, he'll be in charge of this case. It's a jurisdictional problem," he continued. "Do you understand how the police forces work here?"

"No more than I need to," I said.

Bari grunted. "Probably smart. Well, we've got three kinds of police in this country: the Garde Républicaine, the Gendarmerie, and the Sûreté.

"I've seen the Garde," said Lindy. "Aren't they the ones in the red berets who stand outside government offices?"

"That's right," said Bari. "They're really just security guards. And the Gendarmerie, which I belong to, is basically paramilitary. That's one of the reasons I joined after I finished the army – I could transfer rank and seniority across."

"And the Sûreté?" I said.

"The Sûreté is the municipal police force." He paused. "And Dabo is their chief."

"So why is he so nervous about you showing up in his office?"

Bari made the sharp sucking noise that Senegalese use to express disgust or contempt. "Dabo's nothing but a *nyama-nyama*, an incompetent fool, typical of the kind of leadership the city police have right now. He spends most of the day trying to make his telephone work. Half his men are on the take, half the rest can barely read. He works mainly for the politicians and the business interests – he's a *lèche-bottes* out of the old school."

"Maybe he's a bootlicker," I said, "but that still doesn't explain why he's nervous."

Bari sighed. "To a man like Dabo, procedure is everything. Malick was acting unofficially and without authorization, and he was on Dabo's turf. The Gendarmerie's a national police force, you see, not a local one. We can't get involved in city crimes unless we're asked in."

"And you weren't asked."

"Of course not. And we won't be, even with Malick dead. Dabo knows what my unit's investigating right now. He'd be happier with rabies."

"What do you mean?"

Bari smiled thinly. "Malick and I were starting to put together data on organized crime in the country. Who's involved, and how they're connected to people both here and in other countries. One way or another, we were going to be looking at some of the people that pull Dabo's strings. He's been aware of our investigation for some time, but he's never wanted to help us out. And he doesn't want us getting involved in his cases, either. So when things happen in the city, he takes care of them quietly, in his own way. Malick was working on something that made Dabo very nervous."

"And now that Malick's dead, he's got a problem he didn't want."

"Exactly."

"You said Malick was working on something. Was that what got him killed?

"I don't know," Bari said softly. "It was something important, that's all he told me." He looked at me. "And you can help me find out what it was."

"Me? How?"

"Malick was friendly with an American at your embassy – one of the clerks. He went to the embassy the day before yesterday. When he came back he was excited – all he'd say was that he'd found out something, and that he wanted to check on a guy; someone who'd just arrived in the country. If we can find out who that person is, we may have a clue as to what happened."

I shrugged. "So why not check with the immigration officials at the airport?"

Bari shook his head. "Hundreds of people arrive in Dakar every day. We need a name fast, and you can get it for me." He paused. "Go to the embassy and see his friend. Find out what he told him. Whatever it was, it probably got him killed."

"Do you really think he learned something from this guy at the embassy?" I asked.

"I'm sure of it," Bari replied. "I didn't see Malick yesterday," he continued, "but he called me from the airport at noon. All he said was 'I've found who I was looking for – tell you all about it tomorrow.'" Bari paused. "And this morning, you found him on the beach."

Lindy's eyes were wide. "And you think the person he was looking for – the one he found at the airport – is the one who knifed him?"

Bari shrugged. "I don't know, mademoiselle." His eyes hardened. "But when I find him, I'll be sure to ask him. Depend on that." He scrawled a telephone number on the restaurant receipt and handed it to me. "Call me when you find out something, all right?"

I nodded. "You've got it."

* * *

We stood there in the parking lot, watching him drive off. Lindy Greenwood turned to me. "Look, why don't we go somewhere and talk?"

"Talk? About what?"

"Anything. Let's go for a drink. Coffee. Tea. Dinner. Whatever."

I looked at her. "It's too early for dinner," I said. "It's only eleven o'clock."

She blew an exasperated sigh. "God, first that jerk Dabo, now you. Don't be an idiot, okay? I want to talk to you – find out more about you."

"Why?"

She pushed hair out of her eyes. "I should have thought that was obvious, for crying out loud. Look – you come along and rescue me on the beach, right? Then it turns out you just happen to know this guy N'Dour. Then you promise to help him. Don't you think I'm curious about all of that?"

"I don't–"

She kept right on talking. "You're interesting, you're good-looking, you speak good French, and you've been around. You even know the difference between apes and monkeys. You don't meet men like that very often. At least I don't."

I was staring at her now.

She grinned back. "Maybe you're a jerk, but maybe you're some kind of hero. How will I know unless I get to know you better?" She paused and folded her arms. "Now, is that too much to ask?"

I blinked. "Ah, no. No, I guess not. Do you always move this fast?"

Her eyes sparkled. "You take it when it comes. I'm going back to the research station soon, and for all I know, you're booked out to Paris on the midnight flight. So what about it?"

"What about what?"

"Do you want to go somewhere? Get a drink or something? There's a lot I want to ask you."

"I was, ah, going to the embassy, actually."

"How about afterwards? What are you doing for lunch, for instance? That place N'Dour mentioned – the one on the receipt? I've seen it before; it's right near my hotel. Why don't we try it? What was it called?"

"The Dragon d'Or," I said. "The Golden Dragon. Look, I–"

"So meet me there at one, okay?" She put her hand on my arm. "We'll have lunch and talk. I won't bite, I promise."

She stepped into the street, put two fingers in her mouth and blew a long, loud whistle. A taxi slid to a halt in front of us.

She opened the door and paused, watching me, her eyes dancing. "Come on," she said. "Let's at least have lunch. Why not?"

I'm sometimes a little slow on the uptake, but I'm not entirely clueless. A definite current was beginning to flow between us. "Sure," I said after a moment. "Sure, why not?"

She smiled. "That's the spirit." Then she got inside and shut the door.

I watched her taxi speed off down the street. "Sure," I repeated softly. "Why the hell not?"

CHAPTER FOUR

In the old days, American Embassies were friendly places, but that was long ago, in a galaxy very far away. Today, the older embassies have been remodeled to make them more 'secure', and the newer ones are designed by descendants of the guys who did the plans for the Bastille and the Tower of London. And these days, nobody's bothering to hide the barbed wire, the jacklights, and the surveillance cameras.

I gave my name and showed my passport to the marine guard on duty and signed the book. Then I lifted my arms while he frisked me and passed a metal detector over my clothing. Even though the security procedures wouldn't have made a professional terrorist even pause for breath, I was a good sport and kept my mouth shut while the gunnery sergeant ran me through the drill.

He finished patting me down and returned my passport, and then handed me over to the next marine. This one was seated behind a double pane of bulletproof glass, his M16 conspicuously clipped to the wall next to him, although how they expected the poor guy to shoot anybody from inside a glass cage was beyond me. I don't make foreign policy, I just have to live with it.

"Help you, sir?" His voice echoed through the intercom.

It reminded me of those self-serve gas stations out on the strips where at night somebody sits locked in a booth the size of a closet and works the drawer that you put your money into, watching your eyes all the while, waiting to see if you're the one who's going to do the stickup that night. Maybe that's what these marines do when they get too old for embassy duty, I thought.

I told him the name of the man that Bari had given me. The marine nodded and murmured into a telephone at his elbow. A moment later, the phone buzzed back. He listened, glanced at me and spoke quietly into the mouthpiece. Then he looked up. "Man you wanted to see? He's been reassigned. Want to talk to his boss?"

I considered for a moment, and then nodded. Might as well get this over with. The marine spoke again into the mouthpiece, hung up, and fished out a visitor's pass for me to wear around my neck, and pushed it through the slit in the glass.

"Down the hall, fourth office on the right. Arnold Shacklady, Chief of Security. You gotta turn your pass in and go through a search again when you leave."

The buzzer sounded and I pushed through the big door and into the embassy.

Embassies are strange places. Technically, they are pieces of the home country's territory which just happen to be surrounded by a foreign country. Culturally, they are a bizarre kind of force-field bubble in a strange environment, designed primarily to care for one of our most peculiar social classes. These are the people we call diplomats, our last remaining vestige of the feudal system.

I spend little time in embassies, and even less time, if I can help it, with diplomats. Diplomats are a world unto themselves; they work and live according to arrangements which are a thousand years old, following rules which not only tolerate privilege and inequality, but celebrate them. For some reason, Americans in particular seem to take to this arrangement with enthusiasm, eventually coming to believe that their diplomatic lifestyle is not only normal, but essential.

I walked slowly down the corridor until I found the door the marine guard had indicated and went in. There was no one at the desk, so I helped myself to a chair and sat down to take a look around.

It was the standard government office with the standard Sears office furniture. There were standard certificates of merit and a standard three-month federal calendar on the wall, together with what looked like a standard personally signed photograph of the current president.

A man came out of the next room. He was about sixty, tall and bony, with an unhealthy light-yellow complexion that spoke of too many hours in front of the VCR. "You Mr. Donovan?" He didn't offer to shake hands.

I nodded, looking him over. His mouth was pursed and wrinkled-looking, as if he'd just bitten into a green mango, and his carrot-red hair was going thin on top. He had on a powder-blue seersucker suit, a rep tie, and a white button-down shirt. I couldn't see his feet, but wingtips sounded like a safe bet.

He sat down behind the desk. "I'm Arnold Shacklady, Embassy Chief of Security. The man you're looking for is no longer working with us, I'm afraid. What can I help you with?" It was said with a smile, but Shacklady's eyes were watching me closely.

Briefly, I described the situation to him. When I finished, Shacklady frowned. "Let me see if I understand what you're after. You want to know what my assistant blabbed about to this cop, the one who got beat up, is that right?"

"Knifed. Killed, actually."

"Whatever." He waved dismissively. "Well, I need to tell you that the guy who gave out the information has been put on report for breach of procedure. Right now, he's back in Washington, explaining himself to the IG."

"The IG?"

Shacklady gave a thin smile. "The inspector general, Mr. Donovan. He'll be lucky to get off with a reprimand. I run a tight little ship here."

"That's certainly good to know," I said, keeping a smile on my face. "Mind telling me what the information was?"

Shacklady grunted, pushed himself out of his leather armchair, and disappeared into the next room. He returned a moment later with a thin manila folder, holding it carefully between thumb and forefinger, the way you might hold a dead rat by the tail. He sank down into his chair, flipped open the folder and glanced through it, his lips working slowly as he read. Finally he closed it, centered it precisely on the desk in front of him, and sat back.

"Nope."

I looked up. "I beg your pardon?"

"Nope, Mr. Donovan, you don't get this information. See, this file's government property, and you're not supposed to pass out what's in it to just anybody, let alone one of the locals here."

I thought about all this for a moment. "So you're not going to let me see it, either."

Shacklady nodded. "You got it. Just because my assistant was a damned fool doesn't mean I have to be. He had no authority to do what he did, and I wouldn't be surprised if we don't see him back here again." He paused. "But that's really none of your business, the way I see it. So the answer's no, Donovan."

"Is the material classified?"

"No, it is not. He'd be under arrest if it had been."

"Then can I ask why you won't let me see it?"

"You can ask. And I could give you a couple different reasons. Or none at all." He leaned forward and tapped the folder. "The simplest way to explain it is this: if you gotta ask to see what's in here, then you're not authorized to know." He sat back. "Basically, see, you're not an official American. That's the problem."

I looked at him. "Not an official American?" I pulled out my passport. "You mean this isn't real? Damn, and I've been using it all these years."

Shacklady looked annoyed. "I'm not talking about that, for Pete's sake. You're not *official*, is what I mean. You're not an employee of the US government–"

"Thank God," I murmured.

He ignored me. And that means you've got no status here, no privileges, zip. You're not on the diplomatic list, and you haven't got a security clearance. Hell, you can't even buy toilet paper in the commissary."

I sighed. Clearly this wasn't going anywhere. I thought about telling Shacklady that even though I might not be on his list, he was certainly near the top of mine.

Instead, I leaned forward. "Mr. Shacklady, listen to me. Whether your assistant was right or wrong to give this information out, a Senegalese policeman died this morning because of something in that file in front of you. All I'm asking–"

He waved me down. "Forget it, Donovan. As a matter of fact" – he looked down at the open folder – "the local authorities were given this information, by me, just as soon as I got it. Two days later, I found out it had been leaked. So if your Senegalese cop buddy wants to know more, let him go through his own damn government's channels. He can make an official request."

He leaned back, a tight smirk on his face. "And knowing the way they do things in this country, maybe in a year or two he'll get to see it."

"That's not a very helpful attitude," I said. I was beginning to really dislike this man.

"Stiff cheese, Donovan. That's the way they do it to us." He grimaced. "Takes those damn Senegalese weeks to clear our peoples' duty-free goods through customs, more stupid forms than you can imagine. I don't owe them anything. I've done my job by the book, and that's all I'm damn well going to do."

I sighed inwardly, knowing that I'd run out of options. Shacklady was playing it by the book, all right; the one they gave Foreign Service officers, printed in large, easy-to-read type. The man was an authentic toady, and there was no way in hell that he was going to let me see that file, not for love nor money. Originally, a toady actually ate toads for a living; today, the term referred to somebody who did whatever the rules told him to do, regardless of the facts of the situation at hand. Somebody like Shacklady.

Shacklady dropped the file to the desk and stood up. "Anything else I can do for you today?"

I sat and fixed him with a beady eye, wondering how a guy like that could get so skinny on a steady diet of toads, or whatever it was that they were serving up in the embassy snack bar these days. I felt like popping him one on the end of his bony nose, but that could wait. As they say, revenge is a dish best served cold.

What I really needed right now was the folder.

I could see the big grey steel filing cabinets in the next room, with their combination locks and red 'SECRET' labels, and I knew that once the folder went back in there, I'd never see it again. So I was thinking hard as Shacklady steered me out of his office and back into the corridor.

Just then, a fat, bald man in a military attaché's uniform popped his head out of an office three doors down. "Hey, Arnold, step in here a minute, willya? We got another damned problem with the Fourth of July reception, and I need you to look at something."

I caught my breath, smiling at Shacklady to cover my elation. "I can see you're busy," I said. "I'll find my own way out." I glanced down at his feet. "Nice wingtips, by the way."

Shacklady grunted. "Don't forget to turn in your pass." He walked back and started talking to the chicken colonel. Leaving, bless him, the folder sitting on his desk.

I glanced up and down the hall. Nothing but wall posters of American landscapes, a bulletin board and a water cooler along one side. On the other, a fire alarm and an extinguisher, an empty office, and the men's room. Think, Donovan, think.

Glancing into the empty office, I spotted a telephone on the desk, and a split second later, an idea lit up my mind, just like those light bulbs in the comics. Perfect, I thought, ducking inside. I had about a minute to get this right. Starting now.

I ducked into the empty room. Beside the telephone was a list of internal numbers. I scanned the possibilities, finally choosing 'Communications Room.' I punched in the number.

"Yo," a male Midwestern voice responded, sounding sleepy and bored.

I put my handkerchief over the receiver. Don't try this one at home, folks, I thought. "Leesin, foreign peeg." I spoke in low, deep tones, trying to sound like Count Dracula.

"We gonna blow op you embassy, right now. Better get movin." It came out sounding more like Cheech Marin than Dracula, but what the hell, making a good impression's the main thing.

"Whaaat? Say, who the hell is this?"

I looked up at the door. If anybody walked in right now, my financial worries would be over; the Feds would be providing room and board for a good many years. This is what happens, I thought, when unofficial Americans are allowed to use the phones.

"We the People's Army, peeg." I dropped my voice to a whisper. "Bomb gonna go off in four minutes exactly."

"Wait, now. Wait just a goddamned—"

"Four minutes," I repeated. "Power to the people, mon; down with the official Americans." I hung up.

No time to waste now. I came cautiously out of the office and disappeared into the men's room, just as a siren started up somewhere close by. I went to the towel dispenser on the wall and grabbed a double handful. Twisting the paper towels into crude torch, I lit the end with my trusty Zippo. When it was flaming nicely, I poked it at the sensor for the sprinkler system, high up on the ceiling.

Ten seconds later, water erupted from the outlets, dousing the torch. I dropped the soggy paper and opened the door. The sprinklers in the corridor had gone off as well, and secretaries shrieked as they scampered for shelter, holding papers over their hairdos.

I went down the corridor, casually pulling the fire alarm as I passed it. Bells began to ring throughout the building, adding a nice touch of panic to the siren's piercing wail. From somewhere up ahead, I could hear orders being shouted through a walkie-talkie.

Everyone was piling into the corridor now, heading for the doors, vainly trying to dodge the sprinkler streams. I ducked back around the corner and peeped into Shacklady's office. He was gone, but the file was still where he had left it. In five seconds I had opened the folder, scooped up the few sheets inside, and slipped them inside my shirt.

Then I joined the line of people being led outside by the marine guards. Needless to say, no one was being searched. Houdini couldn't have done it better.

Five minutes later I stood across the street, blinking in the sunlight and watching Shacklady wringing the water out of his seersucker jacket.

And now, a beer and a quiet place to read in.

CHAPTER FIVE

Just on noon now, and the tables at the Café de Paris were starting to fill up. A shaven-headed Toucouleur waiter wearing baggy Muslim trousers and a pair of plastic shoes slit to accommodate his wide feet materialized beside me.

"*Une petite*," I said.

He grunted approvingly and shuffled away.

Dakar as observed from its sidewalk cafés is one of life's great free shows; a veritable human smorgasbord. Sleek Africans, robed, briefcased and Italian-shod, walked together with Europeans, Levantines and Indochinese. Beggars and saints, cheikhs, charlatans and shylocks, taxi drivers, shoeshine boys, hawkers selling beads and sunglasses, and here and there, a drunk coming off an all-nighter and looking for breakfast – all passed by a few feet away.

The best, of course, were the women.

For grace and beauty, Senegalese women are rivalled only by their Somali and Ethiopian sisters. They are tall and slim, with pointed breasts, narrow hips, and high tight rumps balanced on long slender legs. Their skin glows gunmetal-blue in the sunlight, and their eyes are feline and slightly slanted. They tattoo their gums to appear more beautiful, and they like to wear their hair in elaborate snakelike arrangements decorated with cowrie shells and beads.

They are hot-blooded and sharp-tongued, with a vocabulary that would make a Boston cabdriver blush. They can also cook, and since they believe that hot pepper is an aphrodisiac, dinner at your girlfriend's might wind up taking the roof of your mouth off.

Right now, there were hundreds of these rare creatures passing by a scant few inches from my nose, intoxicating my senses with their perfume. One of them caught me looking and showed me the tip of her pink tongue, her eyes sparkling with mischief. I grinned at her. She giggled, spit elegantly through the gap between her front teeth, and kept moving.

"*Enlève ça, chef.*" The waiter had materialized beside me, a bottle of Stork beer in one hand and a bowl of roasted peanuts in the other. He was using his tongue to point to the ashtray, brimming with butts, on the table in front of me.

I lifted the ashtray as he put the peanuts down. He clamped the beer bottle between his legs and uncapped it in one deft motion, using the edge of a large spoon which he had produced from somewhere within the folds of his baggy trousers.

I paid for the beer and tipped him fifty francs.

He grinned, showing me teeth stained from a lifetime of kola nuts. "*Merci, patron*." Scooping up the ashtray, he flung its contents over the top of the potted plants onto the sidewalk beyond, narrowly missing a beggar squatting there. Then he laid the cap carefully back atop my beer bottle and shuffled away.

Nothing beats good service, I thought, as I took a large swallow of beer. It was cold and very good. Inside the bar, someone had put Françoise Hardy on the jukebox, and as the first few bars of *Tous les Garçons et les Filles* drifted out, I pulled the papers I'd stolen from the embassy out from under my shirt and unfolded them.

The first sheet was an official State Department cablegram, marked 'immediate.' I sat up, pushed my beer glass aside, and got ready to pay attention.

Diplomatic cables carry one of four designations: routine, priority, immediate and flash. The routine ones stay in somebody's in-tray until there's nothing better to do. Priority cables are more important, but nothing to get up in the middle of the night about. But if an 'immediate' came rolling in over the wire, feet would be coming off the desktops and hitting the parquet all over the embassy, and if the word 'flash' appeared, you'd hear the ugly wet sound of you-know-what hitting the fan blades as the real panic started, because something big and bad had happened somewhere in the world, and there was incoming on the way.

I grabbed a handful of peanuts from the tray on the table, and began to read.

SECSTATE WASH DC
AMEMB DAKAR 8707
PRIORITY
STATE 080791
DISTRIBUTION: NO DIS
1. FBI HAS INFORMED STATE DEPT THAT CLAUDE ANDRE DIEUDONNE AKA TI-CLAUDE IS EN ROUTE TO SENEGAL. DIEUDONNE IS A HAITIAN CITIZEN WITH A US WORK PERMIT. BACKGROUND MATERIAL BEING SENT TO YOU VIA FAX TODAY.
2. FBI RECORDS SEARCH INDICATES DIEUDONNE MAY HAVE STRONG UNDERWORLD CONNECTIONS IN HAITI AND US. SUSPECTED OF COMPLICITY IN MULTIPLE INSTANCES OF EXTORTION AND MURDER. JUSTICE DEPT CONFIRMS THAT DEPORTATION PROCEEDINGS WILL PROBABLY BEGIN WITHIN THE NEXT THREE MONTHS.
3. DIEUDONNE OBTAINED VISA FOR SENEGAL ONE WEEK AGO. NOW BOOKED ON PAN AM 341 TO DAKAR WEDNESDAY FOURTEENTH ETA YOFF AIRPORT 0600 ZULU.
4. FBI UNABLE TO ASCERTAIN MOTIVE FOR TRIP. REQUEST YOU INFORM HOST COUNTRY SECURITY OFFICIALS OF DIEUDONNE'S ARRIVAL AND ADVISE THEM THAT FBI CONSIDERS DIEUDONNE ARMED AND DANGEROUS. FBI REQUESTS FOLLOWTHROUGH AS APPROPRIATE. MESSAGE ENDS.
SECSTATE

I read it twice, then flipped to the next page. A second cable, this one very short. It was the reply, addressed to 'SECSTATE WASHINGTON' and it didn't even have a paragraph number, because it was only one paragraph long.

INFORMATION RECEIVED. PASSED TO BOUBAKAR DABO, SENEGALESE POLICE COMMISSAIRE. NO INVOLVEMENT OF US MISSION BEYOND THIS.
SHACKLADY

The date on the second cable was three days ago. Shacklady had been telling the truth; he'd passed the message along, straight by the book. And that meant that Dabo had known about Ti-Claude Dieudonné's visit before Malick had.

Which is why, I realized, Dabo wants all of us off the dance floor for this one. He'd gotten the word from the embassy, and didn't follow up. But in the meantime, somebody else from the competing service did follow up, and got killed for his trouble. And because it happened inside city limits, Dabo gets to deal with it. Not good.

I glanced at the rest of the sheets. They were bad fax copies of some photographs and FBI notes that had come in together with the cable. The photos had been taken with a long-range telephoto, and showed Ti-Claude – 'Little Claude' – to be a thin black man of average height and build with a large bushy Afro, a pencil moustache, and a sharp, rodentlike face. In one of the photographs Ti-Claude was smiling, showing two very prominent front teeth.

I looked at him carefully. No doubt about it; it was the guy on the beach. The guy who'd knifed Malick N'Diaye, stolen my car, and taken a shot at me. He looks just like a rat, I thought. And he's got a lot to answer for.

The notes were perfunctory. Ti-Claude Dieudonné had arrived in the US some five years ago, and was suspected of being a contract killer for the big crime families in New York and Baltimore. Informed sources said his specialty was headhunting – finding and killing individuals for a fee. His preferred weapon was the stiletto, but he'd use whatever was at hand, including, in one instance, an electric carving knife. That sent shivers down my spine.

He was suspected of at least five murders, and had been arrested three times on suspicion of murder, but never convicted. Deportation proceedings were entangled in legal red tape, but moving slowly.

And now he was here in Dakar. I folded the papers thoughtfully and stuffed them back in my shirt pocket. The missing piece was the motive. Why the hell would a Haitian fly all the way from New York to West Africa to knife a policeman on the beach in the early morning?

There was more to this, as they say, than meets the eye. But I was damned if I could see what it was.

People on the sidewalk were hurrying now. The air had changed subtly, growing thicker and more fragrant, taking on a greenish-yellow cast. I looked at the sky, and saw that the rain was finally on its way.

I sat quietly sipping the last of my beer as the first drops fell, splattering loudly on the pavement, sending the last passers-by sprinting frantically for cover. Seconds later, the downpour began, a thundering drumming noise as tons of water spilled out of the sky.

It was the very start of the wet season, the time in Africa I liked best. Massive, brooding rainclouds would hang motionless over the country for days at a time, suddenly releasing their rain in a flood. In minutes the rain would end, and the city would be dry again, considerably cooler and somewhat cleaner.

I ordered another beer and listened to the music on the jukebox inside the bar, watching the rain-haze on the roofs of the cars parked along the street, letting my thoughts run together like a triple-decker ice cream cone left out in the sun.

It's good to be back in Senegal, I thought. Senegal was an outpost, the kind of place I felt most relaxed in. The people were proud and elegant, their environment an outback landscape of thorn and baobab that Georgia O'Keeffe would have liked. And out here on the outposts, life was fine: the sun was brighter, the wind fresher, and the beer had a special taste. If I stayed here long enough, I'd recover.

But it was pretty clear to me that this wasn't going to be the quiet, restful vacation I'd planned on. I'd started the morning without a care in the world, and since then I'd encountered a dead policeman, a pretty blonde, and a rat-faced car thief who was both a killer and a lousy shot. I'd been reunited with an old wartime buddy, and because I'd agreed to help him, I'd tried to set the American embassy on fire.

Shit. How could the day get much more complicated?

But despite all this, it was good to be back in Dakar, and especially good to see Bari N'Dour again. He and I had enjoyed some good times together. Of course, it had taken a dirty little war going on just over the border in the south to introduce me to Bari, to get me involved with the place and the people, but I'd never regretted it. Through Bari, I'd come to know the kindness of the Senegalese, and the open space and freedom of the bush country, its baobab trees rising from the red laterite like ancient totems. And in between flights to the combat zone, Bari and I had explored Dakar's back streets.

Dakar was one of the world's great cities, vibrant and alive, its European facade concealing a richness and variety that few of the diplomats and tourists even suspected. Wolofs, Toucouleurs, Mandingues, Sereres and all the other Senegalese ethnic groups existed side by side with Lebanese and Syrian traders from the Levant, Mauritanian Berbers from the northern deserts, Portuguese Creoles from Cabo Verde and Bissau, Viets and Khmers left over from the Indochinese wars, and a dozen others.

In the neighborhoods, the nights were full of music and celebration. We'd watched Wolof *sabars* in Grand Dakar and Fann, where the staccato drumbeats would suddenly quicken pace while the pumping feet of the dancing women sent puffs of dust into the air as the crowd roared and clapped, and people tossed their headscarves into the arena in tribute to the dancer's skill. And in the suburban backyards of SICAP and Dieuppeul, there had been Cap-Verdian *coladeras*, with mountains of spicy food and swarms of small children darting everywhere. The old ladies, brown and wizened like nuts in their faded print granny-dresses, would sit smiling on the sidelines and smoke their pipes and gossip while the men, bottles of Negrita rum balanced on their heads, shuffled and swayed to the music of a live pachanga band.

But I could see that things were changing. Senegal was different now to what it had been only a few short years ago. The Senegalese had always been poor, and of necessity they were good at doing more with less, but after years of drought and bad economic planning, they were running out of less.

The country had been running for centuries using a system of political and religious patronage which made Mayor Daley's Chicago look like first-grade show and tell, but now the system was finally starting to come apart. There was more unemployment, less food, and less money. The city itself seemed older somehow, dustier and drier than I'd remembered it.

The international carpetbaggers had had a good run here, of course – the technicians, academics, diplomats, and businessmen, all professional hustlers in the latest development shell game. But they seemed like vultures now, huddled around a dying carcass.

The money was drying up, and there was a sense that the game was coming to an end. And it was happening all over West Africa. Sweep up the floor, fold up the tables, and send everyone out into the cold light of dawn. Game's over. Time, gentlemen, please.

A group of Wolofs sat down at the table next to me and ordered whiskey-cocas in loud voices. They were smoking black-market Marlboros and wearing second-hand Levis they'd picked up in the market. One of them had on an imitation silk jacket, the kind the guys in Vietnam had favored, with 'Plenty Money This Year' written across the back in big red letters.

Keep hoping, I thought.

I picked up my change and walked slowly down the street, ignoring a *bana-bana* hawker who opened his voluminous boubou to me like a flasher, revealing cigarette cartons and rows of cheap watches.

On the side streets, the drains had overflowed, littering the gutters with the junk which had come floating up out of the sewers, buoyed on the tide of rising water. I stepped across a large dead rat, practically the size of a small dog. Tomorrow, in the hot sun, it would begin to smell. Its large yellow teeth gleamed at me, and I thought for a moment of the photograph of Ti-Claude that I had in my pocket.

I shivered and walked on up the street, toward the Dragon d'Or.

CHAPTER SIX

The narrow streets hidden behind the Avenue Lamine Gueye date from the earliest days of Dakar. A European quarter in colonial times, today's inhabitants are African artisans and workers, together with a few creoles from Cabo Verde. Washing hangs over the balconies, children play in the alleys, and pushcart vendors shout their wares as they move slowly past the doorways. Scattered among the shops and stores are cafés, cheap hotels and late-night bars. And the Dragon d'Or – one of the best Vietnamese restaurants in town.

I walked slowly up the street, taking my time, looking from side to side. I was early for my lunch date with Lindy Greenwood, but not because I valued punctuality. Malick N'Diaye had had a receipt from the Dragon d'Or in his pocket when he'd been killed, and Bari had said that Malick couldn't stand Vietnamese food. So if he'd spent time in a Vietnamese restaurant, it was for something other than the noodles.

I was betting that whatever it was, it involved Ti-Claude, the rat-faced man. Bari wanted to find him, and so did I. After all, if you go around letting total strangers steal your car and take shots at you, you won't keep your reputation for long.

It was siesta time, and most of the activity on the street had stopped. Here and there, sweaty porters pushed wheeled carts piled high with fruit and vegetables up the street toward the market. The smell of rice and fish wafted from the open doorways, and from somewhere on an upper floor, a transistor radio played Arabic music.

The only shops still open were those of the Mauritanians. The Mauritanians never closed, as far as I could tell. Their tiny shops, made of flattened tin cans and packing crates, crouched in the narrow alleyways between the buildings. In the cramped and gloomy interiors, turbaned Maures squatted on the dirt floor, getting up from time to time to sell a box of sugar or a packet of cigarettes. The rest of the time they seemed to spend brewing endless cups of strong, sweet mint tea, reading from the Koran, or chatting among themselves in a Berber dialect which sounded like the desert wind at night.

The Dragon d'Or sat wedged in between a *quincaillerie* on one side and a barbershop on the other, looking bright and freshly painted. '*Cuisine Nord-Vietnamienne*' was neatly lettered over the door. I went through the open door and took a seat by the window.

The owner, a diminutive woman in a flowered cheongsam, greeted me. I asked her for a large Stork. When it came, I pulled out Malick's receipt and showed it to her.

"I remember him," she said after a moment. "He came in twice. Last time yesterday. Sat right over there." She pointed to another window seat.

She shook her head. "Ate nothing, just drank coffee. Five, six coffees. No food."

"Just coffee? He just sat and drank coffee?"

She shrugged. "Waiting, maybe. Watching. What for? Who knows?" She bent to lay silverware on the table, already embarrassed by having told me so much.

I looked up to see Lindy Greenwood coming in the door. She looked radiant in her light summer dress, long blonde hair loose and shining.

She saw me and flashed me a wide smile. "Hey, you came after all." She slipped into the seat across from me. "I was afraid you might change your mind."

"Why would you think that?" I said.

She shrugged. "I don't know. I thought I might have come on a little strong or something this morning." She looked at the bottle of Stork in front of me. "Can I have one of those?"

I looked at the woman in the cheongsam, who nodded happily.

"One beer," she said, beaming at Lindy. "And a menu," she added, sliding it across the table.

I glanced at it, and then at Lindy. "Want to order?"

She gave an embarrassed grin. "I have no idea what to ask for," she confessed. "But I wanted to come here because I'd heard it was a nice place to eat. Besides, it's right across the street from my hotel."

I looked across the street to the flea-bag hotel I'd noticed earlier. A faded and peeling sign on the side identified it as the 'Auberge Jaune' – the Yellow Inn. "That's your hotel?"

She shrugged. "Okay, so it's a dump. But it's cheap, and I'm nearly broke." She bent to the menu. "Do you know anything about Vietnamese food?"

"A little."

I turned to the owner and ordered nems and transparent noodle soup. She smiled broadly, nodded, and walked off toward the kitchen.

Lindy was watching me, a faint smile on her lips. I watched her back. Her skin was golden brown against the yellow of her dress, and her eyes were a deep green, with irises like fractured glass. I felt my chest tighten a little.

Her beer came, and I poured it for her. We sat quietly for a moment, looking at each other. "Well," I said finally.

She smiled and put her hand on my arm. Her fingers were cool and strong. "It's okay," she said. "You don't have to say anything. You like looking at me?"

I nodded.

"Well, I like looking at you, too," she said. "You're cute."

"Cute?"

"Yeah. You know – nice-looking?"

I stared at her, feeling my cheeks slowly growing warm. My God, I thought, I'm blushing.

She took her hand away. "I'm sorry, I've made you go all pink. I guess I am a little forward sometimes. That's my dad's fault, I think. He always told me if I saw something I wanted, to just go out there and get it." She grinned. "I guess that could include people, too, don't you think?"

She sat up and brushed her hair back. "Oh, boy, me and my big mouth. Well, I'll try to behave, okay?" She took a ladylike sip of beer. "What do you want to talk about? The weather, perhaps?" She flashed her eyes at me and giggled.

I choked down some beer, thinking desperately of something to say. "Ah, tell me about rehabilitating chimpanzees," I said after a moment. "Isn't that a somewhat unusual line of work?"

Lindy grinned. "Serious talk, huh? Okay. No, it's not that unusual, not if you're an animal psychologist like me. Interspecies communication is the new field, Max. Can I call you Max?"

"Sure. I told you that already, remember?"

"Oh, right. Well, like I told that guy Dabo this morning, I run a research station down in the game park," she said. "I've got a grant from Emory University, but it's about to run out."

She brushed her hair back. "That's why I came up to Dakar. To make a phone call. Funny to think of travelling five hundred miles to make a phone call, but I'd put in for an extension on the grant, you know, and I had to find out if they'd approved it. There aren't any phones down there – none that call to the States, at any rate – and so I had to come here. Lord knows I needed a change, even for just a couple of days."

"And did they? Approve your grant, I mean."

She frowned. "Nope. I got through yesterday. The budget committee's got problems, no new money for anything this fiscal year. Thought I'd go to the beach this morning to be by myself for a little while." She smiled softly. "Didn't quite turn out that way, did it?"

"So what happens to your project if there's no more money?"

She picked at her beer label, shredding it into tiny pieces. "Well, unless I can find some money somewhere, I'm going to have to shut everything down at the end of the rainy season, throw away nearly a year's work." She sighed. "I'm going back down to the game park day after tomorrow."

"You run this research station all by yourself? What exactly do you do down there?"

"It's officially called a 'cognitive re-orientation experiment,'" she said. "I've got fifteen chimps at the station, and I'm teaching them to re-adapt themselves to the wild again. All of the chimps in camp, you see – except the very little ones who were born since the project began – came from somewhere else. Zoos, labs, or private individuals. They're waste products, in a sense."

"Waste products? What do you mean?"

She looked at me, her eyes serious. "At first, baby chimps are like baby kittens – small and cute and playful. But once a chimp is fully grown – say at about age fifteen – they turn into problems. They're tremendously strong, for one thing. They also go through hormonal changes, so they're not so docile and sweet-tempered anymore. They start attacking people or tearing things to bits, and they're not that easy to control." She paused. "So they're not much good for the circus, anymore. Or for research. And they're certainly not suitable for pets."

I nodded. "And I take it there aren't many retirement homes for unwanted chimps?"

"Right. So I got the idea, last year, to try an experiment – to see if I could re-adapt them to natural conditions. I got a dozen chimps, donated to the Center. Not all are fully mature, of course. Thank God, because I doubt if I could control them if they were. But in one way or another, all of them have outlived their usefulness, as far as their keepers were concerned."

"And how do the chimps feel about being put back into the wild?"

She looked at me. "It's not as if they had a choice, Max. At maturity, they're already basically unfit for human society. So we have to teach them to adapt."

"Sounds like a lot of work," I said.

"We owe it to them." She put down her beer. "For every circus chimp on roller skates, there are a bunch of dead ones. And–"

I raised my hand. "Wait. I don't follow you. Where do the dead ones come in?"

"Do you know how they're captured in the wild?"

I shook my head.

"Well," she continued, "to capture a chimp, you don't go after the adults – they're too wild and strong. You get the babies, the helpless ones. But because chimpanzees travel in bands and because they'll fight to defend each other, you sometimes have to kill most of the band to get one baby chimp. So every chimp that's been captured has probably seen its mother get killed, for a start. And of the babies that are captured, half will die later, on the way to market or in captivity. So the next time you see a cute little chimp on TV, think about how they got there."

"Jesus," I said softly.

"All of the bigger chimps I've got at the research station have been captured in the wild when they were very young. The oldest one's a male named Bobo. Bobo was taken not far from here, in fact – down toward the Guinea border."

She looked at me. "So I'm teaching them to live like real chimpanzees again, instead of like poor imitations of humans. It's tough sometimes, but they're making progress." She paused. "The problem is, they need at least another year, and the way things stand now, they won't get it."

"What happens to them then?"

She shook her head. "That's what I worry about, Max. I'm not sure they're going to make it on their own if I leave them that early. Unless they know exactly what they're doing in the bush, they're going to get picked off fast. That's what the grant extension was for, you see – to buy them the extra time they needed."

Our food came, and we sat quietly for a while, eating the nems. Lindy had never had Vietnamese food before, so I showed her how to cut the nems and wrap them in lettuce before dipping them in the fish sauce.

She made a face. "Tastes great, but God, it smells like dirty socks. What is it?"

"The sauce? The Vietnamese call it *nuoc mam*. It's an acquired taste, I guess. You get to like it after a while. I ate a lot of it when I was in Vietnam."

"I thought they flew in steaks and ice cream for you guys, stuff like that."

"Not in prison camp." I picked up a nem. "This stuff is a whole lot better than what they gave us in the camp, as a matter of fact. But we got a lot of fish sauce, which is high in nutrients – it's what kept us alive." I smiled at her. "I can ask them for a peanut butter and jelly sandwich if you prefer."

"Don't get smart." She put her nem down. "I asked you out because I wanted to find out more about you, but so far, I've been doing all the talking." She leaned forward. "So tell me about yourself, *Mister* Donovan. Where you come from, what you do, and who the hell you actually are. Let's start with the basics, okay?"

"Okay."

"Married?"

I laughed and shook my head. "Not even seriously involved."

"Thank heavens. But you were a football hero in high school, right?"

"Wrong." I spoke around a nem. "I was an Air Force brat; grew up overseas, mostly. Asia and Europe. The international high school I went to in Bangkok didn't have a football team, and anyway, there were more interesting things to do."

She leaned forward, her eyes on mine. "Girls?"

"Better than that, even. Flying. My first summer job was as a kicker." I saw the question in her eyes, and grinned. "A kicker is a guy who kicks stuff out of airplanes. Every day for three months, I stood strapped into the doorframe of an Air America C-47 and used my feet to shove 50-kilo rice bags down onto jungle villages in Laos and Cambodia."

"The hearts and minds thing, I get it," she said. "Wasn't that dangerous?"

"Maybe. Probably. I don't remember. I didn't have a whole lot of sense back then." I chewed for a minute. "Nor later on, come to that. I got my pilot's license, and then out of college, got involved in the war. They kept trying to teach me how to kill people, but somehow I never managed to get the hang of it. Finally, they gave up and assigned me to medivac."

She nodded. "That must have been a lot safer."

"Not so I noticed. I had three crash-landings and a year in a POW camp. After that, I kind of figured my military obligation had been taken care of."

"So what did you do then?"

I shrugged. "What we all did; looked for work. I tried the US for a few months, but I was just a face in the crowd." I took a sip of beer. "So I lit out for the territories. I worked here in Dakar for a year or so, flying relief food around the Sahel during the drought. That's where I met Bari N'Dour."

"This was part of the relief thing?"

"Well, no. What Bari and I did was a little extracurricular, actually. Bari wasn't a cop then; he was with the Senegalese Army, and they were providing covert support to the freedom fighters in Guinea-Bissau, which was under Portuguese control at the time. So I flew food relief for the UN during the week, and helped out the Senegalese Army a little on weekends. You know – guns, medicine, stuff like that. Nothing really exciting."

I took another bite of my nem. "After that, I just kept moving around, flying things here and there. I wound up in New Guinea." I chewed noisily. "And then one day, coming through The Gap north of Port Moresby, both engines cut out at once. I walked out at Woitape a week later, and by then, I'd decided that my flying days were over. So I made a mid-career change. I became a supplier."

"A supplier? Of what?"

I smiled. "Of whatever you want. Wherever it is."

She put down her fork. "I'm missing something, again, right? Is what you do legal?"

"Legal and illegal are matters of opinion," I said. "I'll give you an example. When I worked here during the drought, a lot of people were starving. Know what one of the biggest problems was? Government corruption and red tape. Customs procedures were holding up food shipments, everybody was taking a cut, and in some places, food was being used as a political weapon against opposition parties."

She nodded. "I've heard about that in Ethiopia."

"It happened here, too. So from time to time, we'd load up a plane at night, fly it in low across the border, and land in some farmer's peanut field. We'd pass out the food ourselves, and to hell with the government. Illegal? You bet. And I'd do it again tomorrow if I had to."

I picked up the last nem. "Split it with you," I said.

She shook her head, so I ate it in three bites.

"So these days," I said when I had finished, "I'm sort of a boondocks bloodhound. People send me to paw through the garbage cans on the outposts, the places not many people know about. When I find something interesting, I make a deal."

She watched me carefully. "And what kind of things do you look for?"

I shrugged. "Anything you want. I mainly look for stuff that's lost, stolen or strayed. Often, it's a person. Hostages, runaways, fly-by-nights."

"Seems like a strange thing to do for work," she said.

"It's not work," I said. "Work is what someone else wants you to do. I operate on my own, and I'm good at what I do. I can find things, because I know a lot of the hiding places, and because I'm a natural-born hider myself.

I put myself in someone else's skin, and then it's just a matter of following the tracks."

She looked at me. "Just that easy, huh?"

I gave her my best smile. "No, of course not. Following the tracks is easy. The hard part is dealing with what you sometimes find at the other end of the trail."

She finished her beer and patted her mouth with the napkin. "You haven't mentioned the embassy," she said. "Is that what you were doing there? Following the tracks?"

"The embassy?"

"You know; the information you went to collect. For your gendarme friend, Bari N'Dour." She leaned forward. "So what happened? Did you find out anything?"

"As a matter of fact, I did."

Briefly, I told her about the file. I left out details of how I'd gotten it.

"Seems like Bari's partner walked into something he wasn't expecting," I concluded. "The embassy received this cable from the FBI five days ago, and Shacklady says he passed the information straight on to Dabo. Dabo sat on the information a little longer than he should have. If he'd passed around what he knew, Malick N'Diaye might still be alive."

"And you think this Haitian – Ti-Claude – was the one who killed him? The one we saw this morning?"

I nodded.

"But what would the motive have been?"

I shrugged. "Anybody's guess at this point. You want mine? Okay, here it is. Malick was investigating organized crime for Bari, trying to trace the connections to the outside. Naturally, he'd be interested in something like this. Maybe Malick met Ti-Claude's flight, started to shadow him."

I paused. "That's a dangerous thing to do if the man you're trailing is a real professional, because you're likely to get spotted. And if Ti-Claude came here on business, he wouldn't welcome the attention at all. He might have decided to just get rid of anyone who seemed to be following him."

I brought out the folded sheets from my pocket and laid them on the table. "Anyway, it's just a guess. Bari wanted to know what Malick found out at the embassy, and this is it. My guess is he'll try and find this guy Ti-Claude and bring him in for questioning." I tapped the photograph. "Look at him – with teeth and hair like that, Ti-Claude ought to stand out pretty well in a crowd, don't you think?"

Lindy opened her mouth to say something, but I never gave her a chance to speak. I was looking past her, over her shoulder and out the window at something that had caught my eye. Across the street, the door to the Auberge Jaune had opened, and a man had stepped out onto the sidewalk. My fingers tightened on her arm.

"Max, what is it? Max, you're hurting me!"

"It's him."

"Him? Who?"

"The guy in the photographs. Ti-Claude. He's across the street. No, don't turn around. He's coming this way."

It was unmistakably Ti-Claude. He came slowly down the steps of the Auberge Jaune, his eyes moving from side to side, looking for all the world like a tall, thin rat.

Lindy's eyes were wide. "He's coming here? What are we going to do?"

"Stay put, that's what," I said. "And don't look at him. He only got a glimpse of us before, remember."

By the time Ti-Claude came through the door, Lindy had on a pair of extra-large sunglasses and was studying the tablecloth closely. I had my face hidden behind a section of the morning edition of the *Soleil*. '*Gagnez la Loterie Nationale*,' said an ad in boldface type two inches from my nose.

I kept quiet as a mouse, listening to him ask the hostess for a packet of Gauloises and change for the telephone.

While she was getting the cigarettes, he asked her what time dinner was served.

A moment later, I peeped over the top of the paper to see him speaking quietly into the telephone in the far corner. He nodded twice, spoke again, and hung up. Then he lit a cigarette and went out the door.

I put the newspaper down and took a deep breath. He didn't recognize us, I thought with relief. All good now. But just a little scary all the same.

"Aren't you going to call Bari N'Dour?"

I watched Ti-Claude get into a cab. "Uh-huh. But right now, I'm curious about where he's going." I looked at her. "I'm going to follow him. Want to come?"

Her eyes shone. "I thought you'd never ask."

CHAPTER SEVEN

The whistle in the wheelhouse blew a long blast, and last-minute passengers scrambled aboard. A moment later, the *Blaise Diagne* cast off its mooring ropes and moved away from the dock, its engines throbbing. Lindy and I moved forward to take seats on the open deck, where I could keep an eye on Ti-Claude.

We were headed out of Dakar harbor toward the island of Gorée, riding the commuter chaloupe which left every half hour. I stood at the railing, watching the freighters slip by as we nosed out into the open water toward the island. I looked back at the skyline of the city, brilliant white in the sunshine. The chaloupe was clearing the harbor breakwater now, coming about on its main course toward Gorée, straight ahead across the open water. We rode the outgoing tide, enjoying the cool breeze coming off the water.

Many of our fellow passengers were tourists, out for a sightseeing trip to the island. Most of them, I knew, would be visiting the slavery museum, the restored structure from which human cargoes were dispatched to the plantations and mines of the New World. Others would inspect the ruins of the French fortifications atop the island's seaward bluff, where massive artillery works sat rusting in the hot sun. Ti-Claude, I was sure, was interested in neither.

We had jumped in a taxi and followed Ti-Claude down through town to the port, watching as he got out, paid his driver, and walked out onto the chaloupe's crowded dock. The *Blaise Diagne* was preparing to leave even as we arrived. Keeping him in sight, we hurried to join the throng of passengers queuing for tickets. There was barely time to get on board.

Now the chaloupe was swinging around the small island, and we had a view of the prison at one end and the high bluffs at the other. A narrow strip of beach lay in the middle, the landing dock jutting out from it like a long black finger. The *Blaise Diagne* gave several warning blasts on her horn, and the pitch of the engines changed as the pilot began slowing the chaloupe.

The small cafés and restaurants near the wharf were crammed with people. Further back, the regal bulk of the Chevalier de Boufflers Hotel looked down on the beach. Strollers in bright tourist outfits thronged Gorée's narrow streets, clutching souvenirs and beach-bags. By evening, I knew, the island would once again belong to its inhabitants.

I helped Lindy off the boat. "Now we follow him," I said. "See what he does."

"And then?"

I shrugged. "Who knows? But if you behave yourself, I'll buy you an ice cream later."

She gave my hand a squeeze and laughed, her teeth very white. "You're trying to steal my heart, aren't you? God, I can hardly wait."

"For the ice cream? Or to have your heart stolen?"

"Oh, look, he's going up there."

Ti-Claude was heading straight up a narrow alley that led toward the bluff at the end of the island. We followed at a discreet distance, keeping several groups of tourists between us. He walked purposefully, looking to neither left nor right, taking no notice of the colorful stalls or sidewalk restaurants.

The alley turned a sharp corner. We came around it just in time to see Ti-Claude entering a side door in the wall. Beyond, the alley ended abruptly, opening onto the steep rocky bluff that formed this side of the island, plunging nearly straight down into the cool green water.

I looked at the door through which Ti-Claude had disappeared. It was let into the high wall which ran along the length of the alley, and which blocked the house behind from public view. Much of Gorée is built like an Arab medina, with drab walls concealing the splendor of some magnificent older mansions behind them. Standing on tiptoe, I could just make out the roof of what looked like a large, ornate house.

I thought about trying the door myself, but just then I caught sight of two men, almost concealed in a deep alcove beside the door. They were watching me with hooded eyes. They looked Levantine, not African, and both were wearing jackets and ties. As I watched, one leaned over to say something to the other, and as the material of his jacket pulled tight, I could see that he was wearing a shoulder holster.

Lindy'd seen it, too. "Bodyguard?" she murmured quietly. I nodded. She looked at me. "So what's our next move?"

I glanced around. There was a small boutique right at the end of the alley, set into the wall beside the steep bluff. "Time for that ice cream, I think," I said, taking her arm. "And perhaps a telephone call."

The boutique had ice cream, but no telephone. Bari N'Dour would have to wait a little longer. We ordered chocolate cones, and as I paid, I asked the storekeeper, "Who owns that big house down the street, the one with the guards in front?"

He looked at me for a moment. "That belongs to Rachid Khoury, *monsieur*," he said carefully. "Why do you ask?"

I caught something in his tone of voice. "No reason," I said lightly. "It's a pretty big house, isn't it?"

"Monsieur Khoury is a very rich man," the storekeeper said simply. "He has another house in the city, I believe." He pointed down the bluff to the water, where a seaplane lay moored offshore. "He also has an airplane."

I smiled. "That's very nice. And what does he do for a living?"

The storekeeper's eyes slid away and his face closed up. "*Je n'ai aucune idée, monsieur*," he said quietly. "I have no idea."

Well, thank you very much, I thought. We ate our ice cream slowly, poking through the small shop, looking at this and that, passing the time.

"What if he doesn't come out?" Lindy said finally. "What if he's there for dinner or something? I mean, this is fun in a strange kind of way, but–"

"Shh," I said. "Someone's coming now."

With a creak, the old door was opening. Ti-Claude emerged, carrying a manila envelope in his hand, and as we watched, hurried down the street toward the dock.

I turned to the shopkeeper. "Another ice cream, please. And give my sister here whatever she wants."

"Aren't you going to follow him?" Lindy said. "He might get away!"

"We're on an island, remember? And the next chaloupe's not due to leave for another twenty minutes." I turned back to the shopkeeper. "I'll try the vanilla this time, I think."

Five minutes later, I heard a familiar noise. Looking out the shop's tiny window at the water below, I could see Khoury's seaplane spanking across the waves, rising into the bright sunshine, heading north.

* * *

I stood fifty feet away from Ti-Claude, telephone receiver to my ear, dialing Bari N'Dour's number. His voice came on the line over the hiss and crackle of static that sounded like an army of cockroaches eating the wires. For all I knew they were. I wondered for perhaps the thousandth time why the French had never managed somehow to give their ex-colonies a decent telephone system.

"Max, is that you?" His voice sounded as if he were squatting at the bottom of a deep well. "Good news, Max. Dabo's men scored a coup – they found your car half an hour ago, near the fish market. I'll get it back to you as soon as I can. Listen, are you all right? There was a fire and security alert at the American embassy this morning. What the hell did–"

"Never mind that," I said. "Listen carefully, I don't have much time." I began to explain what we'd seen.

We'd followed Ti-Claude back aboard the chaloupe. Once on the mainland again, we'd tailed his taxi along Dakar's seafront corniche to the government-run Artisans' Village, on the beach at the site of the old fishing village of Soumbedioune. The Artisans' Village is a tightly packed collection of small handicraft shops, and because everything was jammed together, it was easy to keep an eye on Ti-Claude.

At this hour of the afternoon, the place was thronged with tourists. Ti-Claude had spent the last twenty minutes drifting among them, looking at the displays of weaving, gold- and silverwork, and woodcarving, examining the merchandise, chatting with the sellers, moving slowly on down to the next stalls. Right now, he was standing in front of one particular woodcarving shop. He'd been there for the last ten minutes, looking at the various items for sale and talking with the shop owner.

There was a pay phone two shops down the line. Keeping one eye on Ti-Claude, I quickly told Bari everything we had seen earlier that afternoon, on Gorée. When I finished, I could hear him sigh.

"Good work, Max. It's too bad that Rachid Khoury's involved, though. That makes things a lot more complicated."

"You know Khoury?"

"That's an understatement," he said. "I'll explain about Khoury when I see you."

Ti-Claude put down the carving he'd been examining. Nodding absently to the woodcarver, he began drifting out of sight. I signaled for Lindy to follow him. She nodded and moved off.

"So what are you waiting for?" I said to Bari. "You know who Ti-Claude is now, and where he is. Why don't you just get over here and arrest him?"

"It's not that simple. Jurisdiction, remember? This is Dabo's territory, and it's his case. As long as Ti-Claude stays in the city, I can't touch him – not on the basis of what we know so far, anyway." He paused. "So the best thing is to let Ti-Claude run for a day or two, give him some rope and see what he does with it. And in the meantime, try and get something on the bastard."

"Like what?" I'd already guessed what was on his mind, but I wanted him to say it.

"Like the envelope he just got from Rachid Khoury. That would do very nicely." Another pause. "Think you can manage that?"

"Jesus, Bari." I held the receiver to my ear, considering. What the hell, I decided. The sonofabitch had stolen my car and shot at me, hadn't he? So I owed him one.

"Consider it done," I said at last.

"That's the spirit," said Bari. "Don't take any chances, though. Remember – he's still got Malick's gun." He hung up.

I walked over to the woodcarver's stall. "He's looking at the woven mats now," Lindy said in a quiet voice. "Three stalls over on the right."

I nodded.

The woodcarver spied us and came forward. "*Vous désirez?*"

"He was looking at these," Lindy murmured in English, indicating a rack of carved African heads on the display table in front of us. I picked up one of the heads and examined it. It was made of cheap wood, smeared with shoe polish to make it appear like ebony, and I was willing to bet that the woodcarver had an army of ten-year olds out behind the shop manufacturing them by the dozen. They were crude, almost childish, easily the least attractive things in the shop. Does Ti-Claude have such bad taste, I wondered, or is his interest for some other reason?

The shopowner beamed. "Superb quality, *chef*. An excellent choice. For you, a very special price."

I shook my head and handed it back to him. Lindy touched my arm.

"He's leaving," she said. "Come on."

The woodcarver passed a business card across to me. "Next time, *monsieur*, I'll make you a good bargain on something nice. Just ask for me – my name's on the card."

I nodded absently and stuffed the card into my shirt pocket without looking at it. Then I hurried to catch up with Lindy.

* * *

We followed Ti-Claude's taxi slowly back through town. It was six o'clock now, rush hour, and the streets were choked with cars. We were crawling up the Avenue Pompidou, near the sidewalk cafés, when Lindy muttered, "Damn, he's stopping."

I tapped our driver on the shoulder. "Pull up ahead," I said. "And keep the motor running."

"*D'accord, patron.*"

Adjusting the side mirror, I watched Ti-Claude as he left his taxi and walked over to where two young long-haired white guys sat cross-legged in front of the post office steps, begging from the passersby.

I studied them closely. They were most likely Europeans of some kind. They certainly weren't Americans – you can generally tell an American overseas at a hundred yards. They looked to be in their early twenties or late teens, in need of a bath, a good meal, and a course of vitamins. I'd seen many of their tribe. They were spear-carriers in a modern Children's Crusade, following each other along the hippie trail from Morocco to West Africa, and from there vaguely on toward Asia. They were basic Eurotrash playing at being pilgrims, wandering across the poorer countries in search of their private vision of the Holy Grail, leaving parents or loved ones behind. But the road to nirvana often went through some pretty ugly country, metaphorically speaking, and not everybody finished the trip. These two looked like they'd gone about as far as they were going to.

We were too far away to hear what Ti-Claude was saying to them, but whatever it was, he had their undivided attention. He spoke for several minutes, and they nodded frequently. Finally, one of them said something back to him. Ti-Claude smiled, tapped his wristwatch, and stood up, dropping a banknote into the upended hat. Then he climbed back into his waiting taxi and drove off.

"What the hell was that all about?" said Lindy as our driver put the Renault in gear and eased back into the traffic.

"No idea. Maybe he wants to take panhandling lessons."

Dusk was settling down over the city as we followed Ti-Claude's taxi back up the Rue Blanchot. We pulled in behind a peanut truck and watched as he got out and went into the Auberge Jaune. He was pulling a key from his pocket as he went up the steps.

"Jeepers," said Lindy. "Do you suppose he lives there? I mean, that's where I'm staying, for Pete's sake."

A moment later, a light went on in one of the second-floor rooms.

"He lives there, all right," I said to Lindy. "And you need to change hotels."

She looked at me. "Are you serious?"

"You bet I am. This guy's a killer, remember? You shouldn't be anywhere near him until Bari's got him behind bars. Not under any circumstances." I fished my hotel key out of my pocket and thrust it at her. "Take this," I said. "You can use my room tonight. Hotel Atlantique, down near the Place."

"I know where it is," she said. "But–"

"No buts. The room has twin beds, so we don't need to discuss that part of it. I'm going across the street to the Dragon d'Or for a while. Take the taxi and go to the hotel."

She opened her mouth to protest, but I put a warning finger to her lips.

"Don't argue with me," I said. "Just do it. We can come up here and get your stuff tomorrow." I gave her a smile. "I'll be back at the hotel in a couple of hours, and then we'll go out to dinner. Deal?"

She looked at me. "You really mean it, don't you?"

"I really do."

She shrugged. "It's a deal, then. Where do we go for dinner?"

I opened the taxi door and got out. "Your choice. See you in a little while."

I breathed a sigh of relief as I watched her drive off. Now I could figure out how I was going to get into Ti-Claude's room.

And back out again, in one piece.

CHAPTER EIGHT

I checked my watch, stepped out of the alley, and crossed the street to the Auberge Jaune. It had been half an hour since Lindy had gone off to my hotel. Seven o'clock now, early evening, and people were beginning to reappear on the street again. Ti-Claude had left the Auberge ten minutes ago and gone straight across the street, into the Dragon d'Or. I'd watched as the woman in the cheongsam greeted him, led him to a table, and handed him a menu. When she brought him a beer, I decided to make my move.

Unless he was a really fast eater, I had enough time for what I was about to do.

I pushed open the door to the Auberge Jaune and stepped inside. The lobby was cool, dark and very dirty. An ancient Peul wearing sunglasses, a smudged khaki jacket and baggy Muslim pants dozed peacefully in a wicker chair behind the reception desk. Using some sort of remote-sensing radar, he came awake and erect as I approached.

"*M'sieu?*"

His sunglasses were so dark I could not see his eyes. He must operate like a bat, I thought.

"I'd, ah, like a room," I said. I'd hoped to avoid this part, actually, but there didn't seem any chance of that.

The Peul extracted a lemon mouth-stick from the folds of his trousers and chewed it ruminatively, thinking over my statement. While he was doing that, I ran my eyes over the lobby.

Three or four penniless-looking Europeans sat in the lobby's sagging chairs, clones of the two panhandlers we'd seen earlier in front of the post office. The *routards* would all know about this place. Some of them would spend weeks here, doing very little except getting high in their rooms and emerging every other day or so to get something to eat. They were on a grand adventure, but for most of them, it would consist mainly of time spent in bottom-end hotels like this one, complaining to each other about the locals, and exchanging information about where and how to score.

Maybe Lindy had to stay in places like these because of her research budget, but I didn't think Ti-Claude had to. If he was here, there was a reason for it.

The Peul at the reception desk finally spoke. "*Vous n'avez pas de bagage*," he declared.

"I know I don't have any luggage," I said. "It's coming later."

He looked me up and down and sniffed. "*De toutes les façons*," he said, "we have no rooms available."

I sighed. I took a five thousand franc note out of my pocket and laid it carefully on the desk between us. "Are you sure? It would be cruel indeed to force a weary traveler out into the street."

The Peul's hand came up and the banknote disappeared within it, as if it had never existed. "God forbid," he murmured.

From under the counter he produced a key. "First floor," he said, handing it over to me. "*Soyez le bienvenu.*"

* * *

The bed was of the French chain-mail variety, and sagged alarmingly in the middle. Two long narrow windows looked out on a tiny courtyard, from which came the sounds of Congolese music from a tape player and a faint odor of yamba, the mild Senegalese marijuana.

I watched a cockroach edge cautiously out from under the armoire next to the window, and then scuttle fearfully along the wall. There were bound to be mosquitoes, too, in this part of town, and the bed had no nets. No matter, I thought; I wouldn't be staying the night.

It was fully dark now. Time to make my move.

I'd carefully watched the hotel windows when Ti-Claude went inside, noting the location of his room as the light went on. Now I closed the door to my own room, walked to the end of the corridor, and looked out the end window. I watched the street for a moment, noting the patterns. Only a few people moved through the cones of light thrown by the streetlamps. Taxis purred by occasionally, and once in a while, a goods truck rattled past. Across the street, the Dragon d'Or was filling up with customers.

Ti-Claude should be starting his main course about now, I decided.

I moved back up the hall. Stopping in front of Ti-Claude's door, I took a deep breath, reached into my pocket, and pulled out my American Express card. "Don't leave home without it," I said softly.

* * *

The lock was a simple one, and it responded almost immediately to pressure from the thin plastic card. I opened the door and eased myself quietly into the room, my heart hammering. I closed the door carefully behind me, hearing the lock click back into place. Despite the fact that I had done this – and worse than this – dozens of times before, I had the same ice block in the bottom of my guts as always.

It was a little like the feeling that I'd had as a kid the summer I spent with my aunt and uncle in the Midwest, the summer I'd delivered papers to earn pocket money. The first day on the job, I'd been warned, was the hardest. You had to put the papers up on the porch, and when you opened the gate, you didn't know what might be waiting for you in the yard. The yard might look empty and safe, but some of the houses had watchdogs, and they'd let you get inside and then go for you suddenly, without warning.

So it always paid to look around a little. I stood just inside the door and calmed my breathing, listening to the night, getting used to the place. The light coming in from the streetlamp outside showed me a room as small and dingy as my own, the bed rumpled but unslept in. The window was closed, the air stale-smelling. I crossed the room, opened the window and left it slightly ajar. Then I turned, ready to begin work.

A suitcase lay opened at the foot of the bed, odd bits of clothing spilling from it. I searched that first, finding nothing. Then I moved to the rickety desk in a corner of the room. Change lay scattered across the top of it. I slid open the first drawer, only to find it empty.

I tried the second. Jackpot.

Inside were several handkerchiefs, three pairs of socks, and a manila envelope. The same envelope, I was willing to bet, that Ti-Claude had gotten at Khoury's house earlier in the afternoon. Carefully, I opened the flap of the envelope, turned it upside down, and shook.

A map and three pieces of paper fluttered to the desktop. The map was of Senegal, the standard sort of thing you could pick up at any tourist office. On one side, the entire country was represented. The other side was a map of the streets of downtown Dakar, with points of interest picked out in red. I scanned the map carefully, looking for marks or notations, but found nothing.

One of the pieces of paper was a sheet of ordinary writing bond. It contained a list written in a precise hand in ballpoint. The writing was the thin, spidery kind that French children learn in school. The list was short, and contained four lines, the words written in capital letters.

'ABDOU FALL' was the first one. 'BIRAM THIAM' was the second. The third line said 'LEVIEUX.' The fourth line said simply, 'TOGOLAIS.'

I studied the words carefully, trying to extract their meaning. Abdou Fall and Biram Thiam were men's names, obviously; but *le vieux* meant simply 'the old man,' and there were millions of those in Senegal. And who was 'the Togolese'?

I picked up the remaining two pieces of paper. One was a double-sided brochure describing the Niokolo-Koba game park, including a simple map of the main roads, the tourist hotel at Simenti, and the airstrip. The remaining item was a train timetable for the Dakar-Bamako express.

I spread the items out on the desk and stared at them, willing them to make some kind of sense. When nothing happened after a few minutes, I sighed and checked my watch. I'd been inside Ti-Claude's room for fifteen minutes, and now it was time to take a bow and move offstage before he came back.

I replaced the envelope in the drawer, trying to remember its exact position, and hoping that he hadn't left any telltales to signal a search. What the hell, I thought, pushing the drawer shut, it doesn't matter; this guy is finished as soon as Bari N'Dour gets permission to interrogate him. It won't make any difference if he knows I've tossed his room.

And then I heard something that froze my heart. The sound of a key being inserted into the lock of the door.

I had perhaps five seconds to get out of the room.

I went out the window like greased spit, not knowing or caring what lay on the other side. I was only two floors up, after all, and the worst that could happen was that I'd break every bone in my body as I fell to the sidewalk below.

Which would be a gold-plated bargain compared to what would happen if Ti-Claude caught me in his room.

The ledge outside the window was less than a foot wide, and had probably been mortared together at around the same time as Lincoln was drafting the Gettysburg Address. In places, it had crumbled away almost entirely. I stood spread-eagled, thirty feet above the street, and listened to Ti-Claude's footsteps approach, praying that he wouldn't remember that the window had been latched. Praying, too, that he wasn't about to lean out and feed the pigeons.

Below me, the street was mercifully quiet. So quiet that I could hear the latch on the window click shut, hear his footsteps retreat. Hear the door shut as he went out again and into the corridor. All this above the hammering of my heart.

I looked up into the night sky. Thank you, I thought, whoever you are.

There was a drainpipe on the corner of the building, and I started to edge toward it, inching my way along, keeping my body carefully balanced on the ledge. Below me, I heard the front door of the hotel open. I turned my head and saw Ti-Claude walk out into the street and stop, looking from side to side. A zebra-striped Peugeot taxi turned the corner, honked happily in greeting, and pulled up beside him.

I watched its taillights disappear into the evening. Great. That little caper took ten years off my life, and all I have to show for it is a list of names.

I sighed and edged closer to the drainpipe.

* * *

Ten minutes later I was sitting at the bar in the Dragon d'Or, finishing a double whiskey. The trembling in my hands was almost gone. Another five minutes, I thought, and then I'll call Bari N'Dour. Just then I looked up, and what I saw made me change my mind.

The zebra-striped Peugeot was back. And parked right outside the hotel. I stood up, threw some money on the bar, and went out the door, whistling softly.

Like any good Dakar taximan, he spotted me the moment I came out the door. "*Hssssssst. Chef! Ici, chef! Hssssssst.*"

I walked across the street. The taximan was a sleek, fat Wolof wearing a Modibo Keita cap and an off-white grand boubou with yellow embroidery. I opened the door, and slid into the back seat.

The inside of the cab was decorated with cutouts of French rock stars from the pages of *Paris Match* and *Salut les Copains*, strings of plastic beads, and a large, tinted photograph of the Grand Caliph of the Mouride Islamic Brotherhood, seated in full regalia on what looked like a magic carpet. From a radio-cassette under the dash came the sound of religious chanting.

The license taped to the dash identified the taximan as Modu Gaye, 43 years old, of Sicap-Baobabs. He gave me an incurious glance through the rearview mirror. "*Fann, bokk?*" he said, in the fashion of taximen the world over. "Where to?"

I had Modu figured for someone who would respect the traditional formalities, so I dug in my pocket, found a five thousand franc note, and laid it flat on his meaty shoulder. His eyes went down to the banknote, and then up to meet mine. I don't think I've ever seen someone's eyebrows go so far up.

I dredged up the few words of Wolof I remembered and spoke softly and respectfully in his ear. "*Asalaam aleikum, suma mak.*" I used the form which meant 'elder brother'. "I greet you by your last name and your first and ask if your body is at peace?"

Modu didn't miss a beat. His pudgy hand closed gently around the money, and a second later, it had disappeared into the folds of his boubou. "*Djaam rek*, little brother," he replied. "Peace only. I greet the people of your house. What do you require?"

Bingo. I shifted into French now. "Your last client — the one you picked up here. Where did you take him?"

His face turned towards mine, and in the glow of the restaurant's sign I could see his gold teeth glinting. "The black man?"

I nodded.

"I took him to the post office," he said. "And at the post office, we picked up two more passengers."

I remembered the two Europeans begging on the sidewalk. "Two toubabs with long hair?"

His eyebrows went up again, and he grinned. "Not relatives of yours, I hope. The toubabs smelled. And," he added, "the black is not even an African."

"Where did you take them?"

He clucked in disapproval. "I took them to Yaye Ganaar's."

In the darkness, I smiled to myself. If Ti-Claude and the two Europeans were headed for Yaye Ganaar's bar, then they were headed into territory I knew well. Yaye Ganaar's – well, well. I fished in my pocket and found another banknote. Modu watched me carefully as I unfolded it.

"Let's go," I said, giving him the money. "And may Allah light your path."

Modu jammed the taxi into gear. "*Bissimullahi*." My head snapped back as we roared down the street into the darkness.

CHAPTER NINE

Modu drove me at terrifying speed through the dark side streets, heading down into the tough area around the port. We bounced over potholes and swerved around meandering animals until he finally slammed the cab to a halt, halfway down a dimly lit alley. "*Voilà*," he said.

We had stopped in front of a lighted doorway curtained with brightly colored plastic strips. Somewhere inside, Little Millie Small was belting out *My Boy Lollipop* on the jukebox. If West Africa ever sets up a Music Hall of Fame, that song will be one of the first to be nominated for inclusion.

Two sleepy cigarette and kola nut sellers squatted on the sidewalk, talking quietly. A few feet away, a huge Wolof woman was cooking brochettes for sale over a charcoal brazier. The place looked and felt exactly as it always had, right down to the music.

"Don't bother waiting," I said to Modu. "I might be a while."

He shrugged. "*Comme tu veux,*" he said. "I make the rounds here a couple of times a night."

I pushed through the plastic curtain, pausing to let my eyes accommodate to the dim light. There were few customers tonight – three or four European men, a dozen Africans, and a squad of local girls. No sign of Ti-Claude or his two toubab friends.

The girls stared at me as I walked slowly to the bar, and one or two smiled shyly. Such accomplished actresses should be on stage, I thought; in Dakar, a shy bargirl was the ultimate oxymoron.

The bar's centerpiece was a large neon sign advertising Kronenbourg beer. Underneath it, a tight-lipped, sharp-faced métisse looked up from her newspaper. "*A boire?*"

I nodded, ordered Stork, and paid. Then I pulled out one of my cards and pushed it across the bar. "Give this to Yaye Ganaar, will you?"

She looked at me for a long moment. Finally she shrugged, moving off with catlike grace through a door behind the bar. In a moment she was back, tilting her head sideways to indicate that I was to enter. I picked up my beer and went into the back room.

Yaye Ganaar sat enthroned in a huge, overstuffed armchair, smoking a bone pipe filled with acrid black tobacco and playing *mariage* with four old men. I entered quietly and greeted everyone in turn, shaking hands and murmuring "*salaam aleikum.*" The responses were automatic; no one looked up from their cards. Two of them moved aside slightly on their bench to let me sit down.

Yaye Ganaar was even bigger than I'd remembered. Swathed in a dozen yards of expensive cloth and sporting a towering red wig and billowing headscarf, she resembled a three-masted Yankee clipper under full sail. Like most Wolof women, she wore her wealth, and the rings, bracelets and necklaces she sported must have been worth thousands. Her palms, lips and feet were dyed orange-red with henna, and her gums were tattooed bright blue. She'd told me once that she'd had three husbands.

I wondered if any of them were still alive.

"*Ndeysaan*, it's little Max, after all this time." She smiled, her gold teeth glittering in the smoky light of the room. "Where the hell have you been hiding?" She leaned forward, peering at me. "Married yet? No, I see not. Married men have a look about them."

She cackled gleefully as she began to deal again. "Plenty of women out in the bar, Max. Take your pick." She paused. "You in or out?"

"I didn't come for cards, mother," I said, grinning. "Or for women. I'm looking for some people."

Her eyes narrowed as I described Ti-Claude and the two Europeans. "I remember them," she said. "They were here not long ago. The rat-faced black and the three toubabs." She slapped a card down on the table.

"Three white men?"

"That's what I said, didn't I? Two filthy ones, and another with a moustache." She sniffed. "At least he looked as if he knew what a shower was for."

She turned and pointed out the one-way mirror into the bar. "The one with the moustache came early and waited for the others, in that booth over there, against the wall. They talked for a few minutes, and then he left. The black and the two filthy pigs stayed behind for a while." She made a noise of disgust. "The toubabs had hair down to

71

their shoulders. I've seen them before – they sit on the sidewalk by the post office and beg."

She shook her head disgustedly. "They drank Coca-Cola, of all things; I had to send a girl out for it."

She refilled her pipe. "Toubabs," she said thoughtfully, "are not what they used to be."

"Tell me about the black one," I said. "What did he do here?"

"Do? The black was even worse than the toubabs – he drank nothing at all. He isn't from here – I've never seen him before."

She turned to me, her eyes snapping. "And I'll tell you what else he did, Max. He hurt one of my girls."

She indicated a plump girl sitting against the wall in the far corner of the room. "Ami over there tried to get him interested in her, but they got in an argument instead. She says he hurt her arm, so I told her to take the night off."

"If they didn't want women," I said, "and they didn't want to drink, what did they want?"

Yaye Ganaar sniffed. "*Yamba*. They wanted yamba. The black one wanted Ami to get some for him. When she refused, he twisted her arm."

I sat up a little straighter. "Yamba? Marijuana?"

She shifted on her chair and puffed herself up in indignation. "I told them to look elsewhere. 'This is a social club, *messieurs*,' I said to them. 'Not a damned opium den.' Finally they left."

"Where did they go?"

She shrugged. "Who knows? I told Ami to get rid of them." She peered at me through the pipe smoke. "Why all the questions, Max?"

"It's important, mother. I need to find him."

She looked at me for a moment, and then nodded. "Yes," she said. "He's a bad one, isn't he? I could tell. But he's dangerous, Max; I can tell that, too."

"I'll be careful," I told her quietly.

She sighed. "Ask Ami, then." She turned. "Ami, *waaye!*" Her voice could pierce sheet steel.

The girl looked up. "*Naam.*"

"*Kaaye!*"

Ami stood up and shuffled across the floor, wearing a suspicious frown and rubbing her arm. Yaye Ganaar spoke rapidly to her for a moment in Wolof. Then the girl turned to me and spoke in French.

"They went down the street," she said. "To the Jardin d'Attractions. The black one, he was bad – *très méchant*. He hurt my arm when I told him we didn't sell yamba here."

Yaye Ganaar began to deal out the cards again. "*Ah, oui, le Jardin d'Attractions,*" she said. "Plenty of yamba there." She sniffed. "Plenty of syphilis, too. Sure you don't want to play?"

I stood up. "I've got to be going," I said. "Thanks for the information."

I kissed her goodbye on both cheeks and headed out the door.

"Max."

I turned. "Yes, mother?"

She fixed me with a beady eye. "Be careful, Max. Don't do anything stupid."

* * *

The Jardin d'Attractions was only two streets over, but a world away. If Yaye Ganaar's was a friendly neighborhood brothel, the Jardin was an industrial-strength whorehouse.

I stopped just inside the beaded curtain. Franco and the OK Jazz were on the jukebox singing *Infidelité Mado*, but I couldn't afford to sit and enjoy the music right now. I needed to figure out what had happened to Ti-Claude and his two companions.

I also needed to make sure I came back out the door in one piece. The Jardin had a rock-solid reputation as one of Dakar's toughest bars, a meeting place for the hard core.

The word on the street had always been that for the right price, anything could be bought or sold at the Jardin, and that sex, drugs, and contraband were only the more legitimate side of the business. So I took a moment to look around.

It was the usual late-night snakepit, a red-lit hell worthy of a John Carpenter movie. In the smoky gloom, pinpoints of light glinted from glasses, bottles, and metal fixtures. The clientele tonight was a mixture of European and African men, and everyone was getting along just fine. Most of the bar's customers, in fact, seemed far too wasted to notice such subtle differences as skin color.

Three drunk French paratroopers slumped over the bar, arguing with a tall Fulani girl. Over in one corner a small group of street hustlers played baby-foot at the machine, and in the booth next to them, two Wolof girls were gently exploring the anatomy of a fat African in an expensive business suit.

A couple danced by with beer bottles in their hands. The man had a Czech ski cap pulled down over his eyes and a tattered Mamba beer T-shirt. To the great delight of his girlfriend, he was belting out the chorus of that old Senegalese favorite, *'Tjeboudienne, munumaa ko baaye.'* Roughly translated, it means 'I can't stop eating rice and fish.'

Everyone in the place was stumbling around in the dim red light like extras from the cast of *Night of the Living Dead*, and over it all were the smells of marijuana and cigarette smoke, sweat, spilled alcohol and blocked toilets. A woman pushed past me wearing silver metallic eyeshadow and an orange wig done in a high, tight hairstyle that made her look a little like the Bride of Frankenstein. I shivered and wondered what happened to these people after midnight.

I didn't intend to be here to find out.

I moved to the bar. Behind it stood a statuesque Senegalese drag queen with an elaborate hairstyle and the longest set of painted fingernails I'd ever seen. Her mouth was a deep red slash, her eyes heavily made up and topped with frosted false eyelashes.

"Hello, darling," she said as she approached. She had a leer as wicked as Mick Jagger's, and eyes that glittered like ancient ice. "Welcome to our little establishment. I'm Elisabeth."

She held out her hand in a limp gesture of exaggerated camp. When I took it, she stroked the inside of my palm with her thumb, while she ran her pink tongue lightly around her lips.

"Have you come for one of the bitches, dear, or are you looking for – something else, perhaps?" Her eyebrows went up archly. "I hope you're not the type that likes rough stuff." She giggled coyly. "I'm still recovering from last night."

I reached into my pocket. Bari N'Dour is going to pay all of this back to me, I thought grimly as I took out another five-thousand-franc note and pushed it across the bar toward Elisabeth. "No thanks," I said quietly. "I'm after information."

Her face registered no surprise. She left the money where it was and stared at me, calculating the odds. I stared back at her. All I need is for her to open her mouth and say the wrong thing, and then I'll have to fight my way out of here. Come on, sweetie, I thought, show me some heart.

Elisabeth looked at me for a few more seconds. "*Waxxal, nakk,*" she said finally. "So talk."

I nodded. "I'm looking for a Haitian and two white guys. They were in here earlier. Have you seen them?"

"The *noir* who looks like a rat and the two dirty hippies?"

"The same."

Elisabeth took the banknote and stuffed it down the front of her dress. "They were with Fatou," she said finally. "Over there." She stuck out her long pink tongue at a girl sitting alone, two seats down the bar from me. "Come on, I'll introduce you."

Fatou was tall and the color of baking chocolate, her hair done in long tight snakes and piled high on her head. She had a spectacular figure, with jutting breasts and buttocks which strained through the tight see-through blouse and imitation leather miniskirt she wore.

She sat and stared at nothing in particular, swaying quietly to some internal beat. She was high as the jet stream, riding on something a lot more powerful than the local beer.

I sat down next to her and was immediately enveloped in a thick cloud of Bint el Sudan perfume. I cleared my throat. "How about a drink?" Not the world's snappiest line, but I'd scored before with less.

She nodded absently.

I looked at Elisabeth. "Beer," I said, and pushed another banknote across the bar. "And get something for yourself."

Elisabeth winked and walked off into the smoky distance, twitching her narrow butt.

Fatou sat docilely in a world of her own. After a moment, she reached out and grasped my fingers. She slowly raised my hand to her eyes and brought them into focus. "*Tiens*," she murmured, rubbing my skin. "Another toubab, my lucky day." She turned and looked at me. "You're clean, too."

I waded right in. "I want to know about the Haitian and the two whites," I said.

Fatou snapped awake as if she'd been stung. "You a *flic*?" she snapped.

Elisabeth arrived with our beers. I handed Fatou hers and took a sip of mine.

"Don't be silly," I said. "When was the last time you saw a white cop in here?" I waited for a couple of beats. "I understand they were interested in buying something. I'm interested in buying something, too, mademoiselle."

Fatou probably hadn't been called mademoiselle for years. She looked at me, and then poured her beer down in one long gulp. "You want yamba?" she said. "That's what they came in here for."

"Not yamba," I said. "Information. I need to know–"

Fatou's eyes widened. She grabbed my shirt and pulled me forward, just as a beer bottle whizzed past my ear and shattered on the wall. I turned, aware of the sound of raised voices over the general din of the crowd. The Fulani girl at the other end of the bar was yelling at one of the French paras.

"That's my friend Rokhaya," Fatou whispered. "She's been having trouble with those three all night."

Rokhaya's face was a mask of scorn. "*Ça, alors, tu vois?*" she said in a voice loud enough to hear in Casablanca. "You're drunk as a pig, *évidemment*. And you expect me to go to bed with you?" She laughed harshly. "*Jamais de la vie!* Never! The last time you were in here, you got drunk, too. You tried to fuck Aminata, but you fell asleep instead. She told me all about it. And when you woke up, you wouldn't pay her."

She stepped back and looked the para up and down. "I'll bet can't even get it up."

The para's face hardened. He was on a serious wallbanger, at the stage where he had the idea that he was a bulletproof movie star with a fortune in his pocket, and this wasn't the kind of fan letter he wanted to get.

He lurched forward, grabbing Rokhaya by the arm. "*Sale connasse,*" he growled. "*Je vais te–*"

She pulled free and slapped him hard across the face, rocking his head back. "Come on, big boy," she taunted. "You're going to what? Are you really a man? Or just pretending to be one?"

The drunken para drew himself upright, holding the bar rail with one hand, grabbing the end of his moustache with the other. "Of course I'm a man, you filthy little whore! See these whiskers?"

"*Oooh, là, là!*" Rokhaya stepped back two paces and lifted her skirt high. "See this?" To no one's surprise, she wasn't wearing underwear. "Even *ma petite chatte* here has more whiskers than that."

"*Bravo!*" cried Fatou, leaning forward and clapping her hands in glee. She nearly fell off the barstool.

Elisabeth had trotted down to the end of the bar by this time. She took the drunken paratrooper by the shoulders and turned him around, patting him on the cheek.

"Don't pay any attention to nasty old Rokhaya, dear," she said in a soothing voice. "Of course you can get it up. I'll even help you if you want. Now, if you'll promise to be a good boy, I'll give you a free beer. Would you like that?"

She poured him out a fresh Stork. The paratrooper took a gulp and made a face. "This beer," he said in a loud voice, "tastes like shit."

Rokhaya's eyes lit up. She smiled, looking as if she'd just swallowed a flashlight. "Well, *chéri*," she said, "I guess you'd know all about that, wouldn't you?"

"That's enough!" screamed the Frenchman, and threw a wild hook at her.

Elisabeth, her good deed done, shrieked and disappeared under the bar. Rokhaya ducked under the punch, which carried the para off the barstool entirely and onto the floor. He struggled to his feet, bellowing with rage. Grabbing Rokhaya's blouse, he drew his fist back.

I started forward, but Elisabeth beat me to it. She reappeared suddenly from behind the bar, rising up like Poseidon from the sea. In her hand she clutched a bottle of Marie Brizard blackberry brandy, which she proceeded to bring down hard on the para's head.

He dropped as though poleaxed. As his comrades started roaring, the rest of the patrons in the bar stopped what they were doing and began to slowly shuffle toward the source of the excitement, strange fires building in their eyes.

Fatou hopped off her barstool. "Time to go," she announced, grabbing my hand and pulling me toward the back door. "*Ça va faire du vilain.*"

"Things are indeed getting pretty ugly," I agreed, following her out the door and into the dark alley. Behind us, the roaring was getting louder.

CHAPTER TEN

The alley was cloaked in an almost palpable darkness, under which swirled the mixed odors of vomit, spilled beer and urine. Fatou navigated through the murk as if by instinct, steering smoothly around heaps of garbage and junk. I stumbled along behind, clutching her hand like a blind beggar in the marketplace.

There was a staircase at the end of the alley, and she started up.

"Wait a second," I said. "Where the hell are we going?"

She smiled in the darkness, her teeth flashing like the Cheshire Cat's. "*Chez moi*, of course. Come on, there's nothing to be afraid of."

I'll bet you say that to all the boys. This isn't smart, I told myself. This is a mistake; not smart at all. But it's the next step. The way ahead, the open door. So go ahead and walk through. I shrugged mentally and started up the stairs.

We climbed two flights, to the top of the building. At the top of the stairs there was a louvered door. I swatted mosquitoes while Fatou fumbled under her tight blouse for the key and maneuvered it into the lock. Entering, she groped on a side table for matches, and lit two candles.

The room was as hot as an oven, and about as well furnished. There were two metal chairs and a low table, plus a wide mattress on the tile floor. There was a young woman, covered in a cloth *pagne*, sleeping on the mattress.

"That's Koumba. She lives here, too," Fatou said as she disappeared into the next room.

Koumba turned over and slowly came awake, sitting up and rubbing her eyes. She was attractive, with wide, luminous eyes, an upturned nose, and hair braided in simple cornrows decorated with beads and cowries. She had a tiny waist and a pair of miniscule pink nylon briefs which concealed nothing. Her loose *pagne* parted in front, revealing full breasts. She caught my glance and smiled, lying back on the mattress so that her breasts were fully exposed.

She winked at me and stretched, her pink tongue showing briefly between her pouting lips.

Relax, I told myself. It's a whorehouse, remember?

Fatou reappeared, minus her blouse and bra. She sat down cross-legged on the mattress beside Koumba, her mini hiked up around her waist, her spectacular breasts pointed straight at me. In her hand she held a crumpled paper bag.

She opened the bag and dumped a dozen rolled cones of newspaper onto the mattress. "That's what they bought, *chéri*. Interested?"

I picked up one and sniffed it. It wasn't terribly strong, but it was yamba, all right.

"Five hundred francs each," Fatou said. "So. How many do you want?"

Koumba came and sat on the arm of my chair, slipping her arm through mine. "Yamba king-size," she said with a giggle. I realized that she, too, was stoned. She turned and gave my ear a little lick. I could smell the sleep on her body, feel the tight skin of her breast on my upper arm.

"How many did the Haitian buy?"

Fatou laughed contemptuously. "Only two. He gave them to the two toubabs who came with him. The dirty ones."

"What happened then?"

She shrugged. "They left. All they wanted was the drug. No drinking, no fucking." She rolled her eyes. "*Ça, alors.*"

Koumba had been working on my shirt. She undid the last button and slipped it off my shoulders. Then she started on my belt. "But you're different, aren't you, *chéri?*" she murmured. "I can tell. Come on; we can smoke first if you want, have some fun with you afterwards. You, me and Fatou: *une partouze.* You interested in that?"

Fatou picked up one of the cones and bounced it on her flattened palm. "How many?" she said. While she was waiting for my answer, Koumba pulled my zipper down and put her hand on my crotch.

"Hey, wait a second," I said.

Koumba giggled. "Come on, man. Buy the grass and let's get started. *On baise, oui?* Come on, *chéri*, take a look." She pulled the elastic band of her briefs down, flashing me a glimpse of pubic hair.

"How many, man?" repeated Fatou. Her voice was all business now. Koumba may have been hot for my bod, but Fatou's motives were purer. She just wanted my money.

Well, this is a fine mess, I thought. And there seems to be only one way out. I dug out my money, and their eyes widened at the sight of the roll. Mistake number two, I thought. But too late for that now.

I peeled off a thousand francs and put it on the table. "Two cones, then," I said with a smile. Great, said a small voice deep inside my head; you're now officially part of a drug deal.

"Two?" In the candlelight, Fatou's eyes went hard and sharp as she looked at the single crumpled banknote, and then at me. "That's it? Two? That's all you want?"

Koumba let go of my trousers and sat up. "*Duul, waaye,*" she said under her breath.

Shit is right, I thought as I stood up. My trousers fell down around my ankles. I had on my new boxer shorts, the ones with pictures of Donald Duck on them, but neither of the women seemed impressed.

I looked around for my shirt. "Listen," I began, "don't take this the wrong way, okay? I just want to–"

But Fatou wasn't interested. She turned. "Alioune!" Her voice was a hard-edged bark.

Behind me, I heard the door open. Oh-oh. Could it be that a new guest is about to join our little party? I turned to see a large man inching into the room, clutching a knife.

I smiled at Alioune, showing him all my teeth. "*Bonsoir.*"

Ignoring me, he raised his eyebrows at Fatou. "*Fu mu nekk, xaalis-bi?*"

"The money's in my pants pocket," I said in French, answering his question myself. I kicked off my sandals and stepped out of my trousers, wrapping them carefully around my right hand. "You're going to have to guess which pocket it's in."

I stood there in my boxer shorts, keeping my right arm out in front of me. I smiled. "But guessing should make it more interesting, don't you think?"

Alioune grunted and started toward me, swinging the knife in wide arcs. I parried with my trousers and backed up slowly, looking right and left. There was a window with wooden shutters across the room to my right, but the easiest way to go, I decided, was straight out the door, which meant straight through Alioune.

I bumped up against the wall and stopped. Bracing myself, I waited until Alioune swung again. Then I took a deep breath and brought my foot up into his crotch, trying to kick a late-night field goal. Alioune let out a high-pitched hoot and fell over. Koumba and Fatou were scrambling out of the way now, clearing the decks for the next act.

It wasn't long in coming. There were footsteps on the stairs outside, and two more men appeared in the doorway. So much for my way out. Alioune was getting up from the floor, his face a mask of pain and anger, and Fatou was yelling something at the two men in the doorway. One of them started moving toward me.

Know when to hold, the song says; know when to fold. And know when to run like hell. It was definitely that time.

I had no idea what was on the other side of the shuttered windows, but that wasn't the important thing. The important thing was that I knew precisely what was on this side of the window.

I picked up a chair by its leg, feinted once at Alioune, and turned, fixing the position of the window in my mind. Then I bent, blew out both candles, took the chair with both hands and heaved it through the shutters.

There was a splintering crash, together with screams and curses from the pitch-black room. I dove for the window, grabbed the frame on the way out, and paused, blinking into the night, trying to get my bearings.

There was a low roof ten feet below me. I jumped, landed on my feet, and took off running along the rooftop. The open night air was cool relief after the closeness of Fatou's apartment, and adrenaline coursed through my body, giving me the idea that I could run forever if I had to.

It wasn't really necessary. A hundred yards along the roof I found a fire escape leading to the ground. Taking the steps three at a time, I found myself back on the same street as the Jardin d'Attractions.

The party inside had just ended. A dark-blue police salad wagon had pulled up outside the door, and people were being hustled out of the bar and into the back of it. I watched the French paras being frogmarched out, and then Elisabeth appeared, stepping regally between two cops. She winked at me just before she climbed inside.

I stood in the street in my Donald Duck underwear and watched the police van drive away, its siren rising and falling. I looked down at my trousers. They were sliced to pieces, but at least my money was safe.

A car pulled up beside me and hissed. It was Modu, the taxi driver. He looked me up and down. "Having a good time?" he said at last.

I smiled. "Modu, old friend," I said in a weary voice, "how much for that handsome boubou you're wearing?"

* * *

Half an hour later I stood on the narrow balcony outside my room at the hotel. The moon had risen, and in the soft light, I could see Lindy sprawled out across the bed. She appeared to be wearing one of my shirts as a night-dress.

On the table were the remains of a shawarma sandwich, all that had ever materialized of the dinner I'd promised her. She'd been fast asleep when I came tiptoeing in, and I left her that way, preferring to save my apologies and explanations for the morning.

The night was cool, the city quiet. Out beyond the harbor I could see the lights of Gorée Island, and beyond, the navigation lights of a freighter standing off the entrance to Dakar harbor. Overhead, the stars were bright; there would be no more rain tonight. The Southern Cross winked invitingly at me from down low on the horizon. I yawned, took a deep breath, and closed the shutters.

I fell asleep quickly, but slept uneasily. I dreamed of the large grey sewer-rats which lived under the streets of Dakar, with their shoebutton eyes and large, sharp yellow teeth. They looked very much like the photograph of Ti-Claude that I had stolen from the embassy. In my dreams, the rats stared at me, their little eyes bright, as if they wanted to tell me something. But being dead, of course, they could not speak.

CHAPTER ELEVEN

At eight o'clock the next morning, we were all seated at a back table in the Dragon d'Or, eating croissants and drinking strong coffee. Between bites, I was giving them a slightly edited version of my night out.

"First the embassy caper, now this. You should have known better," was all Bari N'Dour said when I had finished.

I spoke around a mouthful of croissant. "It was for a good cause," I said. "And besides," I added, "it could have turned up some interesting information."

"But it didn't," Lindy pointed out. "All you found out was that Ti-Claude and those two Europeans bought some grass and drank some Coke. Big deal. There's hardly any mystery in that." She looked at me. "In fact, the biggest mystery is exactly how you lost your clothes, but I won't go into that right now."

"Let's not," Bari agreed. "And let's not talk about what happened at the embassy yesterday, either. Much as I'd like to," he added.

Lindy turned to me. "What happened at the embassy yesterday? You didn't say anything about this."

"I'm not supposed to talk about it," I said, with a sidelong glance at Bari.

"Forget the damned embassy," said Bari. "Let's talk instead about what you found in Ti-Claude's hotel room." Bari held up his notepad and read off the list of names I'd given him. "Abdou Fall, Biram Thiam, the old man, and the Togolese." He scowled. "Who the hell are these people?"

"Let's start with an easier question," I said. "Who exactly is Rachid Khoury? He's the one who gave Ti-Claude the envelope, after all."

Bari nodded. "I can answer that one. Rachid Khoury is a Lebanese businessman. He lives in a big villa on Gorée – the place you saw yesterday. He's a millionaire – he owns a fleet of trucks, some movie houses, and a lot of real estate. He also has an import-export business which deals in a little bit of everything, all the way from cement and wooden poles to airport art."

"This doesn't tell us much," I said.

"That's only the legitimate side of his business, Max. He's also involved in organized crime, although we don't know just how. We have an idea that he's into bribery and price-fixing, maybe other things, too," Bari said. "But because we can't prove it, we can't nail him."

He picked up the sheets I'd stolen from the embassy. "That's why Malick got excited about Ti-Claude, you see; because of the connection with US organized crime. Now it looks as if there's a link to Khoury, too."

"You mean there's an underworld here?" said Lindy. "Like we have in the US?"

Bari nodded. "What we call 'organized crime' in this country has three different parts. One part is the French crime establishment, which operates mainly out of Marseilles and Corsica. They're not based here, but you'll see them around from time to time. They like to hide out in West Africa when things get hot in Europe. In the main, they leave us alone, and we leave them alone – that's INTERPOL business.

"Then there are the local crooks – our own *petits voyoux*, the thieves and scam artists. They're unimportant. We know most of them, we understand how they work, and we can round them up anytime. But it's the third element – the Lebanese – that are the real problem."

He bit off the end of his croissant. "Some of the Lebanese have been here for over a hundred years. Most of them are solid, honest citizens, but a few aren't. A few, like Khoury, have gotten rich, legally or illegally. Many of the Lebanese here are related to each other through marriage, and all of them have other relatives outside the country – in West Africa, Europe, or the US. There are maybe four or five big Lebanese business families here – Haddad, Khoury, Nassif and a couple of others. We think at least a couple of them are into illegal dealings."

"What kind of illegal dealings?" I asked. "Drugs?"

Bari shook his head. "No. Contraband, mainly. Cigarettes, radios, car parts – stuff like that. Cigarettes and radios may not strike either of you as the big time, but they're worth millions in a country like this. Enough to get killed for, I'd say."

I pushed my coffee away. "So arrest both of them; Ti-Claude and Khoury both. What more do you need?"

Bari shook his head. "Not yet. Not without more proof that something's going on. Khoury's an important man in this town; he's got half the Hôtel de Ville in his pocket. Unless we have something very solid, Dabo's going to let him go. That's why I was hoping that you'd turn up something in Ti-Claude's room."

He paused. "But none of this really matters, because Khoury's not in the country anymore. He flew out to France yesterday afternoon after his meeting with Ti-Claude." He picked up a sheet of paper. "And late last night, he took the Air France flight from Paris to New York."

"New York?"

Bari nodded. "Khoury's got a brother there; they trade with each other. Khoury goes over three or four times a year. He's not expected back until next week."

"That still leaves Ti-Claude," I said. I gestured across the street to the Auberge Jaune. "We all know he's in there. Why don't you just pick him up and sweat him?"

"I've already explained that to you," Bari said patiently. "I'm outside my jurisdiction. The Gendarmerie's got no authority inside the region of Cap Vert; we're a national police force, not a local one." He paused. "The case, I'm sorry to say, is still under Dabo's control."

"You mean you can't even bring this guy in for questioning?"

Bari checked his watch. "I'm meeting with my boss in half an hour. If I can convince him that this is serious enough, he might be able to pressure Dabo to sign an authorization for us to pick Ti-Claude up."

"What do you think your chances are?"

"Excellent, if I can get the paperwork ready in time." He leaned forward. "Can you keep an eye on the hotel until then?" He caught my expression. "Hey, I brought your car back this morning, didn't I? That should be worth a small favor, *n'est-ce pas?*" He stood up. "What about it? I need to be up at the Palais de Justice in ten minutes if I'm going to get the forms on this signed."

I sighed. "Sure. What's another few minutes at this point? You're coming straight back to take him in, right?"

"Absolutely." He put some money on the table. "Have some more croissants and another cup of coffee. I'll be back within the hour. Call me if anything happens in the meantime."

* * *

Five minutes later, Lindy grabbed my arm.

"Ti-Claude just came out of the hotel," she said. "He's got a shoulder bag – looks like a serious excursion. Oh-oh; he just got into a taxi."

Cursing, I gulped the last of my coffee and followed her out the door, the keys to my car in my hand.

The morning rush was already over, and it was easy going as we followed Ti-Claude's taxi around the Place de l'Indépendance and down towards the train station.

"Think he's planning on leaving town?" said Lindy. "Maybe we'd better call Bari now."

"Not yet," I said. "Let's see what he does first."

Ti-Claude got out of his taxi in front of the terminal and paid the driver. I pulled my little Renault into the main parking lot, found a shady eucalyptus tree, and killed the motor. We sat quietly, watching to see what would happen.

There was little activity at the train station at this hour of the morning. In front of the garish colonial-style terminal, a few women sat behind small piles of peanuts, hot *kany* peppers, and long, stringy manioc, waving lazily at the flies. Sleepy porters lounged nearby, their pushcarts upended. As we watched, Ti-Claude strolled toward the line of taxis parked at the entrance to the station. Most of the drivers were grouped in a loose circle under a nearby tree, sipping mint tea, smoking, and reading the morning newspapers.

Ti-Claude walked along the taxi rank until he came to the men under the tree. He stopped and spoke to one of them, who in turn called to another. The man got up, hoisting his boubou around his broad shoulders, and walked over to Ti-Claude. The two men talked for a moment, obviously bargaining, and then shook hands. They walked together to one of the taxis in the rank. Ti-Claude got in, and the cab moved off slowly.

I put the car in gear and pulled out into the street, following about a hundred meters behind. Ti-Claude's taxi moved up through the Place, turned right on Avenue Pompidou, and stopped in front of the post office.

I slowed to a crawl.

"It's those two white kids again," said Lindy. "Look, they're getting in with him."

The taxi went straight up Pompidou to the Marché Sandaga. The two Europeans sat in the back, Ti-Claude in the front, next to the driver. They turned right on Lamine Gueye, heading toward the autoroute.

"Where the hell are they going?" I muttered.

"Looks like they're leaving the city," Lindy said. "Bari will like that; now he can arrest him." She squeezed my arm. "And then we can go play."

"I wish Bari were with us now," I muttered, running the lights by the bus station, trying to close the gap. "I don't like the way this is shaping up."

We were out on the autoroute now, picking up speed fast. The city center was falling behind us, nothing to be seen in the rearview mirror now except the tall emerald spire of the Grand Mosque. Overhead, pedestrian crosswalks flashed by, their sides painted in large green and white ads for Air Afrique. Pink and purple bougainvillea interspersed with brilliant red flamboyants lined the road, making the freeway almost attractive. The effect was marred, however, by the missing sections of concrete wall which revealed the squalid bidonville slums behind, scant yards from the expensive cars roaring by at high speed.

Ti-Claude's taxi shot down the broad highway without stopping, straight through the town of Rufisque and out the other side, picking up speed again as it passed the Bata factory, heading north on the main highway to St. Louis.

"Listen," said Lindy, "I really think you ought to call Bari now. I mean *now.*"

"You see a phone booth anywhere?" I glanced down at the dash. We were doing 90 kph now, near the limit of the little Renault's engine, and we had less than half a tank of gas.

The landscape was changing now, as we moved further out of the Cap Vert region. The palms and filao trees of Dakar had given way to sand and thorn-bushes, and here and there, forests of baobab trees reared up high above the flat bush. I've always thought baobabs were a little supernatural, and apparently the Senegalese felt the same way. Out in the more remote villages, Bari said, they still buried their griots in the hollow trunks of the baobab.

Our little Renault roared along, barely managing to keep the taxi in sight. We were catching the heavy traffic from the north now, big Berliet and Mercedes trucks whose drivers believed in the time-honored Senegalese principle of *au plus fort la raison*, which on a narrow two-lane road meant that they could drive pretty much how and where they pleased. From time to time a blue and yellow *car-rapide* stuffed with passengers would flash by, baggage piled high on the roof.

Fifteen kilometers later, Ti-Claude's taxi slowed and turned left. We followed.

"Where does this road go?" said Lindy.

"Back out to the coast," I said. "It ends at a little fishing village. Maybe they've decided to go to the beach for the day."

We stayed back a quarter of a mile as they sped over the rolling hills toward the ocean. Fifteen minutes of fast driving brought us to the crest of a hill above the fishing village of Kayar. Ahead of us, I saw the taxi turning off the main road and onto a track along the beach.

Kayar is a sleepy village of Wolof and Lebu fishermen, with a wide beautiful beach, spectacular surf, and several small restaurants catering to the weekend tourists from Dakar. The high point of the day is the arrival of the fishing fleet, with the crews of the brightly painted pirogues chanting and bending to their paddles as they drive the boats through the surf to the beach. The fishermen will sell you their catch straight off the boat, at a fraction of market prices. They have tuna, shark, and that fine eating fish that the Senegalese call *thiof* – delicious with either mayonnaise or butter.

In front of us, the paved road ended abruptly. Ti-Claude's taxi kept going, grinding its way down the beach along the sand track, tires spinning.

Lindy looked at me. "Should we follow them?"

I shook my head. "Too easy to get stuck. That track probably just goes down the beach a few hundred yards. Let's park here."

We pulled up next to a small *bar-relais* which had obviously seen better days. A faded wooden sign outside said '*Auberge des Palmiers*.' The bar lay crouched within the shade of a cluster of straggly palms, as if hiding from the heat.

I pushed open the door to the bar. The *patron* sat behind the counter, a tired-looking Lebanese with a Zapata moustache and sad brown eyes under heavy lids. He looked up from his copy of *Paris-Match* and raised his eyebrows.

"*Messieurs-dames?*" It was almost a sigh.

"The *piste* outside," I said, pointing to the track the taxi had taken a moment ago. "Where does it go?"

"Go? It goes nowhere, *monsieur*." He shrugged. "Merely to the top of that small rise you see there. People sometimes drive along it to find privacy from the village children, but I would not advise you to attempt it. The sand is deep, and you might get stuck. Something to drink, perhaps?"

It was too early for beer. I ordered two *limonades* and passed one to Lindy. "Have you got a telephone?"

He nodded. "In the office. Do you want to use it now?"

"In a moment." To Lindy, I said, "Let's take these outside and drink them. Then I'll call."

The patio was nearly empty. At one of the tables, a quarrelsome French family was finishing an early lunch, their table littered with empty Evian bottles and crusts of bread. Underneath their table, three plump cats waited patiently for them to leave.

There was little activity on the beach at this time of day. The fishing boats were still far out at sea, and would not return until evening. There were a few European sunbathers scattered on the sand near the restaurant, and a cluster of Senegalese children playing listlessly near one of the big wooden pirogues. Ti-Claude's taxi had disappeared, with only the tire tracks in the deep sand to mark its passage.

I walked to the edge of the small patio and squinted northward along the beach. The tire tracks disappeared over a small rise in the sand, heading toward a cluster of scrub and palm about a kilometer away. Its outline shimmered in the heat haze.

I stared into the distance, shielding my eyes from the glare of the sun. "If the track ends over the rise," I said finally, "then they're probably up there swimming."

The French family looked up suspiciously, sniffed disapprovingly at the sound of English, and went back to poking at their food.

Lindy nodded. "Or smoking some of that reefer they bought last night. Want to call now?"

"No," I said after a moment. "I want to find out what they're doing up there."

"You want to go up there, is that it?"

I looked at Lindy and she looked at me. "Yeah," I said. "You game?"

She nodded. "Let's go for it," she said. "We can call later."

* * *

Walking in the deep sand was awkward, and we made slow progress up the track. "I feel like one of the extras in *Beau Geste*," Lindy muttered, wiping her forehead. "This sand is hot, I want you to know."

I nodded, stopped to pick a sandspur off my foot, and looked longingly at the water. Then I straightened up and soldiered on.

Lindy reached the top of the rise first, and stopped. "There's the taxi," she said as I came trudging up. "But something's wrong, I think. What do you make of it?"

I came up beside her and followed her pointing finger with my eyes. Two hundred yards in front of us, the hood of the taxi glinted in the sun, down close to the water. The taxi was off the track, tipped at a slight angle, up over its hubcaps in the deep sand. One of its doors was open.

Ti-Claude was nowhere in sight. Nor was the taximan. Two small figures were huddled together at the edge of the

93

waves, their long hair and dirty clothing unmistakably that of the two Europeans.

I became aware of a high, thin, keening noise. At first I thought it was a seabird's cry, but when I looked up, the hot sky was empty. Then I realized that the noise was coming from one of the figures on the beach.

The small hairs on the back of my neck began to rise. "I think you're right," I said at last. "Something is wrong."

Again the noise reached my ears; long, wailing sounds punctuated by harsh gasps as air was sucked into tortured lungs. As we watched, one of them gave a shrill scream and leaped into the air. He began to run helplessly from side to side in frantic swings, plunging blindly into the shallow water, screaming all the while – an urgent, invariant note of terror and panic. Finally, he fell on the sand and lay there sobbing in exhaustion, flapping his arms helplessly like a slaughtered chicken.

His companion sat motionless a few yards away, staring out at the ocean.

Lindy looked at me. "I think we'd better get down there, don't you?"

We ran toward the water's edge, our movements made clumsy by the deep, soft sand. It reminded me of nightmares, the ones where you're trying to hurry, but can't seem to make your feet move fast enough.

The taxi was between us and the figures on the beach, and I had just come around the end of it, moving fast, when I tripped over something heavy and pitched headlong into the sand. I hit solidly and felt the wind go out of me with a rush of air and a stab of pain. Then I heard Lindy's sharp intake of breath.

I sat up, half-dazed, and looked at what had tripped me. The taximan lay stretched on the sand behind me. His flat-heeled slippers had been kicked off, and his grand boubou was soaked with blood. His throat had been cut, and in the process, his head had been all but severed from his shoulders.

His eyes were wide open and bulging, and his mouth was curled into a grotesque grin. Already, bright green flies had begun to gather around the still-wet bloodstains. The sounds of screaming continued from the beach behind me.

I got slowly to my hands and knees, staring at the mutilated corpse with an almost clinical fascination. The fingers of both hands had been chopped off, scattered beside the body. Next to them lay a bushknife, its blade half-buried in the sand. It was the short, broad-bladed kind used for heavy work, favored by Senegalese farmers for the task of clearing their peanut fields.

I stared at the fingers with numb detachment. The man's hands must have been placed across the taxi's doorwell. Then the fingers were cut off with short hacking strokes of the bushknife. Yes, that would have been the best way to do it, I decided.

I shuddered, leaned forward, and vomited spectacularly and with considerable relief into the sand.

After a moment I got to my feet. Lindy was standing, trembling, looking at the two white kids on the beach, her face ashen with shock. I came up beside her.

"Be careful," she said after a moment. "I think there's something really wrong with them."

One of the Europeans was sitting at the edge of the sand, staring out to sea, his eyes open in total innocence. The other was lying exhausted in the shallow water, crying helplessly as if his heart would break. One wore a faded tie-dye T-shirt, and the other had on what looked like an army surplus shirt embellished with crude embroidery. Both of them were filthy, with matted hair and dirt rings around their feet and ankles.

But the dirt wasn't what was bothering me, I realized; it was the lack of blood. There was no blood on either of them, none that I could see. And the taxidriver had been murdered only minutes ago.

The one sitting on the sand took no notice of us as we approached. I hesitated, and then I touched him lightly on the shoulder. He screamed and shrank back, pulling feebly at his beard and hair.

Lindy looked at me. "What's the matter with them? Drugs?"

"Looks like it," I murmured. "Maybe some bad acid. Maybe something a lot stronger." Whatever it was, they had front-row seats at their own private showing of *Looney Tunes*, projected up against the backs of their eyeballs, following a script written and directed by whatever they'd smoked, drunk, eaten or shot into a vein.

And where was Ti-Claude? I glanced back at the taxi, seeing for the first time the footprints in the sand leading off toward the scrub in the distance. I scanned the dunes with my eyes. Wherever he was, he wasn't far away. He might be still moving, or he might be waiting, watching us from cover, waiting for us to split up, planning his next move.

Lindy followed my eyes. "He's still out there somewhere, isn't he? Now is it time to call?"

I took her hand. "Now it's definitely time. Come on."

Together, we began to run back up the track toward the relais.

CHAPTER TWELVE

Well after dark now, but the heat hung on. We sat around the large table in Dabo's office, sweating in the humidity, and listened as he droned on. I sipped coffee from a paper cup and watched the big fan turning overhead. Lindy sat beside me, looking at her fingernails. Across the table, Dr. Renaudeau from the Hôpital Principal smoked a Gauloise and stared off into space. Only Bari N'Dour appeared to really be paying attention, and to judge from his expression, his patience was nearly at an end.

We had been listening for the past half hour to a detailed account of the afternoon's events, and Dabo showed no signs of stopping. Through the open window I could hear the lilting strains of the evening call to prayer coming from somewhere out in the city.

"They were taken immediately to the Hôpital Principal, as I think I mentioned," Dabo was saying. "Dr. Renaudeau examined both of them as soon as they arrived. They were treated for drug overdose and subsequently, ah, interviewed by several of our staff."

He cleared his throat and lifted a sheaf of papers from the desk. "This is the stenographic record of that interview." He pursed his lips and adjusted his heavy spectacles. "Let me begin—"

Bari leaned forward and cleared his throat. "Perhaps, *mon commissaire*, it would save time if Dr. Renaudeau summarized the more salient points for us. That way, we can cover the medical aspects as well."

Renaudeau stubbed out his cigarette and sat up. Without waiting for Dabo, he began to speak. "They're more or less recovered, except for a slight case of malnutrition, which in the present context, is somewhat irrelevant." He spoke crisply and with assurance.

"It's the drug that concerns us here," he continued. "It appears to be a very toxic variety of what is commonly known as PCP, an alkaloid sometimes used for veterinary purposes." He looked at me. "In the United States, I believe it's sometimes called angel dust. In a high enough dosage, it can produce some extremely unpleasant sensations."

That's putting it mildly, I thought, remembering the one who had run in circles and sobbed. Years ago, a Vietnam buddy had described to me what a mild dose had felt like. All the fire hydrants on Telegraph Avenue had melted and run into the street, he'd said. He could see inside the people who passed him where he lay on the sidewalk, right through their skin to the little clickety gears and wires inside which made them jerk and move like the little Swiss clockwork toys you see at Christmas.

Great stuff: just the thing for smoothing out the wrinkles in your mind.

"Neither of them can remember anything coherent past the point at which they arrived at the fishing village," Renaudeau was saying. "They only remember waking up in the hospital."

"How convenient," murmured Dabo. "Then they have no recollection of murdering the taxi driver."

I leaned forward. "They didn't murder the taxi driver," I said quietly. "Ti-Claude did. He gave them the drug to make it appear that they were responsible, but there was no blood on their clothes or on their hands."

Dabo turned an impassive face to me. "That, *monsieur*, is supposition. Let me remind you, moreover, that you have no official status here. You are here because Brigadier N'Dour brought you, not because I want you here. You will please refrain from interrupting."

He lifted the papers in front of him. "According to the interview, the two young men are in fact runaways from the French Army. Six weeks ago, they left their camp near Toulouse when they heard a rumor that their company was to be sent to French Polynesia to help deal with some of the political disturbances affecting that area. Like many young people, they are somewhat idealistic in a confused way. To avoid participating in what they saw as French overseas imperialism – I'm quoting here, obviously – they decided to run away.

"They made their way out of France, to Morocco and eventually here, overland through Mauritania, in the company of several other young people. They found themselves alone and virtually penniless in a strange city. They eked out a living by begging near the post office, drawing crude chalk pictures on the sidewalk to attract attention and sympathy."

"And how did they meet Ti-Claude?" I asked. "Did they tell you that?"

Dabo consulted his notes. "Three days ago they met the Haitian, on the street. He befriended them, apparently. He brought them to his hotel, gave them food, and even a little pocket money."

"And you don't find that a little suspicious?"

Dabo looked at me. "In our country, Monsieur Donovan, this type of behavior is usually considered normal hospitality toward unfortunate strangers."

"In my country," I said drily, "it's usually considered a setup."

Bari tapped his fingers impatiently on the table. "What about the trip to the fishing village? How did that come about?"

Dabo raised his papers. "He had promised them a meal at the small hotel there. They accepted readily, of course. On the way, he produced some yellow capsules." He paused. "He told them that the capsules contained lysergic acid. Since they were familiar with that drug, they each took one."

"Is that normal hospitality, too, over here?" It was a cheap shot, but the best I could do.

Dabo ignored me. "They stated in the interview that they did not actually see this man Ti-Claude take a capsule, although they assumed that he had. As they approached the village, they began to feel the drug's effects." He put the paper down. "And that's all they can remember."

Lindy spoke quietly. "What's going to happen to them?"

Dabo looked solemn. "They will be treated, of course. And then they will be charged with murder."

I slammed my fist on the table. "Are you completely crazy?" All eyes in the room turned to me. "I've already told you – they didn't kill that taxi driver. Ti-Claude did.

He killed Malick N'Diaye, too. And he's still running around out there while we sit here talking!" I could feel my face growing hot.

I was hot, tired, and sweaty. I hadn't eaten since morning, and there was a raw edge to my voice as I spoke. "Do any of you understand what you're dealing with here? This guy is a professional killing machine, and somebody's wound him up and set him loose. He's off the leash now, and he's going to kill again. Khoury's involved in this somehow, and if you don't—"

Dabo's voice slammed into mine. "Enough! I have already warned you once, Monsieur Donovan, not to intrude into police matters."

His voice dropped into a low, steely register. "Police work is a matter of procedure and logic, not raw emotion. The fingerprints on the bushknife are those of the Frenchmen. As for this man you call Ti-Claude, his role in this affair is far from clear. It is possible that he had nothing to do with this at all, that their story is simply a self-serving way of diverting attention from—"

"Shut up, will you?" Bari's voice was angry and barely under control, filling the hot room. "Let me remind you, *mon cher collègue*, that this case is now under the jurisdiction of the Gendarmerie. It is I who set the agenda here, not you." He opened his notebook. "A list of names was found in Ti-Claude's hotel room last night. Here are—"

Dabo adjusted his glasses. "How did you obtain a list of names? Surely, the proper procedure—"

"*Merde* for your procedure," snapped Bari. "The names are the important thing." He looked around the table. "The taxi driver who was murdered today was named Abdou Fall. His was the first name on the list we obtained. Fall was a Serere from Thies, and he'd been working in Dakar for over fifteen years. His regular beat was the train station, and he picked up cargo as well as incoming passengers. Does anyone know Abdou Fall?"

There was silence in the room.

Dabo pursed his lips. "What is the point of this, if I may ask?"

Bari looked at him. "It's obvious, don't you see? Ti-Claude's got a list, and he's going to kill them all. First Fall, then the others." He looked down at his notebook. "The second name," he said, "is Biram Thiam. Anyone know Biram Thiam?"

Just then a cop appeared in the doorway, his face shiny with sweat and plastered all over with bad news.

Nobody had to ask.

* * *

Out on the beach behind the Artisans' Village, the beam from the lighthouse at Ouakam swept over us every forty-five seconds, an eerie metronome pacing the human tragedy on the sand below. The moon had not yet risen, but the police had rigged some arc-lights on cables, and the photographers were popping flashbulbs as Renaudeau and I walked out along the sand to the abandoned fishing canoe where Biram Thiam's body had been found. Behind us were the barricades they'd put up to keep back the crowd. Beside the canoe, Bari was being briefed by the young cop who'd called in the report.

"We found him by accident," the young cop was saying. "One of the kids in the village had arranged to meet his girlfriend here tonight, out by this old pirogue." He smiled. "They were using it as a place to make out. But tonight, he got here early, and heard some cats making a hell of a racket. He found the body staked out in the sand behind the boat. Here it is."

We rounded the end of the boat and I saw what he'd been talking about: Biram Thiam was staked out in the sand, spread-eagled on his back. The sharp smell of fish came to me, and I saw that the dead man had been smeared with offal from the fishing boats.

The body had been clawed apart in a dozen places, and flesh mingled with fish parts on the damp sand. Something had been eating the corpse, and as I watched, I saw a pair of cats slink between two rocks, their yellow eyes blazing with hunger and cunning. They wouldn't be too particular about what they ate out here in the dark, away from the village.

I took a closer look. It was the man I'd seen in the Artisans' Village the day before. The woodcarver who'd given me his card. I fumbled in my shirt pocket, found it, and read the name. Biram Thiam. Jesus Christ.

I could feel my nausea return in a rush, and I turned away, into the darkness.

"The way the kid told it," the young cop was saying, "there must have been a hundred cats milling around, getting ready for a late dinner."

Bari sighed. "We'll start interviewing the villagers tonight," he said to the cop. He turned to Dr. Renaudeau. "Can you do the autopsy tonight?"

He nodded. "I'll go make arrangements." He walked off with the cop, down toward where the police vans were lined up at the edge of the beach.

Bari and I were alone. "It probably happened just after dark," he said. "I'd guess that Ti-Claude waited for Thiam to close up his shop. It would have been easy to get him out here alone, on some pretext or other."

He looked at me. "But why, in Allah's name? Why? Why tie him up like this? Why cover him with fish guts?"

I looked again at the body, a vague thought forming in my mind. "Maybe," I said at last, "he wanted the murder to appear as horrible as the other one."

"You mean the taxi driver?"

"Yes. That one was pretty spectacular, too, you'll have to admit."

"But what about Malick?" he said. "He was the first one killed, and there was nothing spectacular about that, was there?"

I thought for a moment. "Maybe Malick was a mistake, Bari," I said at last. "Maybe he just got in the way."

Bari was silent for a moment. Then he nodded. "All right, suppose that's so. But the question still stands: why make a spectacle of the other killings?" He turned to face me. "Almost as if the killer wanted to make a statement."

"A statement?"

"Make a statement," he repeated. "Send a message." His voice was low and intense. "Send a message, make a statement; isn't that what you say in America?"

I looked at him. "But a message to whom?"

We stood there for a long moment, looking out at the ocean. "I don't know," he said finally. "I just don't know."

I shook my head. "And neither do I, my friend. But I do know one thing: I'm way out of my league on this one. It's all yours now."

I put my hand on his shoulder. "*Maa salaam*," I said softly. "Goodbye."

Then I left him there and went in search of Lindy and something strong to drink that would put me to sleep without dreams.

CHAPTER THIRTEEN

They began coming out from under the cover of the trees as we reached the edge of the forest clearing. I saw first one, then another, and then I realized that there were at least a dozen of them, some of them pretty big. They were on both sides of us now, and coming closer.

I spoke in a low voice. "You didn't say anything about this, you know."

"Shh," said Lindy. "Keep walking normally, and don't show fear. Whatever they do, don't react, okay?"

I counted fifteen of them now. They formed a rough skirmish line, almost encircling us. A couple of them had gotten between us and the Land Rover now, and I wondered if we could outrun them if we had to make a break for it.

"Smile," she said quietly. "Keep moving. Try to act like you know what you're doing."

Then the biggest one bent down and picked up a heavy stick. I stopped walking. As if on signal, so did everyone else.

The big one had a shock of snow-white hair running up the side of his head, and he was obviously the leader. He tapped the stick against the ground experimentally a few times and looked at me. Then he leaned forward and began moving slowly from side to side across the balls of his feet, letting the stick swing easily from his hand. His yellow teeth were exposed in a big grin as he watched me closely.

If he comes at me with that thing, I thought, I won't have a chance. I was just on the point of breaking for the Land Rover when Lindy spoke.

"Bobo," she said calmly, "don't be an asshole." She stepped forward, hands on her hips, and glared at the chimp. "I might have known you'd try something like this."

Bobo looked from me to Lindy and back again, a slightly sheepish expression on his face. He began hooting in a low voice, tapping the stick on the ground nervously. With his free hand, he reached up to scratch his crotch. The other chimps watched us, their eyes bright with anticipation and mischief.

Lindy turned to me. "It's because you're a strange male, you see. Just a stupid macho thing, that's all. Bobo thinks he's got to test you out."

I looked at the chimp, then back at her. "And what do I have to do to pass?" I said.

"Nothing. Bobo's a coward, really. When he starts displaying like that, just hold your ground. If he doesn't get any reaction out of you, he'll lose interest."

I stood and watched as Bobo began to breathe rapidly, with short grunts.

"He's starting his display now," said Lindy. "He'll get all the others stirred up as well. Chimps love to see a good fight. Don't do anything, just stand still. I'll handle this."

Bobo's grunts got louder and faster, until they erupted in a frantic burst of pant-hooting. He banged the stick on the ground fiercely, and took two steps forward. One or two of the younger males were beginning to sway now, too.

"Okay, hold it right there, folks." Lindy bent over and picked up several large laterite rocks. "Honestly," she muttered, "the crap I have to put up with."

A rock in either hand, she advanced on the chimps, tossing her hair back impatiently. They moved back uneasily, muttering to themselves.

She swept the chimps with accusing eyes. "I've told you all before to be nice to guests. Remember the long talk we had about that?"

The chimps looked at her with solemn, serious faces.

"Max is my guest now," she continued. "Nobody's going to misbehave in front of him." She glared at Bobo. "Especially not you. Now put the stick down; put it down right now."

Bobo held his ground, stick in hand, teeth bared, as Lindy began to walk toward him. He let her come to within a few feet, and then he dropped the stick and ran off a few yards, just out of range. He turned and began to jump up and down, hooting loudly. Just for a second, I could have sworn he flipped her a bird.

Whatever the gesture was, it certainly got a reaction. "That's it," Lindy shouted. "Now you're going to get it, you stupid furbag!" She pulled her arm back as if to throw the rock.

With a piercing cry, Bobo fled to the safety of a tall tree, zipping up the broad trunk. The rest of the chimps exploded in noise and movement. With sharp cries of fear and excitement they ran in all directions.

I stared in amazement. Suddenly, a small chimp launched himself into my arms and clung desperately to me, overcome by the drama around him.

In seconds it was over. From his perch in the tree, Bobo smoothed his fur and chattered miserably to himself, darting fearful glances every few seconds at the ground below where Lindy stood, shouting furious abuse at him and brandishing the rock.

After a moment, she dropped the rock and walked back toward me, her eyes glowing with excitement, her broad mouth curved in mischief. Her khaki shirt was stained with sweat and red laterite dust. Brushing her hair out of her eyes, she scooped the baby chimp from my arms and cuddled it, making reassuring noises and calling the others to her. They came, silently and respectfully, and sat around her while she held the small one and lectured them on manners.

"Now pay attention," she told them in a quiet, serious voice. "This is my friend Max, and he'll be with us for a week or two." She looked at me. "Say hello, Max."

I looked at the chimps, and the chimps looked at me. "Hi," I said.

There was no reaction, only guarded interest.

Lindy raised a warning finger, like a schoolmarm. "I will be very angry if anyone starts playing tricks on Max. You are all to be extremely nice and well-behaved. Otherwise, you'll get thumped, just like numb-nuts over there nearly did." To underscore the point she picked up another lump of rock and chucked it in Bobo's general direction, producing a stream of apologetic chatter from the tree and more nervous glances from the group on the ground.

"No tricks, I mean it. Now come on; we should get on to camp." She walked into the forest, still carrying the small one.

I followed; Bobo stayed behind in the tree. I felt a small hand in mine and looked down to see another chimp falling in beside me. He grinned and nodded, as if to say, 'It's all right, she's not really mad anymore.' Hand in hand, we walked through the trees toward camp.

"Wasn't that, ah, excessive?" I asked her as we picked our way along the path.

"Not really. Chimps are tough, and you have to be pretty direct to get them to pay attention. You probably saw that I wasn't trying to hurt him; just scare him a bit." She pointed ahead on the path. "Here we are. Pretty ritzy, huh?"

The research station lay nestled in among the tall trees, a hundred yards back from the clearing. It was a low structure made of large laterite stone blocks, mortared together and framed with crudely poured concrete posts. The roof was heavy-gauge galvanized iron secured with half-inch U-bolts. There were thick bars on the windows. Lindy took a large key from her belt and opened the heavy iron door, holding it for me as I slipped inside.

"What was this place before you took it over?" I asked. "An ammunition dump?"

She laughed. "I had it built specially for the project, in fact. It has to be strong, otherwise the chimps would tear it apart to get inside." She indicated the door. "They'd have demolished a wooden door in a matter of hours. Even now, I have to be careful; they'll find their way in if you give them the least opportunity. They love the food, of course, but they also like to play with the gadgets and drink the medicine."

I looked around. The 'house' was divided into two rooms, one a combined kitchen-storeroom, where we now stood, and beyond that, a larger bedroom-office. There was a wide, low bamboo bed with a mosquito net neatly folded above it, and a desk against the wall, strewn with Lindy's books and papers. A radio-cassette sat on the shelf, together with a small collection of tapes. Against the other wall was another set of crude shelves containing an assortment of clothing.

Dozens of objects hung from the roof and the wall on nails and bits of string – cameras, binoculars, water bottles, flashlights, old clothes, pictures, mirrors, maps and other useful objects. Against one wall stood a rifle. In the dim light, the place looked like a tropical version of the Old Curiosity Shop.

I nodded approvingly. "Nice," I said. "I wouldn't mind living here myself. How long have you been out here?"

"Almost a year. I've had visits from other researchers once in a while, but most of the time, I'm on my own." She looked around. "Like now. The tourist hotel at Simenti shut down for the season last week, just before I went up to Dakar. In another couple of weeks the rain will close the roads, and then I'll be stuck in here until November when things dry out again."

I whistled. November was five months away; a long time to be on one's own. Especially here. Lindy's research station was right in the middle of one of the biggest remaining chunks of wilderness in West Africa, empty of people but teeming with wild animals.

And a long, long way from help, should she ever need it.

She must have read my expression. "It's not so bad, if that's what you're thinking. I'm not afraid of the animals. The only really dangerous predators around here are the two-legged kind."

"What do you mean?"

She hefted the rifle. "Poachers. From Mali and Mauritania. They come for meat and ivory, and sometimes to catch live animals to sell to the European zoos. Last year, thirty of them came in from the north, in half a dozen big trucks. They killed two park guards and wounded three others. The army finally had to come in and get them."

"A rifle isn't going to do you much good against that kind of trouble," I pointed out. "And you don't even have a radio."

She shrugged. "I can take care of myself, Max." Her eyes twinkled. "I may only have one rifle, but I've got a hell of a lot of ammunition." She snapped her fingers. "Oh-oh, the supplies – I almost forgot. We'd better get the Land Rover unloaded before the chimps do it for us."

* * *

We spent the next forty minutes unloading what we'd bought from Tambacounda. Most of it was food for the rainy season – bags of beans, rice, and sugar, together with cases of cooking oil, canned pineapple and evaporated milk.

"We'll make another trip in a couple of days," Lindy said as we hauled the boxes through the forest and into the camp. "I want to be well stocked by the time the rains cut me off."

Remembering the drive out from Tambacounda, I could understand her concern. We'd left the dusty capital of Eastern Senegal four hours ago, heading east along a bumpy dirt road. We entered the park at Niokolo, where a dozen baboons perched silently on the steps of the deserted ranger station and watched us go by.

Inside the park, the road had rapidly deteriorated, becoming a muddy and overgrown track which wound like a snake through the dense bush and hard laterite pan as it pushed further into the forest toward Mount Asserik and the research camp beyond. I'd had to grip the dash with both hands to keep from bouncing.

Senegal as a whole is as flat as a pool table and about as interesting, but here in the eastern region, the hills climbed steadily toward the flanks of the Fouta-Djallon Range in neighboring Guinea. Asserik was one of half a dozen high plateaux in the region, rearing up a thousand feet above the relatively flat terrain below. When I'd flown this area,

I'd used Asserik frequently as a landmark. Its forested slopes provided ideal cover, Lindy had explained, for troops of wild chimpanzees. And a perfect place for a research station.

Now I sweated in the hundred-degree heat as I brought in the last of our boxes, the ones containing the stuff we'd bought to celebrate Lindy's return to camp and my arrival. Two cases of beer, a bottle of whiskey, fresh lettuce, bread, and two thick steaks.

"I'm going to enjoy dinner tonight," I said, as I put the box on the table.

"Enjoy it while you can," she replied as she stacked cans on the hut's bamboo shelves. "Tomorrow it's back to rice and peanut sauce."

She unlocked the big iron door and we stepped outside. Immediately, the chimps surrounded us, loping over from the other side of the compound and swinging down from the tall trees that surrounded the hut. The smaller ones tugged at our hands, wanting to be picked up.

I looked up to see Bobo walking toward me. He stopped a few feet away, looking me over carefully. Finally he came forward and, in a remarkably human gesture, took my hand and placed it on top of his bowed head. I let it lie there for a moment, and then I gently ruffled his fur. He looked up at me and grinned hugely, grasping me firmly around the buttocks. Then he buried his face in my crotch and sniffed deeply.

I gasped, looking at Lindy for help.

"Relax," she said, laughing. "He's just acknowledged you as dominant. Now he's making sure he knows what you smell like for future reference." She smiled. "Congratulations. You're one of the gang now."

She looked down at Bobo. "He thinks I'm his mother, actually – he'll warn me when he thinks there's a leopard in the bush. He was anxious about you, Max, because he thought you might hurt me. He'd react that way toward anyone he thought posed a threat to me."

"So you've got a bodyguard. How'd he get that white streak in his fur?"

Her expression grew serious. "He was shot by the men who captured him. When he was very little. We think he came from nearby, in fact – down toward the Guinea border. He's more fearful and aggressive than most of them, and I think it's because of the trauma he suffered. He flies into a rage, for example, if anyone points a gun in his direction. One of the park guards did it in fun last year, and I had to pull Bobo off him." She stroked his fur. "I don't know what he'd do, for example, if someone pointed a gun at me."

"What would have happened," I said, "if Bobo and I had decided to fight earlier this afternoon?"

"He'd have kicked the stuffing out of you," she said simply. "Chimps are a whole lot tougher than people think. Bobo is four or five times stronger than a human male, and a lot faster."

"Then why didn't he just go for me?"

"Well, size intimidates chimps, for one thing. You're big, so the chimps are a little afraid of you. And they know you're with me. I'm basically their mother."

I put a small chimp that I'd been carrying back on the ground and picked up another that had been clamoring for attention. "And you're teaching them all to be real chimps again," I said. "Does it work?"

She pointed to some crude nests of sticks and grass up high in the trees which ringed the camp. "See those? I taught them how to make nests in trees. They were all sleeping in the clearing, down on the ground, when I started. No chimp in the wild does that – they'll be dinner for the snakes and big cats if they do."

She walked over to one of the trees and grabbed a low branch. Pulling herself up effortlessly, she began to climb. As she made her way toward one of the high nests, she continued to talk. "They didn't know about nests, so I showed them. Came out here with them and built one while they watched. Then I spent a week sleeping in the damned thing, just so they'd get the idea."

I stood in quiet amazement, shading my eyes with my hand to watch her progress. "And did they?"

"Oh, sure. But they thought it was too much work. I'd help them build nests, they'd spend a few nights in the trees, and then they'd go back to sleeping on the ground. I tried everything – threats, persuasion, you name it. Even threw firecrackers out the window of the camp at night to scare them. Then one night a panther came by, and suddenly they all decided they really ought to be sleeping in the trees."

She was far above me now, looking down, her long hair framing her face. The other chimps had joined her now. They crouched on the branches beside her, swaying back and forth and making soft contented grunting noises. One of the small ones had hopped over beside Lindy and was grooming her hair, running quick fingers through it in search of lice to eat. Absently, Lindy began to groom the fur of the animal on the other side of her, humming as she did so.

I watched her for a moment. "Have you ever thought," I said finally, "that you could use some rehabilitation yourself?"

She laughed and gently pushed the chimps away. Then she swung fluidly down from branch to branch, dropping the last eight feet to land cat-like beside me. She gave me a quick kiss, and the chimps hooted and grunted approval.

"Maybe," she said. "And how would I go about getting myself rehabilitated?"

I grinned. "What you need," I said, "is a man around the house. I'll start by cooking you a nice steak for dinner tonight. And after dinner I'll sing you some songs and tell you some bedtime stories."

She cocked her head. "And then?"

"And then I'll tuck you in."

She laughed, a sound like temple bells. "I can hardly wait."

* * *

"The main question, I guess," I said as I washed and cut the lettuce in the camp's makeshift kitchen, "is whether or not it's working. Are they getting rehabilitated?"

Lindy was laying out the table, pushing books and papers down to one end, setting out silverware and plates. "Yes and no," she said over her shoulder. "They can learn the patterns well enough, and they seem to understand why they're learning them. But I'm having a lot of trouble with them right at the moment."

"Trouble? How?"

Outside, dusk was gathering in. She got the big Petromax lantern down from its hook and started pumping it up. "Well, basically, I think they really just don't want to go back to living in the forest." The Petromax ignited with a soft whump. "Take Bobo, for example. Most of the chimps here stay pretty close to home, but not him. He's been seen miles away, over by the tourist hotel, rooting around in the trash for scraps."

I scratched an insect bite on my arm. "I can understand that," I said. "Most of us humans prefer security and safety to uncertainty and danger. Who can blame the chimps for wanting it that way, too?"

"Even if it means living in a cage?"

I opened a can of tuna to add to the salad. "Hey, look at the people living in a so-called developed society. What is it the French say? *Métro, boulot, dodo* – take the train, go to work, go to sleep. For most people that and television are all there is."

"But not people like us," she said.

I grinned at her. "No, not for people like us. But Lindy, don't forget – we're craaazy." I rolled my eyes, making her laugh.

I wiped my hands and brought the salad to the table. "And that, *ma chérie-coco*, is why we're together," I said. "Insanity loves company, after all. Now, what will you drink with your dinner? Warm beer or warm whiskey?"

* * *

We stayed at the table after dinner, sipping our beer and talking. Rain fell gently outside, and the Petromax in the corner was hissing softly. I was warm and dry and well-fed, a little sleepy from the beer, almost ready to call it a night. I thought of the chimpanzees outside in their nests of sticks in the trees with the rain coming down and maybe a few pairs of bright yellow eyes peering hungrily at them from the deep bush just beyond the camp, and I couldn't blame them for wanting to be like real people.

I took a sip of my beer, listening to the rain on the tin roof. "What happens if I get caught in here by the rains?" I said after a while.

She gave me what I think was meant to be an evil smile. "Then, my friend, you get to stay here with me until the end of November."

I was looking at the rise of her breasts under her cotton shirt and thinking that maybe a few months in the bush with Lindy wouldn't be such a bad idea at all, when up at the edge of my vision, I saw something move. I looked up and saw a bright green snake coiled around one of the rafters. As I sat frozen to the spot, it dropped on the table between us.

There was a crash, and plates flew in all directions. I looked down to see Lindy's bushknife deeply embedded in the tabletop, and on either side of the broad blade, half a snake.

I hadn't even had time to let go of my beer.

"Cripes," I said after a moment.

"Practice makes perfect," she said, pulling the blade out of the wood. "The snakes come in looking for frogs. The frogs come in to get the mosquitoes. The mosquitoes come in to get us. So this is just completing the cycle."

I stared at the two halves of the snake. "That's a green mamba, isn't it?" The tail was still twitching.

"Yes, it is." She stood up. "And if you'll get rid of it, sweetie, I'll get us both another beer."

I picked up the pieces of the snake and took them to the barred window and tossed them out. There'd be nothing left in the morning, I knew; if the driver ants didn't find them, some other hungry creature would. I stood by the window and listened to the rain while I looked out into the blackness of the forest.

We're inside a fortress here, I thought – an oasis of light and relative safety inside an area of thousands of square miles of total wilderness. The rainy season was slowly descending on the area like a giant cloak, blocking off the outside world and its paved roads, its government of laws, its mundane certainties. The research station would shrink against the background of the tall trees which ringed it in, and time would slow down, become bush time. Humans would be outsiders, frail and small against the bulk of the forest.

Inside the borders of the park, the rules of the game, the underlying pattern of existence, would shift; it would be a time of reliance on inner resources, of being extra careful, of hoping that nothing went wrong, that nothing unforeseen cropped up.

That nothing bad happened. Because if it did, all you'd have were your own resources. And if you scream for help in the forest and nobody hears, do you make a noise at all?

Lindy hummed quietly as she strung the mosquito net over the wide bamboo bed. "Don't bother doing the dishes," she said. "Just leave the plates on the table for tonight." She moved close to me, and her warm lips brushed my ear. "Now hurry up and let's get under the mosquito net."

I unbuttoned her shirt and pulled the tails out of her jeans. "Lindy, I–"

She put a finger to my lips. "Just do it, okay?"

CHAPTER FOURTEEN

I woke at sunrise and lay quietly in bed for a while, listening to the forest sounds as the day began. Pale green light filtered in through the windows and slanted across the bed. Finally, Lindy stirred and opened her eyes. "Oh, great, it's tomorrow," she breathed.

She rolled over, looked at me and smiled. "Still here, huh?"

I smiled back. "Still here. Who gets to make breakfast?"

"Wrestle you for it," she said.

* * *

We breakfasted on toast and kinkiliba tea. Then I shook a hunting spider out of my boots, got dressed, and went outside.

The chimps had been up for hours. They greeted us effusively as we came out of the hut, clustering around and making small grunts of pleasure and anticipation. "They're looking forward to their walk," Lindy explained. "We go out for a couple of hours every morning. I usually take them down into the valley to look for food. Afterwards we can have a bath and sit around – it'll be too hot later to do much."

"Fine," I said. I picked up my shoulder bag, and we started off into the bush. The forest had been washed by the night's rain, and now it sparkled in the light, the colors vibrating softly in the crystal sharpness of the early morning.

It is a very Mediterranean light. In the hot lands, however, such a light only comes rarely, and only in the morning. In an hour or less, the sun would climb higher in the sky, dragging heat like a blanket across the forest. The air would lose its tang, and by noon, the bush would look like a washed-out color photograph, the blinding glare of the sun overwhelming and flattening everything.

But for now we enjoyed the morning's coolness and light as we moved easily through the high trees along the side of the broad river valley that stretched away to the south of the camp, towards the mountains in Guinea.

After twenty minutes, Lindy stopped. "Time for breakfast," she announced.

"We just ate," I pointed out.

"Not us, silly. The chimps."

She pointed to a large anthill just off the trail. In West Africa, the ants come equipped with a pretty decent set of pincers, and in the dry season, they'll form huge, long ribbons along the ground as they snake through the forest – or through your house – in search of food and water. They also build nests which look like something out of science fiction – tall skyscrapers of yellow-red mud, some of them twenty feet high.

"Ants for breakfast?"

She grinned. "Watch." She picked up a stick from the ground and thrust it into the entrance to the nest. The chimps had surrounded the anthill now, and were grunting excitedly and jumping up and down. Almost immediately, ants boiled out and began running up the stick.

"Hey, careful," I said, stepping back. "Those bite."

"Relax. They won't bite you if you're careful." She held up the stick and began to lick ants from it, eating them the way a kid would lick chocolate sprinkles from an ice cream cone. I started to open my mouth again, but closed it when I saw that all the chimps had found sticks, too, and were busy poking them into the anthill and devouring the ants which emerged, licking their fingers carefully.

Lindy finished her ants and handed her stick over to a small chimp to use. "Well," she said, "what do you think of that?"

"They, ah, learned that pretty fast," I said carefully. I was watching Lindy's mouth as she chewed up the last of the ants.

"They learned it before, that's why. I just wanted to see if they remembered. Why are you looking at me that way?"

I looked at the chimps and then at her. "Lindy, people don't— I mean, real people don't eat ants. At least, not normally. I mean, I don't think I've ever seen anyone do that before, and—"

"Oh, pooh. Ants are perfectly all right to eat. So are termites and grubs. People all over the world eat insects, and just because your friends don't is no reason to think that they're not acceptable food."

She went back to the anthill and borrowed a branch from one of the chimps. "Go ahead, try one," she said, handing it to me. "It won't kill you."

I stared at the stick. "Well, thanks for the offer," I said at last, "but I think I'll stay with shrimp and lobster."

She stood up, brushing off her shorts. "Shrimp are basically sea cockroaches, Max," she said. "Any entomologist will tell you that."

* * *

We might be something out of Tolkien, I thought as I picked my way over a fallen log. We're giants, and the chimps are the hairy-footed hobbits. Above us, the trees were taller now as we moved further away from camp and down toward the Gambia River.

In the branches overhead, dozens of brightly colored fire finches darted to and fro, and now and then, a flight of green parrots swooped low. Thick vines and creepers hung down across the path, and the forest was filled with bird and insect noises. Once, the chimps spotted a band of green monkeys in the trees off to the right, and we paused while the two groups exchanged greetings and insults before moving off again.

Half an hour later we reached a wide bluff overlooking the river. Stepping out onto the edge, I saw the forest open out below us, stretching off into the distant haze. Below, the Gambia curved lazily around and disappeared off to the west, on its way to the sea hundreds of miles away.

As far as the eye could see, there were no buildings, no smoke, no sign of humans. The only noises were the twittering of birds and the low drone of insects. The smell of the forest rose up on the heat – a green, fresh smell of rain and renewal, with an underlay of decay.

Lindy came over and stood beside me. Together we stared out at the green carpet which stretched endlessly out ahead of us before losing itself in the mists of the rising mountains on the border, far to the south. The chimps, busily engaged in a game of tag, ignored us. I put my arm around her. "How big is this place?" I asked her.

"The park itself? About two million acres. We're more or less in the middle of it."

"And how many people are in it right now?"

She looked at me, grinning. "There are a couple of park rangers over at Simenti, but everyone else has gone home. You and I are probably half the population right now."

"Simenti's where the hotel and the airstrip are, right? Is it far away?"

"Not that far. Twenty kilometers as the crow flies, over on the other side of the mountain. But it takes me three hours to drive there, even when the road's decent. Bobo can do it in under two hours. He goes over there sometimes when I'm away from camp and bums food from the rangers and the tourists."

"You mean there's nobody else? Just us and a few park rangers?"

She pointed down to the southeast. "At the edge of the park there are a few Bassari villages, over by the border.

But even in Bassari country, you can drive for hours and not see anyone."

She turned away and whistled for the chimps. "Come on," she said. "Ready for a bath?"

"Sounds good," I said, fingering my damp shirt. "But where?"

"In the river, of course." She pointed down the slope. "It's shallow down in this part, and shady. Come on." She swung her bag back on her shoulder and we moved off down the trail.

In a few moments we had reached the Gambia. We were on the outside of a wide bend, well shaded by the trees. In the middle of the river was a cluster of large flat rocks. "That's where I bathe," she said, pointing to them. "The chimps don't like water, thank God, and so they don't come out there."

She put down her sack and started undressing. A moment later we were wading cautiously out into the cool water, carrying our clothes and the rucksacks. "If we leave anything where they can get it," Lindy explained, "they'll either steal it or eat it. Bobo ate a whole bar of soap once."

We reached the rocks in the middle of the river and set down our loads, easing our bodies fully into the water. It was cool enough in the shade to raise goosebumps, but delightful to lie full-length in the hot sun. On the far side of the rocks it was deeper, and I did a few flat dives. Some of the chimps had appeared on the bank now, and they cheered each time I hit the water.

She looked curiously at my body. "I didn't notice those scars and things last night," she said. "Where'd they come from?"

"Differences of opinion," I said. "Same thing that makes horse races interesting." I lay back in the water. "This is better than a pool," I said, feeling the slow current wash my body. "What about crocodiles?"

"Upstream there are plenty," she said, soaping her hair. "But they don't usually come down this far. Anyway, the chimps will tell us if they spot one." She handed me the soap. "Here. Wash my back, will you?"

I washed her back while I watched a flock of parrots playing in the trees above us. On the bank, the chimps had settled down to a scratching and grooming session. When I was through, she washed my back. Then we washed each other's fronts.

"What," I said at last, "did you have in mind for this afternoon?"

She laughed. "Lunch first. You need to build up your strength." She splashed me then, and dove into the water, sleek as an otter.

* * *

It was cool on the top of Mount Asserik, quiet and peaceful. We had left the chimps behind; they were afraid to cross the clearing. Lindy and I sat on a grassy ledge overlooking the clearing where the Land Rover was parked, taking turns using the binoculars.

We could see for miles in all directions, the deep green of the forest canopy unbroken except for the broad channel of the river. The distant mountains at the edge of Bassari country near the border were clear and sharp, and we could see rain clouds spilling down their sides, moving slowly out onto the flatter country near the river.

"Isn't this wonderful?" she said in a dreamy voice. "I'm beginning to wonder if I'll ever want to go back to Atlanta."

The sun felt good on my bare chest. I closed my eyes in the warm sunlight and tried to imagine the world out there beyond the forest. "Going back," I said finally, "might be a little difficult. I remember how it was when I came back from Vietnam. The air at home smelled funny, the cars and machines made too much noise, the concrete sidewalks hurt my feet, and the tall buildings blocked the sun. There weren't any animals around except cats and dogs. There was canned music in all the stores and shops, and a lot of crazy people on the streets."

"Wow, that sounds just terrific," she murmured.

"It passes," I said. "Stick with it for a couple of weeks, and things will click back into place."

She turned. "You mean I'll just go back to being like everyone else? Is that what I can look forward to?"

"You don't have to approve of it," I said. "Or even like it. Just accept it; use it. The city is a jungle, too, and urban living is a survival skill. Once you've learned to live out here, Atlanta ought to be child's play. How many of your friends would be able to cope with green mambas at dinner, or ants for breakfast?"

She smiled. "I'll be sorry to go. I guess I just feel a lot more alive out in places like this. No Muzak, no freeways, no fast food."

"No television," I said.

"No billboards."

"No traffic."

"No crazies."

I sat up. "Well, not exactly. Don't forget what happened in Dakar."

She put a hand on my shoulder. "That's the city again, Max; not here. Let's not talk about Ti-Claude, okay? I'm talking about here, in the forest. Things are real out here, Max; the highs are higher, and the lows are lower. Taking a bath in the river, for instance. What's special about that? Well, for me, it's the high point of my day. And nothing feels better than that bath."

"Nothing?" I said innocently.

"Stop trying to distract me," she said, pushing my hand away. "Anyway, you know what I mean. It's just plain old muddy river water, but it's the best thing in the world. When I'm out here by myself, I have a can of sliced pineapple every Saturday night. I mean, I make a ceremony out of it. And it's the best damn pineapple I ever tasted."

She turned to face me. "Do you understand? You must have noticed it yourself — how out here on the edge of things, your hearing improves, your eyesight gets better, that sort of thing?"

I nodded. So much of what she was saying was similar to my own experience. "I do know what you mean," I said after a moment. "Learning that you can survive without television or fast food kind of changes you, doesn't it? You become independent; a survivor. Not many of us are, these days. We're a little like the chimps you're teaching — comfortable, overfed, and a little bland."

She rolled over on her stomach and plucked at the edge of the blanket. "I sometimes wonder, though," she said, "whether being self-reliant really matters. Can't technology take care of most of that for us? Does it matter that kids who learn to rely on calculators sometimes forget how to do long division?"

I watched a hawk circle far above the clearing, searching for prey. "Living out in places like this is like practicing a form of long division, I think," I said at last. "You sharpen your mind and your body, and you develop skills you never knew you had." I ran my finger slowly down the curve of her waist, feeling her firm, warm skin. "And that's important for people. Maybe for society, too, in the long run. Hell, I don't know. How did we get on this subject, anyway?"

She laughed and sat up on the blanket, running her hands through her hair, fluffing it out. Then she stretched luxuriously. "I've got an idea," she said. "We've got a couple of hours before we should be back at camp. If you've finished philosophizing, maybe we could practice another survival skill together."

She began to run her fingers lightly across the hairs on my stomach, her eyes bright, a lazy smile spreading across her face. "What I have in mind isn't nearly as difficult as long division, and it's a lot more fun."

* * *

"Better cover up, Max, or you'll get sunburned."

I reached over, pulled on my shirt, and fell back on the blanket. Peace and utter exhaustion are a fine combination.

I turned my head and looked at Lindy. She lay still, her face and shoulders still flushed, a faint smile on her face. Her hair was spread out in every direction. There was a large pink bite mark on her right shoulder, and I wondered how I had managed to do that.

We were lying side by side, holding hands and staring up at the wide sky, letting the high clouds race through our empty minds. It felt very good to have the sun on my body, to feel the light breeze, to be here with her.

She opened her eyes. "Shit," she said quietly.

"What is it?" I murmured.

"Something's coming," she said. "Something with an engine. Hear it?"

I listened. After a few seconds, I heard it too, very faintly.

"It's a car or a truck, and it's coming this way," she said quietly. "Damn."

Ten minutes later a blue jeep with a canvas top entered the clearing below us. I raised the binoculars and focused. The jeep stopped behind our Land Rover and two men got out. One of them was Bari N'Dour.

"Uh-oh."

"What's wrong?"

I handed the glasses to Lindy. "Take a look. It's Bari."

"Bari? What on earth's he doing here?"

"I don't know. But something tells me it's not good news. Let's get our clothes on and get down there before they shoot one of the chimps."

"Welcome back to the real world," Lindy muttered as she got to her feet.

CHAPTER FIFTEEN

We sat in a backyard bar on a Tambacounda side street, drinking cold Stork out of big bottles. Birds and insects called softly from the tamarind trees, and pachanga music played softly from the transistor radio behind the bar. As we sipped our beer, we watched the animals.

The bar owner had a veritable menagerie, including goats, sheep, guinea fowl, two horses, a loud flock of geese, and half a dozen enormous pigs. Right now, one of the pigs was trying to mount another, and the mountee was squealing loudly, whether in protest or pleasure it was difficult to tell.

"Great floor show," murmured Lindy. "Was this worth the drive, or what?"

I wiped laterite dust from my sweaty face with a handkerchief. It was well after sundown now, but the heat hadn't dropped much. I turned to Bari. "Run it by me again," I said. "How did you find him?"

"We've had people watching at the train stations, the airport, the bus stations. One of them spotted Ti-Claude early this morning, boarding the Bamako express. When the train stopped in Thies, I managed to put a man on board. His name is Bakary, and he comes from Tambacounda. At the stop in Diourbel, he telephoned me and confirmed that Ti-Claude was on board. He's watching him now."

Bari checked his watch. "The train's due in any time now – if it hasn't broken down." He smiled. "I drove down from Dakar as fast as I could. It wasn't hard to beat the train."

"Why didn't you just get Bakary to arrest Ti-Claude in Diourbel?" Lindy asked.

Bari shook his head. "Too risky. The train's packed, as usual. We could easily have a hostage situation and people dead."

I nodded, remembering the bodies of the taxi driver and the woodcarver.

"All you need to do is formally identify him and make a short statement," Bari continued. "It's just a legal technicality. Otherwise, we'd have to bring you up to Dakar. This way, it's over immediately."

"And then we can go back to the park?" said Lindy.

Bari smiled. "Of course. You can drive back later tonight if you want to."

I shuddered, shaking my head. The trip to Tambacounda had been hours of torture over the washboard track that passed for a road, eating Bari's dust as we followed him. The bumping had been severe enough to loosen fillings, the noise so loud as to inhibit conversation.

It had been just sunset before we crested the final small hill and saw Tambacounda spread out before us, its red-tiled roofs peeping up through the tree canopy. Capital of Eastern Senegal, Tambacounda was a town of some thirty thousand whose main claim to fame was the fact that the Dakar-Bamako express train stopped there twice weekly on its way to the border.

It had been the equivalent of a day's work to get here. I wasn't about to turn around and repeat the trip in the dark.

"We'll stay the night," I said.

"Have there been any more murders?" Lindy spoke quietly.

Bari shook his head. "None that we know of. But we've turned up some interesting information on both the woodcarver and the taxi driver. The two men knew each other, and were often seen together, according to our sources. And both of them have previously been arrested –

the taxi driver, twice – for selling goods stolen from the port."

I sipped my beer and wiped big drops of condensation from the bottle. "Not much to go on, is it? Any connection between the two men and Rachid Khoury?"

"Well, that's interesting, in fact," Bari said. "There's no connection at all. In fact, both men were involved with another Lebanese – a man named Samir Nassif."

"Nassif? Who is he? How does he figure in this?"

Bari shrugged. "He's a businessman like Khoury, but clean, as far as we can tell. One of his sidelines is African art, and it turns out that Thiam, the woodcarver, sold him pieces from time to time. And the taxi driver sometimes worked as a *boukiman* for Nassif."

Lindy frowned. "A what?"

"A bagman," Bari said. "The guy who collects for a moneylender. *Bouki* means 'hyena' in Wolof."

I turned to Bari. "Any luck on the other two names?"

"The old man and the Togolese? Nothing." Bari shook his head. "But once we arrest Ti-Claude, we'll get the whole story. The other two names are details. We've got him cornered now; that's the important thing."

I didn't like the image of Ti-Claude being cornered, but this wasn't the time or place to bring it up. So I sipped my beer and watched the pigs and listened to the music. And tried not to think about Ti-Claude, coming toward us now, riding the train across the savannah flatland, drawing closer by the minute.

Bari put a fresh beer in my hand. "But let's not talk about that. Are you enjoying yourself down in the park? What have you been doing for fun?"

I weighed several possible answers in my head, finally giving him the one that seemed the most straightforward.

"Learning to eat ants," I said.

Off in the distance, I heard the train whistle, drifting out of the humid darkness.

* * *

The single bright eye of the train stabbed harshly through the night and down along the shiny metal tracks to where Bari, Lindy and I stood waiting on the station platform.

Although it was just past midnight, the station throbbed with life. Scores of people bustled to and fro, and in the darkness small kerosene lanterns shone dimly, their guttering flames outlining the mango and peanut ladies seated on the concrete platform. *Bana-banas* and medicine men squatted beside them, their wares spread out, arranged to tempt the weary and hungry travelers who would arrive aboard the approaching express train.

Wooden chicken-cages sat atop heaps of piled baggage, and to the side, tethered goats and sheep waited nervously, their long ears twitching. Ragged-trousered porters milled through the crowd, cloth bundles and cheap cardboard suitcases balanced on their heads. Inside the small, lighted office beside the shuttered waiting room, the *chef de gare* sat alone, moving papers around on his cluttered desk and smoking a Gauloise.

Up against the station building, in the interstices of shadow between the flickering lights, out of the way of passing feet and hooves, several old beggars slept, their thin cloths pulled up over their faces. The Bamako express came twice weekly; these men would be here every night.

The train's horn blared, causing the chickens to squawk with fright. With a deep bass thrumming noise, the big Alstom diesel sailed majestically into the station, its front painted in the national colors of red, yellow, and green. Hot oil and grease swept along in its wake.

With a drawn-out screech of brakes and a sigh of compressors releasing, the express came to a shuddering halt, its cyclops eye still shining, probing the inky blackness beyond the station.

I brushed at a stray mosquito, stepped around a goat, and moved closer to the edge of the platform. There were four passenger cars, two wagon-lit sleepers and a long line of boxcars. People began to spill from the doorways, colliding with a wave of fruit-sellers hurrying in the opposite direction. Two huge Wolof women grunted down the steps of one of the sleeping cars, balancing enamel bowls wrapped in cloth on their heads. They were met with squeals of delight and much kissing and slapping of palms by two more women, equally large, waiting on the platform. All four roared off cackling into the darkness, continuing to exchange greetings in loud voices.

Next came a clutch of emaciated and dour Mauritanians, their dirty white robes clutched protectively about them as they stepped down. Each man carried a thin vinyl briefcase in one hand, a tin teapot in the other. Soon they were lost in the crowd, only their electric blue turbans visible.

Bari gripped my elbow. "Come quickly," he hissed. "Something's gone wrong." He had another man with him.

"Wrong?" I asked.

"We've lost him. Come on – in here."

We crammed into the office of the stationmaster. He stood up, glaring at us, but Bari flashed his identification at him. "*Fous le camp*," he said. "Out, now."

Bari turned to me. "This is Bakary," he said, indicating the man with him. "He was our man aboard the train." He nodded to the man. "Tell him what you just told me."

Bakary's face shone with sweat under the yellow bulb. "I had him in my sights, the whole time, *au nom de ma mère*, all the way from Thiès. Then, just outside of town here, he got away. There's a rail junction half a kilometer up the line, where the spur from the peanut factory joins the main line. The train has to slow down while the switches are thrown."

He took a deep breath. "I was sitting at the end of the car, where I could keep an eye on him. Suddenly, he grabbed his bag and went out the door. I followed him. I assumed he was going to the toilet, but when I got there, he was gone." He bowed his head miserably. "He must have jumped from the train."

Bari looked grave. "We've seriously underestimated him, I think. And now he's loose, somewhere in town. We've got to find him. And fast."

He turned to Bakary. "If we can cordon off the town, there's a chance we can trap him before he gets away. We'll have to set up roadblocks. How many ways out of town are there?"

Bakary thought for a moment. "Three main roads, plus the rail line and the airstrip. One road goes back to Dakar, one goes north to the Mali border, and the third goes southeast, to Kédougou. The only other ways out are by rail or air. There's a freight train through here every day, and an Air Sénégal flight twice a week; tomorrow, in fact. He could probably sneak aboard the train without too much trouble, but he'd need a ticket for the plane."

Bari nodded. "We can put men at the station, of course. We should also watch the airport. Where do you get tickets?"

"*Chez Le Vieux*, of course," answered Bakary. "He's the Air Sénégal agent."

"What's his name, this old man?"

Bakary laughed. "Le Vieux *is* the old man's name. Everybody makes that mistake at first. He's a Frenchman, runs a store, just up the street. Chez Le Vieux. He–"

Bari turned to look at me. "That's it," he whispered. "Le Vieux. The third name. It has to be him. Let's go, and pray we're not too late."

* * *

We raced up the street toward the commercial section of town, where Le Vieux had his store. The town was deserted and asleep. A few stray dogs wandered along in the shadows of the closed shops, sniffing hopefully at the piles of garbage in the alleyways, and here and there, a dim kerosene lantern marked the presence of a night *gardien*, bent over in watchful sleep in a darkened doorway.

"Le Vieux's been here for more than thirty years," Bakary was saying. "I remember him when I was a small boy. People say he was a deserter from the French Army, but who knows? No wife, no kids. He's hard-working and friendly, and people like him. He's the local agent for Land Rover, Peugeot, and Citroën, and when Air Sénégal began service, he handled tickets and cargo for them. Slow down; this is his store. The house is around back."

We were too late, of course. I knew it as soon as I saw the open gate at the side of the house.

"Stay in the truck," I said to Lindy.

"But–"

"Do it."

We advanced slowly into the yard, Bari holding his service pistol at the ready. The wide veranda doors were slightly ajar, and from within, lights blazed.

We began to search the premises. The shop had been closed for hours, and the cash register had not been disturbed. Le Vieux's bedroom was still perfectly in order. The easy chair's upholstery still held a dent where Le Vieux had been sitting, and on the table beside the chair lay car keys, some loose change, and a Fleuve Noir crime novel. In the ashtray lay a heavy briar pipe. It was still warm to the touch.

Bakary stuck his head around the door. "In the kitchen," he said. "Come take a look."

Like the rest of the house, the kitchen, too, was immaculate. Except for the large countertop beside the stove. On it sat an empty wooden crate, and beside the crate, several dozen pineapples had been hacked to bits, pulp and skin scattered everywhere on the walls and the floor.

Bari examined everything. "Pineapples?" he said. "What the hell is the man doing with pineapples?"

"Le Vieux sold pineapples," Bakary said. "He had fresh fruit and vegetables flown up from Kédougou once or twice a week. Pineapples, fresh lettuce, bananas, that sort of thing."

We found Le Vieux in the cold room of the store, off the kitchen. The heavy insulated door was open, and the refrigerator's compressor was straining to maintain the temperature inside the freezer against the heat creeping in from outside.

Le Vieux hung suspended from a meathook, next to a butchered steer carcass. The point of the hook had been forcibly driven through his neck, and the body hung a foot off the floor. A small puddle of blood was collecting underneath.

Le Vieux wore leather sandals, shorts, and an open-necked shirt worn outside the belt. He looked to be in his early sixties, a trim, tanned man with strong features and a full head of silver hair. His face was distorted in pain, and I wondered if he'd died before Ti-Claude had stuck the meathook through his neck. I hoped so.

Bari felt the body. "He's still warm. This must have happened just a few minutes ago."

I nodded. "So he's not far away."

From outside, I heard the noise of a car starting up and a screech of tires. Bari shot me a glance. "Is that–"

I was already running toward the door. Outside, Lindy and her Land Rover were gone. In the distance, I could see red taillights moving swiftly down the street.

I ran back inside, snatched up the keys from Le Vieux's bedroom table, and threw open the garage doors. Inside was a battered Peugeot 504 station wagon. "Get in," I said to Bari.

"What the hell do you think you're doing?"

I was already behind the wheel. "I'm going after the sonofabitch, of course," I shouted at him. As the Peugeot's engine roared to life, I flicked on the lights. "You coming or not?"

"Wait." He turned to Bakary. "Go to the Gendarmerie, wake up the *commandant*. Get some people behind us as fast as you can. Don't lose a moment." He got in beside me. "Let's go."

The 504 roared out of the garage and onto the main road. I could still see Lindy's taillights in the distance. But I could see something else as well.

The Dakar-Bamako express was pulling out of the station. I could see its bright headlamp moving, picking up speed, approaching the level crossing. Lindy's Land Rover was racing to get there first.

"*Nom de Dieu*," whispered Bari. "He's not going to make it." The train blew a long warning blast, and its headlamp caught Lindy's Land Rover squarely in its beam as it bore down on the crossing.

Then the Land Rover was gone, swallowed up in the darkness on the other side, and I slammed to a stop as the train moved across my path, its whistle still splitting the night.

I sat helplessly, cursing and slamming my fist against the steering wheel as the long train thundered by, cutting us off from Lindy and Ti-Claude, who were now moving down the road out of town, picking up speed with every passing second.

CHAPTER SIXTEEN

Years ago, I'd followed this road from the air, using it as a reference point as I flew east across the Falémé River and into Mali with loads of relief food. On the maps, it is indicated with a thick red line and the words 'National Highway Number 7.' From five thousand feet up, the road appears wide, smooth, and important.

On the ground, however, the road is an exercise in creative imagination more than anything else, I thought grimly as I fought the wheel and pressed the accelerator to the floor. It was little more than a laterite track, strewn with potholes, ditches and an occasional tree branch. We were making about eighty kilometers an hour in Le Vieux's ageing Peugeot wagon, roaring through the dark, barely under control, and Bari was having to hold on to the dashboard with both hands to keep himself in the seat.

The worst was the washboard, an endless series of ripples set precisely eight inches apart, running across the road. This waveform pattern can shake a light car to pieces within hours. Over a period of a few years, it will do roughly the same thing to your kidneys and vertebrae. There's only one really practical way of dealing with washboard, and I'd learned it years ago in Asia: drive like the proverbial bat out of hell.

The idea is to get going fast enough to smooth out the ripple effect. Most vehicles had an optimum speed for this, depending on their weight. Somewhere between seventy-five and eighty kilometers per hour, the Peugeot attained 'warp speed', and began to plane across the surface of the ridges. Right now, I was steering Le Vieux's station wagon as I would a speedboat – very gently, with plenty of allowance for drift.

We were flat out now, belly to the ground. The noise was deafening, and Bari and I could communicate only by shouting. Fortunately, I didn't have too much to say – I was far too busy trying to keep the car on the road.

Every now and then, our headlamps revealed the outlines of a wrecked car or truck on the shoulder, mute testimony to what the road could do to an inexperienced or inattentive driver. The road went straight through the forest, heading southeast toward the border. There were no more villages now, no signs of human habitation, only the tall trees and an occasional pair of red eyes peering out at us from the undergrowth. Ti-Claude was too far ahead of us now to see his lights, but the dust raised by Lindy's Land Rover still hung in the air, unmistakable proof that he had recently passed by. He couldn't be more than a few kilometers in front of us, I reckoned.

I pressed my foot harder to the floor, coaxing more speed out of the old Peugeot.

It seemed to be growing more humid by the minute. It was going to rain soon, and that would put us at a major disadvantage. The rains in the early part of the wet season tend to be heavy and intense, and if the rain went on for any length of time, it would turn the road into a mass of *poto-poto*, the slippery mud which was so dangerous to drive on. It would also hide the deep potholes in the road, making it impossible to avoid them.

Lindy's Land Rover, on the other hand, was built for such road conditions, with all-terrain tires, four-wheel drive, and an extra low gear ratio. All we had in our favor now was the fact that there was only one road – only one escape route – and that Ti-Claude was going nowhere fast.

In fact, he was driving straight into the most remote and rugged part of the country, a virtual dead end. A hundred kilometers away lay the border town of Kédougou, and beyond it, the Guinean frontier, where Ti-Claude would be lucky to avoid getting shot on sight.

Why is he heading toward Kédougou? It made no sense. Better to have struck out for the open spaces of Mali, the flat and empty Sahel wasteland where someone resourceful could hide for months, rather than straight into the mountains on the border with an unfriendly country.

We had no more insight into his motives now, I realized, than we had at the beginning. All we had was a chain of circumstance and violence which began with Rachid Khoury, and linked a cop, a taxi driver, a woodcarver and a French shopkeeper together in violent death. And now, I feared that another link in the chain might be forged, here on the road to Kédougou.

There ought to be a pattern, I thought. If one person dies, you know there's danger. When the second person dies, you know it's not accidental. By the time the third person dies, you ought to be able to see the outline of a pattern.

So there's got to be a method in this madness, I told myself as I pushed the Peugeot on through the night. Maybe so, my self answered back. But there's also madness. Don't forget that.

Bari tapped me on the shoulder. "Listen," he roared above the engine noise. "I just remembered something. There's a water crossing up ahead – where the Gambia River cuts across the road. We ought to able to get him there."

"How?" I shouted back.

"The bridge is closed for repairs," Bari said. "You have to cross on a ferry. It takes time, half an hour at least. Even if he's started across, we can get him."

"So he's heading into a trap. How far ahead is the river?"

"Another fifty kilometers, I think." He took his pistol from its holster and checked the clip.

It wasn't what I'd call an ideal setup, meeting Ti-Claude in the middle of the night on a riverbank, but it was better than nothing. Like a dog chasing cars, I wasn't too sure what I'd do when we caught Ti-Claude, but right now, it was an academic question; first, we had to catch him. I pressed harder on the accelerator, urging the car on.

Five minutes later, it began to rain.

* * *

The wipers were all but useless against the sheeting rain, their clicking a metronome feeding my frustration and anxiety. Visibility was down to a matter of yards now. I kept the speed up as high as I dared, maneuvering the Peugeot around the obstacles I could see, taking it on the nose for the ones I missed. The ruts and holes in the road had filled up with water, creating vast mudholes of uncertain depth and breadth. By Bari's reckoning, we were less than twenty kilometers from the river now.

"Can't you get some more speed out of this thing?" Bari shouted above the roar of the engine and the rain. "We can't be very far behind them now."

The combined din of the road and the rain was nearly intolerable, a deafening racket which had penetrated into the center of my brain and was shaking my nerve endings to bits.

I turned to him. "What the hell do you think you're riding in, the Concorde?"

"Watch out!" shouted Bari.

I snapped my eyes back to the road ahead, but it was too late. We were on a sharp bend, moving – I now realized – much too fast for the rain-slick washboard, now transformed into the tropical equivalent of glare ice. The steering wheel turned to mush in my hands, and a second later, our tires broke loose. The Peugeot began to drift, slipping sideways, out of control.

Our headlights swung to reveal a thick tree branch across the road. Beyond it, an enormous mudhole extended into the darkness beyond.

"Hang on!" I shouted.

We skidded wildly for a moment, and hit the branch. There was a splintering crash, a shock, and then, with all the grace that several thousand pounds of steel can muster, we took to the air and sailed majestically into the middle of the mudhole.

There was a splash, and then deep silence, broken only by the sounds of the rain and the ticking noise coming from the hot engine.

"*Merde, alors,*" said Bari quietly.

"You can say that again," I said after a moment.

He looked at me. "Once is enough, I think. Are you all right?"

I nodded. "I think so." I rolled down the window and peered out. The Peugeot was lying in a pool of water up to the top of its tires. The windshield and the entire front of the station wagon were covered in mud. The engine was stalled and the lights didn't work. And it was pitch black outside.

I forced open the door and stepped out, promptly going in up to my knees in the muddy water. "Have we got a bushknife in there?" I called to Bari. "Any tools at all? Maybe I can cut some tree branches, push them under the wheels."

Bari searched the interior. "Not a damned thing," he said after a moment.

I got behind the wheel and tried the ignition. The starter ground uselessly for a few seconds, and then died. The motor was wet, the exhaust system flooded. I climbed back out and stood in the rain and the mud and thought hard. The moon was up but largely obscured by the rainclouds, and the steady downpour drowned out the forest noises. The effect was something like taking a warm shower in the dark with your clothes on.

The river crossing at the Gambia was only a few kilometers away, but it might as well have been in Timbuktu. The other cops and soldiers from Tambacounda would get here eventually, but by that time, it would be too late: Ti-Claude would be across the river. And once on the other side, he had all of Eastern Senegal to hide in.

This is happening to someone else, I thought; not to me. The warm water dripped down my face and I could just see the dim outlines of the forest canopy rearing up on either side of the road. I am in the middle of bloody Africa, I thought, on a deserted road through no-man's-land, chasing a maniac who's killed four people, taken shots at me, and kidnapped a woman I am very fond of. I came to this country for a vacation. How on earth did I get into this mess?

Then I saw lights coming through the forest.

"There's a truck coming," I said to Bari. "No, two trucks. It's the Gendarmerie, from Tambacounda."

Now, over the noise of the rain, I could hear them. Heavy vehicles, moving slowly through the bush, their yellow headlamps flickering through the trees.

Bari pushed his way through the mud and stood in the middle of the road. "That's a piece of luck, at least," he said. "We'll leave the station wagon here and go with them. It's not worth taking the time to pull it out. We'll still be able to catch Ti-Claude."

The two vehicles were rounding the bend, catching us in their headlamps. I recognized the lead vehicle as a canvas-topped jeep. It seemed to be towing a heavy trailer of some kind. The second truck was an old Dodge Power Wagon. Bari stepped out onto the road, his hand raised, a smile on his lips.

The trucks stopped thirty feet away, engines ticking over, steam rising from the hoods, pinning us with their high beams.

Bari shaded his eyes against the glare. "Max, go up there and tell them to turn their damned lights off!"

I nodded, walking up to the cab of the first truck. There were at least two people inside, but somehow, they didn't look like gendarmes. For one thing, they were light-skinned. And for another, they were both wearing ragged turbans.

I glanced down at the front of the truck and saw the distinctive green and yellow of a Mauritanian license plate. When I looked up again, I noticed the animal carcasses strapped to the top and sides of the truck.

Uh-oh, I thought. These guys aren't Good Samaritans, and we're not in Kansas anymore.

The door of the cab opened, and a Mauritanian stepped out onto the running board. He cradled a Sterling submachine gun in his arms.

"Run!" I screamed at Bari, and threw myself to the side.

The Mauritanian snicked the clip home, raised his weapon, and began to fire.

CHAPTER SEVENTEEN

Beside me in the darkness, Bari raised his pistol. I put my hand on his shoulder. "Not yet," I whispered. "Let's think about this for just a minute."

We lay behind a fallen log, half-buried in the underbrush, watching the Mauritanians as they grunted and heaved at their jeep, which lay mired up to its axles in the mud. Behind the jeep, the Dodge Power Wagon sat on solid ground, its headlamps slicing through the rainy darkness, clearly outlining the laboring men as they strained to free their jeep. Our Peugeot lay uselessly off to the side, tipped at an angle, half-buried in a lake of mud.

I tugged on Bari's sleeve, and we moved back a little. We could try to pick them off one by one, but if we fired on them, we'd give away our position. The rain was still coming down, although not as hard now. It was very dark in amongst the trees, and I knew that as long as we stayed there, we were relatively safe. Safe, but no nearer to the Gambia River and Ti-Claude.

There were six of the poachers, as far as I could tell. Two had been in the lead jeep, four in the Dodge truck behind. The Dodge was a flatbed truck with stake sides, full of butchered meat, and even through the rain, I could smell the fresh blood. The jeep had a trailer attached to it, a metal box with high sides. Although it was possible that there were men inside, I was betting that it contained more animal carcasses.

The Mauritanians had fired several long bursts in our direction, but they hadn't slowed down, apparently figuring that we weren't worth pursuing. They'd been so interested in shooting at us, however, that they hadn't noticed the mudhole. The lead jeep had gone straight in, and now one of them sat behind the wheel and raced the engine while the other five pushed from behind, trying to get the wheels unstuck. From time to time they glanced around, trying to see if we were still out there in the darkness somewhere.

But they were armed, and therefore cocky and overconfident. I knew we could take them; I just needed to figure out how.

Their first surprise burst of gunfire had sent us diving for cover, but that didn't mean that we were afraid of them. This was too much like a game that Bari and I had played before, down in the border areas around Guinea Bissau. Right now, we held all the cards: we knew where they were, but they didn't know where we were. I wanted to keep it that way, until we had what we needed.

We needed only two things, I decided: an equalizer, and a way out. Both of them were right in front of us.

So I lay in the mud and watched the vehicles, grinning to myself in the darkness. This was the best kind of game, in a way; good, clean dog eat dog.

I moved closer to Bari. "They're going to get that jeep out of the mud in a few more minutes," I whispered. "Think you can drive it when the time comes?"

He nodded.

"Then follow me." I began to crawl forward on my belly, up behind the Dodge Power Wagon.

I worked my way up past the back of the Dodge until I found what I'd been looking for: the fuel tank. It was big, easily a hundred gallons' worth, and I hoped it was full. Best of all was the rag that served as a cap. I pulled it out and held it up for Bari to see. His eyes lit up, and he nodded.

In front of us, the Mauritanians had almost freed their jeep. Shouting and heaving, they rocked the jeep and its heavy trailer back and forth, finally pushing it up and out of the mudhole. A ragged cheer went up.

"Showtime," I murmured to Bari. Taking out my Zippo, I lit the end of the rag protruding from the truck's fuel tank. We melted back into the darkness.

The Mauritanians walked back toward the Dodge, leaving two men in the front jeep. They were starting to climb aboard when the fuel tank blew with a boom and a roar, turning the night into high noon. Screaming, they scattered into the darkness as Bari and I rushed the jeep.

Bari dragged the driver out by the neck and got behind the wheel. I pulled the man on my side out, spun him around, ripped his Sterling off his shoulder, and kicked him into the mud. The Mauritanians had spotted us by now and were racing back toward the jeep, knees pumping under their kaftans. I fired a burst in their general direction and shouted for Bari to get moving.

Bari pointed back at the trailer. "What about that thing?" he said. "We can't—"

"Just drive, will you?" I squeezed off another burst. "I'm doing all the work here."

He slammed the jeep into gear and we lurched off down the muddy track into the night, scant yards ahead of our pursuers.

Bari drove like a maniac with hot coals up his ass, pedal hard to the floor, tires skidding wildly from side to side in the mud and water. I held on with one hand to the side of the jeep and admired the burning truck. Well, that's the end of that.

Or maybe not. In the hellish light from the burning truck, one thing was now very clear: we weren't really moving fast enough to get away. If we couldn't squeeze some more speed out of the jeep, the poachers who were chasing us on foot would catch up.

The trailer we were dragging was the problem. It was heavy and awkward, a sea anchor holding back our progress as it slipped and slid along through the mud. I began to edge back along the side of the jeep, holding the Sterling in one hand, trying to see if I could uncouple the damned thing. Whatever was in the trailer, it stank to high heaven.

Three of the Mauritanians were still behind us, running like greyhounds. I fired another burst, which went wide, and then there was nothing but a clicking sound. I glanced around, searching frantically for more ammunition clips. I could see nothing but a rusty bushknife lying across the back seat.

I looked back at the Mauritanians. They were gaining on us.

"Faster!" I shouted at Bari. "You've got to go faster!"

"Impossible," he shouted back over the engine's roar. "I've got it floored! It's that damned trailer – it's too heavy! Can't you do something?"

"I'm trying, dammit!"

I threw the useless Sterling at the nearest Mauritanian, catching him across the nose. He howled in pain and dropped off. The other two kept coming, drawing ever closer.

Fighting for balance, I stood on the back of the jeep. Grabbing the swaying top of the trailer, I levered myself up and peered inside. From below in the darkness there was a deep coughing growl, and a thump as something shifted position. Something alive, and big. I caught a glimpse of two enormous yellow eyes, and then a huge paw came up, nearly taking my face off.

I turned back to Bari. "Ah, listen, we've got–"

"Save your breath!" he shouted. "Just do something about that trailer!"

I reached down and grabbed the bushknife. Holding the blade between my teeth like a pirate, I edged back along the side of the swaying trailer, hanging on for dear life to the top lip, and hoping I wasn't about to get my fingers chewed off.

Our two remaining pursuers were concentrating their effort on running, and it was working. We were going as fast as we could, and they were faster. Inch by inch, they were closing on us.

The closest Mauritanian was less than ten feet away from the back of the trailer now, and coming up fast. I reached the trailer doors, and looked up to see a gleam of triumph in his eyes as, without breaking stride, he unlimbered his gun.

Holding on with one hand, I hacked at the rope holding the trailer doors shut. One stroke, two, three, and suddenly the rope parted and the doors swung open. Two huge lions, their manes bristling with anger, bounded out of the trailer and landed directly in the path of the oncoming Mauritanians.

Freed of its load, the jeep shot forward into the night.

Carefully, I crawled forward and collapsed into the seat beside Bari. He laughed and slapped my thigh. "Whatever you did back there," he said, "it worked. What was all that crap in the trailer, anyway?"

I looked at him. "You probably wouldn't believe me if I told you," I said, taking a deep breath. "So just drive, okay?"

* * *

Ten minutes later, the engine died. We coasted to a halt at the side of the road, Bari cursing steadily as he ground the starter again and again. I picked up a flashlight from the dashboard compartment and got out.

After a moment, I called to Bari. "Here's our problem," I said.

He came back to where I shone the light on a row of bullet-holes low down on the chassis. Two of them had ripped into our fuel tank.

Bari looked at me. "There's no reserve tank, I suppose?"

I shook my head.

"Then we walk," he said.

I looked up the muddy track into the darkness. The rain continued to pour down. "How far do you think it is?" I said after a moment.

"To the river? Ten or fifteen kilometers," he said.

I checked my watch. "It's 3 a.m.," I said. "If we walk fast, we can be there a little after sunrise."

He smiled at me, his teeth gleaming in the darkness. "Then we'd better get started, don't you think?"

CHAPTER EIGHTEEN

I sat on the riverbank in the steaming heat, exhausted, and watched the pontoon ferry approach. It was not yet seven o'clock, but already the sun was an incandescent ball, sending harsh reflections off the blue-green water of the Gambia as it churned swiftly past. I felt like the football at a Super Bowl game.

Below me in a shallow eddy of the river, a Malinké woman wrapped in a bright cloth printed with the smiling face of Senegal's president sang softly as she washed her baby in the water. As she moved her broad hips, the president's face, stretched tight across her buttocks, seemed to be trying to speak.

Behind me, Bakary was speaking to Bari. "...and we found them all huddled together, up in the crotch of a tree, near the burning truck. They were actually glad to see us, I think. One of them kept jabbering incoherently, some wild story about man-eating lions waiting in the forest. We couldn't get much sense out of any of them, so we made them help us clear the road, and then we sent them back to Tambacounda under guard."

Behind the three Gendarmerie Land Rovers, a small crowd of people had assembled for the crossing. A Fulani herder with a young zebu heifer, a clutch of petty traders with their sacks of goods, and a dozen women with small children, all of them waiting patiently for the ferry, on their way to some local market. I noticed a beautiful Bassari woman in the crowd, her eyes full of laughter and mischief. She wore beads and porcupine quills in her hair, and a small silver triangle dangled from her pierced nose. She caught my eye, grinned, and turned away to whisper something to her companions.

Bari and I had staggered out of the forest shortly after dawn, wet, muddy and exhausted, only to find the ferry moored on the opposite bank. Ten minutes later the three Gendarmerie Land Rovers from Tambacounda had arrived, bringing Bakary and five other men. He explained that breakdowns, mud, and their encounter with the Mauritanian poachers had been the causes for their delay.

It really doesn't matter, I thought numbly as I gazed out at the river; Ti-Claude and Lindy must have crossed hours ago. By now, they could be anywhere.

The ferry was almost at the bank now. It was an ancient, rusting pontoon-style boat with ramps at either end, large enough to hold a car or small truck and a few dozen people. Its greased cable hummed tautly overhead in the morning air as the crew pushed it along with their long bamboo poles, keeping the craft at an angle to the current to add a bit of headway.

With a grinding noise it drew up on the sloping mudbank, dropping its hinged front with a clang. Shouting and gesturing, the crew maneuvered the first of the Gendarmerie vehicles aboard.

Bari turned to Bakary. "We'll take this one," he said, "and cross first. You and the others follow on the next trip."

The rest of the passengers streamed on behind us. The Fulani herdsman was the last to board, hauling vainly at the rope attached to his recalcitrant heifer, which refused categorically to mount the ramp. Finally, half a dozen of the market women simply picked up the wretched animal and carried it, bawling, to the front of the ferry. It lay looking miserable and embarrassed as we cast off and poled slowly back into the main current.

The crew chief was a lean, grizzled Malinké, dressed in rags and wearing an ancient bush-hat of French Army vintage. He stood at the front of the ferry, using his pole to keep the craft at the proper angle.

As I approached, he eyed my filthy clothes and wet boots with a combination of amusement and suspicion.

"Did you take a Land Rover across last night?" I asked. "Green, with a white top?"

"*Bien sûr, patron,*" he said, exposing a mouthful of blackened stumps. "Took them across myself. The *noir* with the big teeth and the white lady." He pushed hard against the current with his pole and shouted something to his men. "But not last night. It was this morning."

My mouth dropped open. "This morning?"

He looked at me. "I just said so, didn't I? Big-teeth was in a hurry, I think. He came to the riverbank in the middle of the night, in the rain. I was on the far side, at the compound of my second wife." He grinned. "My first wife lives on one side, my second on the other. It works pretty well, I find."

He spit into the water and raised his pole. "Anyway, he sent a boy in a pirogue to get me, together with a thousand francs." He shook his head. "It was pissing down rain, and the river had risen. When the water's swift, the cable sometimes breaks. I wasn't going to risk that for a mere thousand francs." He glanced down at the water and spit again. "And besides, there are crocodiles. Lots of them."

He leaned into his pole. "No, he spent the night on the bank, him and the toubab woman. I took him across not half an hour ago. Just before you and your friend over there showed up."

* * *

We bounced off the ramp and roared up the bank, heading down the road at high speed. We had only forty kilometers to go to reach Kédougou. The land was hilly now, with sharp curves and steep descents. Overhead, the sun was bright and hot.

In the distance off to the south, we could see the ramparts of the Fouta-Djallon range, a carpet of folded green ridges rising up to a series of flat-topped buttes. That would be Bassari country – rugged bush only sparsely inhabited, just at the frontier with Guinea.

In the road ahead, two big vultures struggled up from the carcass of a large black snake, their ponderous wingbeats narrowly missing our windshield. A large troop of baboons capered across the road, causing Bari to curse loudly as he braked. The males loped away from our billowing dust cloud, showing their fangs and screaming at us over their shoulders as they raced for the safety of the tall trees.

We met only one other vehicle on the road, a huge Berliet truck loaded with goods and passengers, heading for the ferry. The passengers cheered and waved as they flashed by in a cloud of dust, their colorful robes and headscarves giving them the look of a circus troupe. On top of the swaying truck was a mountain of baggage tied on with rope and string – sacks of rice, baskets, pots, suitcases, trunks, and bamboo cages containing chickens and guinea hens. Two *apprenti-chauffeurs* clung precariously to the top of the cab, holding aloft a gourd of palm wine and grinning. Across the front of the cab, yellow letters a foot high proclaimed '*Dieu Est Grand*.'

God is indeed great, I thought. And if he – or she – has any sense of fair play, he'll let us catch Ti-Claude. Please,

God, let Ti-Claude have a breakdown. A flat tire – anything. Just let me catch the bastard on the road.

We passed through a small Malinké village, a torpid collection of thatched huts hiding behind millet-stalk fences. Bari held the horn down as we roared through, scattering goats and chickens in all directions, making the small children scream and clap with delight. Under the central *bantaba* palaver trees, the elders held their prayer beads still and watched us with incurious eyes.

* * *

Half an hour later the first building appeared, a low-roofed government compound with a flagpole and a rusted sign reading '*Police Frontalière de Kédougou*.' Bari braked hard and swung the Land Rover through the gate, skidding to a stop in front of the door.

A fat *garde* emerged from the doorway, straightening up and saluting as he caught sight of Bari's uniform. Bari ignored him and charged past into the office, his muddy boots thudding on the cement, his voice raised in an angry shout for the officer of the day.

I came through the door a moment later to find him confronting a sweating officer seated at a littered desk.

"I don't need a damned *ordre de mission*, I tell you!" Bari shouted, pounding on the man's desk. "He's killed four people and kidnapped a European woman, and now he's here in town! Didn't they radio you from Tambacounda?"

The officer spread his hands. "Who knows? Our radio hasn't worked for three days. There's no electricity in the whole town – the generator's busted. They say the pilot's bringing spare parts on the mail run today."

Bari slammed his fist on the desk, making the papers jump. "*Merde!*"

"A European woman, did you say? With blonde hair?" The fat *garde* spoke from the doorway. "I saw such a woman go by not twenty minutes ago. In a Land Rover.

Green, with a white top. Someone else was with her – a black man, I think."

Bari nodded. "That's them," he said grimly. "We'll have to block the roads, then do a house-to-house search." He turned to the officer. "How many roads are there out of town?"

"Two," the man replied. "One goes out by the agriculture station, east toward Fongolimbi. The other is the road west, to Bassari country and Guinea. It crosses the Mamacounda creek near the Catholic mission."

"Can you telephone them, find out if someone's used the road in the last few minutes?"

The officer shook his head. "*Pas possible.* The telephone system's out, too. It all depends on the generator, you see."

"*Putain.* All right, get your men together. Once we've got the roads blocked, we'll have to search the town."

Bari turned to me. "Max, take the Land Rover and go to the Catholic mission. Find out if they've seen anyone. I'll get a vehicle from here and talk to the people at the agricultural station. I'll meet you at the mission as soon as I can."

* * *

I drove Bari's dark blue Gendarmerie vehicle slowly down the rutted track that served as the main road through town. Kédougou was a typical frontier settlement, little more than a large village, a negligent collection of huts and tin-roofed houses squatting back away from the fierce sun under the shade of kapok and mango trees. From behind the compound walls came the morning sound of Africa; the monotonous thumping of women pounding grain in a wooden mortar.

Even at this early hour, scores of people thronged the road, on their way to market. They waved as I bumped past, flashing me smiles and shouting greetings. There were tall, aristocratic Fulani, the men in flowing robes, the women dressed in traditional tie-dye indigo set off with huge gold earrings. There were also numbers of smaller, darker Bassari and Tandanké, the women bare-breasted and wearing cowrie shells, beads and coins woven into their hair. The men were plainer, and wore simple black cloth wraparounds and rubber-tire sandals. All of them carried long bushknives.

I heard an engine overhead, and looked up to see the green-and-white Air Sénégal mail plane banking low over the river, starting its approach to the airstrip beyond town. Of course, I remembered; the gendarme in Tambacounda had said that there would be a plane today.

* * *

The Catholic mission sat on the edge of town beside the creek, shaded and quiet. As I drove up, I passed a line of small children in their best clothes marching single file along the walkway, headed for Sunday school, their catechisms neatly balanced on their heads.

Behind its low walls, the mission compound was clean and tidy, with flowers planted in the borders beside the cinder-block buildings. There was a large church, a classroom block, a dispensary, and two large residences for mission staff. Scattered around the periphery of the compound was a collection of thatched huts, obviously used for boarders and patients.

I parked the Gendarmerie Land Rover inside the gate and got down. I could hear the sounds of children singing from the school building. Two European nuns dressed in white robes, sun helmets and sensible blocky shoes were walking across the dirt yard toward the dispensary, prayerbooks in their hands.

I found the priest having breakfast on the veranda of his house. He was tall and thin and somewhere in his sixties, I decided, although it was difficult to tell. He had a long white beard and steel-rimmed, round glasses, and wore a billowing grey soutane.

He stood as I approached, his hand outstretched. The bright eyes behind the glasses contained warmth and intelligence, and a certain amount of watchful curiosity, but his broad smile was genuine. "Père Daniel," he said simply. "You are welcome."

As we shook hands, I realized that he looked very much like the pictures of God that I had constructed in my mind when I was a small child – an old, kindly man with a robe and a long white beard.

He poured me strong coffee and offered freshly baked bread. I accepted both gratefully – I had eaten nothing since yesterday, I realized. As I ate, I explained who I was and why I had come. He listened gravely, showing no surprise. He shook his head slowly when I had finished.

"Horrible," he said quietly. "Kidnapping is a dreadful crime – absolutely barbaric. And you believe that this man – Ti-Claude – came here to kill someone? Someone here?"

I nodded. Just then, we were interrupted by the sound of a car turning in at the mission gate. A moment later, Bari stood on the veranda. "I've just come from the agriculture station. No one's been out along the Fongolimbi road all day. We've set up a roadblock there, and I've given orders to do the same for the road across the creek."

He turned to the priest. "I trust that Monsieur Donovan has explained the situation, *mon père*," he said.

"Yes," the priest replied. "But I'm afraid I can be of little help. No one has been down this road all morning." He swept his arm past the compound to the small bridge, and the distant hills on the other side. "We see everyone who goes by. There has been no one, I assure you."

"Then we've got him," Bari said with satisfaction. "The gardes are putting men into position now, all around town." He smiled grimly. "Once the exits are blocked, we'll start a house-to-house search. We will shoot on sight if necessary. Please inform your staff here that we will be searching the mission compound, and tell them to cooperate with the soldiers when they come."

He shook hands with the priest. To me he said, "I'm setting up a command post at the *préfecture*. Come along when you've finished here. This shouldn't take long; we have him boxed in now."

I nodded, watching him roar off. But we had him boxed in before, I thought.

"You were talking about the Haitian," the priest reminded me. "You said he might have come here to kill someone. Do you have any idea who?"

I shook my head. "That's what I was hoping you'd tell me, *mon père*. You know the people here. Is there anyone who doesn't – well, doesn't fit? Who stands out in some way?"

The priest smiled as he poured me more coffee. "There are many such people here, *monsieur*. This is a border town, full of misfits. Full of people from somewhere else. Some of them come here on legitimate business, and some – well, some come for other reasons."

"Other reasons? What other reasons?"

He looked at me. "Kédougou," he said, "is the smuggling capital of Senegal. Most outsiders don't know that, but it is true. Practically everyone here is involved in it, in one way or another." He lit a Gauloise and threw the match over the veranda, where two scrawny chickens rushed toward it hopefully.

"Smuggling here is of two kinds," he continued. "There is the serious kind, and the everyday kind. Which are you interested in?"

"Tell me about the serious kind," I said.

He paused to wipe his glasses on the hem of his soutane. "Well, a small town like this lives on rumor, you understand. Now and then, stories circulate about strangers who arrive in the night from far away, bringing things to sell or exchange."

"What things?"

The priest shrugged. "Gold. Diamonds. Game poached from the national park." He lowered his voice. "Sometimes even people. Mauritania only abolished slavery a few years ago, and it is said – even today – that once in a while, a convoy of slaves arrives, on its way north."

He puffed his cigarette. "Long before the French came here, there were rich gold mines in the Bambouk, to the north near the Falémé. They provided wealth for the empires of Mali and Songhay. It is said that the mines never entirely petered out, that the location of the gold seams is a well-kept secret known only to a few, and that gold continues to be mined." He paused. "It is also said that this gold comes through here, on its way to the jewelers of Dakar and Nouakchott."

"I'd heard of the gold mines," I said. "But diamonds? I didn't know there were any in Senegal."

"There aren't," he said. "The diamonds are stolen from the mines in Sierra Leone and Liberia, and find their way to Dakar. Did you know that Dakar is one of the diamond centers of the world?"

I shook my head.

"It's true. And many of these diamonds, if the rumors are true, come through Kédougou."

He sighed. "But rumors are merely *courants d'air* – breezes that blow through small towns like these. Gold, diamonds, slaves – who knows? The everyday kind of smuggling, however, is open and practiced by almost everyone. It concerns mundane things, items which happen to be cheaper in one place than another. For most of these people, you see, borders are merely a theoretical concept. They trade watches, transistor radios, cloth, sandals, shotgun shells, even matches – anything that's cheaper on one side of the border than the other. They bring the contraband across on foot, at night, and sell it quite openly in the market."

Just then we heard another vehicle pulling into the compound. I turned, expecting to see Bari again, but glimpsed instead an open-sided jeep with the words 'AIR SÉNÉGAL' painted on the side. A European wearing a bush-pilot's uniform got out and walked briskly toward us.

He was a young Frenchman with a lover-boy moustache, his thick black hair slicked back thirties style. Playing the role, I thought, as I noted the fashionable leather boots and the expensive sunglasses. I'd seen hundreds like him, working the bush airlines all around the periphery, playing *Terry and the Pirates*. If it weren't so hot, he'd probably be wearing a leather jacket and a silk scarf.

The priest made the introductions. "Monsieur Donovan, Raoul Bigard. Bigard does the twice-a-week run from Dakar. Down in the morning, back again straight away."

"*Salut.*" Bigard's handshake was perfunctory. He turned to the priest. "I'm running late, *mon père*; I had to deliver those damned generator spares. No passengers today, I see. Any cargo for Tambacounda?"

Père Daniel gestured to a dozen wooden crates stacked in the corner of the patio. "Just the usual. Oh, and the mail. Let me get it." He disappeared into the house.

I helped the pilot load the crates into the back of the jeep. After a moment, Père Daniel returned holding a small packet of mail.

"I almost forgot this," he said, handing Bigard a crumpled envelope. "A letter came for you earlier this morning."

The pilot looked surprised. "A letter? For me?"

"A small boy brought it earlier, just before Monsieur Donovan arrived, in fact." He smiled. "A local girlfriend, perhaps?"

The pilot frowned, turning the envelope over in his hands. Then he shrugged. "I'll read it later," he said, getting into the jeep. "Got to go. *Au'voir.*" He roared out the drive and towards the road to the airport.

Père Daniel watched him go. "He's lucky to have got all those boxes in his jeep," he said. "Fortunately, pineapples don't weigh much."

I looked at him. "Pineapples? There were pineapples in those crates?"

He nodded. "Why, yes. I send some up almost every week. They go to Tambacounda, to Monsieur Le Vieux. Do you know Le Vieux? He's a very nice man."

I realized I'd never mentioned that Le Vieux was dead. "And where," I said, "do the pineapples come from? Do you grow them here at the mission?"

"Oh, no. They come from Monsieur Demba's gardens. He grows them down by the river."

"Who's Demba?"

"Monsieur Demba owns Kédougou's only bar. It's behind the market, just near the river. He has gardens along the riverbank – he grows pineapples, melons, lettuce, all sorts of things. He sells the vegetables in the market, of course, but also to Le Vieux. Pineapples won't grow in Tambacounda, I'm told, because of the soil."

"And he sends pineapples regularly to Le Vieux?"

"Nearly every week. Bigard takes them free of charge in the plane, if he has the room. Demba's been doing it for years. Ever since he came to town, in fact."

"Where's Demba from? That's a Malinké name, isn't it?"

The priest chuckled. "Oh, he's not from here. And Demba's not his real name – it's something quite unpronounceable. He's Togolese, in fact. Came here about ten years ago. But I don't quite see–"

I didn't hear the rest of his sentence. I was up and running for my vehicle, keys in hand.

CHAPTER NINETEEN

There's no time to find Bari, I thought as I drove fast through town, heart pounding, my knuckles white on the steering wheel. The soldiers would be busy sealing off the roads, getting ready to close the trap, and every second counted.

Demba's bar lay at the end of a dirt track leading to the river. It was a large, fenced compound with a neatly lettered sign saying 'BAR KOBA' and as I drove up, I could see that the gate was open.

I turned in and killed the motor. The compound was still and silent, baking in the hot sun. A covey of guinea hens clicked quietly to themselves as they searched the bare earth for morsels, and from somewhere off near the river a donkey brayed. Moving slowly, I got out of the Land Rover and looked around.

The bar was a long, thatched hangar, done Casamance-style, with chairs and tables spread around inside and out. To the right was a hut made of mud-brick and roofed with tin, and beside that, a low garage. Behind the garage were three smaller huts. I turned slowly, taking in the silence. Then I walked inside the bar.

It was cool under the eaves, and I stepped carefully around three chickens crouching just inside the doorway, seeking relief from the heat. They clucked pettishly at me and fluffed their feathers, settling back down into the dust on the concrete floor. I peered behind the bar. There was nothing there but an old battery-powered record player, several albums, and half a dozen empty beer bottles. Demba obviously wasn't yet open for business. I called softly, but there was no answer.

Walking out behind the bar, I checked the smaller huts. One of them, reeking of urine, was clearly the latrine. The second hut was a storeroom, piled high with sacks of rice, crates of beer and wine, and baskets of onions and peppers. A sleeping cat got up guiltily from the top of one of the sacks and slipped noiselessly out the door, its belly low to the ground.

The third hut contained nothing more than empty beer crates and trash. I closed the door quietly and turned, listening. Something had made a noise, somewhere in the compound. I heard it again, a low hissing sound, coming from the tin-roofed hut.

I stepped up onto the small veranda. The noise was coming from a green metal teapot, sitting on a bed of coals on a tin stove. The water had just begun to boil. I looked around the deserted compound. Who had put the water on? And where were they now?

I clapped my hands together several times loudly. "*Salaam aliekum!*" My voice echoed in the silence. "*Monsieur Demba?*" I waited, the silence seeping into my ears like warm oil. "*Monsieur Demba?*" Something was wrong.

Then I noticed that the door to the garage was ajar.

I moved to the door and slowly pushed it open with my foot. The space inside was dark and dusty, but I could see Lindy's green and white Land Rover parked inside. Just then something cold and hard was pushed into the small of my back, and I froze.

"*Fais pas de bêtise, bonhomme*," a voice whispered in an unmistakable Haitian accent. "Don't do anything stupid, man."

Keeping my hands held high, I turned slowly around. Ti-Claude stood there, his pistol levelled at my chest. In the dim light, his eyes gleamed.

* * *

"Put him in the back with the woman. Nice and easy now. *Doucement, doucement.*"

Ti-Claude's voice was low but menacing. I struggled with Demba's body, dragging it across the red laterite pebbles of the compound, into the garage where Lindy's Land Rover was parked. Demba was big, and must have weighed well over a hundred kilos, most of it soft fat. His hands and feet were bound with wire. He was still alive as far as I could tell, but nobody was going to cover any bets on how much longer he'd stay that way.

I managed to wedge him into the back of the Land Rover. Lindy was already there, also tied with wire, a cloth gag in her mouth. Her eyes darted back and forth from me to Ti-Claude as I settled Demba beside her. Ti-Claude inspected my work, nodding with satisfaction.

"Cover them," he said, handing me a dusty tarpaulin. I nodded and arranged the tarp over them.

He gestured to the driver's seat. "Now get in and start the engine. It's time to leave."

I slid behind the wheel, trying to calm the tremor in my hands and the thudding of my heart. "Listen to me," I said quietly. "The town's surrounded. There are troops everywhere. You'll never make it."

He raised his head and looked at me. His eyes were flat and dead black, opaque and without depth, and he stared at me the way a snake might stare at a bird – no emotion, no feeling, no clue as to what might be going on inside his head. Then I noticed a thin sheen of sweat on his forehead. He's frightened, I realized. He's frightened that he won't be able to get away.

And he's also a killer. He'll kill all of us if he thinks he has to.

"I'll make it," he said quietly. "And you're gonna make sure I do." He spoke in a quiet, deadly voice. "So start this truck now, man."

I turned the key and the engine roared to life. Ti-Claude got in, climbed over the seat and settled in the back. He pulled the tarpaulin over himself until there was just a tiny crack to see out of.

"Okay, Chuck," he said. "Get the truck in gear and move out. You know the road out of town to the south?"

I nodded. "Past the Catholic mission?"

"That one. Head on over there. Drive normally; don't even think about trying to call for help. You fuck up, I'll blow her brains out. Yours too, Chuck. You understand what I'm tellin' you?"

"My name's not Chuck," I said from between clenched teeth.

He gave a dry chuckle, and I felt the barrel of the pistol just behind my ear. "Your name is whatever I say it is. Now shut your fuckin' mouth and let's get moving."

* * *

I stopped the Land Rover a hundred yards from the bridge, on the bank overlooking the creek. I let the engine idle as Ti-Claude peered out from under the tarpaulin, scanning the scene below us.

The bridge was blocked and guarded. Five armed gardes républicaines stood in a group, talking and smoking, their rifles slung casually across their shoulders. Behind them was a barricade hastily improvised from barbed wire and empty oil drums. Beyond, the road climbed the opposite bank and disappeared into the bush, headed toward the mountains in the far distance.

"How do you plan on getting through that?" I spoke softly.

"We're going to drive through it. You and me and Demba and the lady here. We're going to go straight across the bridge, and out the road on the other side. They won't stop a white man in an official vehicle, not if you act like you know what you're doing. So just drive on down there and tell them to open the barricade, and then you go right on through. Don't slow down, don't even look at them.

Pretend you own the goddamn place. Think you can do that, Chuck?"

"What if they tell me to stop?"

"Fuck 'em. You floor it and get the hell across." I felt the muzzle of the pistol cold against the back of my neck. "'cause if you don't, you're dead. You can understand that, can't you?"

I nodded.

He slid back down under the tarp. "Good. Keep both hands right up there on top of the wheel, where I can see 'em. That's right, like that. Now get moving."

The soldiers looked up, squinting into the afternoon sun, as they heard the Land Rover approach. I eased it down the steep bank and pulled up fifteen feet away from the barricade. My hands were gripping the wheel tightly, knuckles white with strain.

A corporal in *parachutiste* camouflage fatigues flipped his rifle off his shoulder and walked slowly toward me, frowning. It was the fat garde républicaine that we'd seen earlier, as we drove into town.

I stuck my head out the window. "*Laissez-moi passer!*" I shouted, making vigorous pushing motions at the barricade.

He stopped, puzzled, and then smiled as he recognized me. He turned to his companions. "It's the brigadier's friend," he announced. "Open up the road!"

The soldiers nodded, and began to pull the barbed wire aside.

"Move it, fucker," Ti-Claude hissed from under the tarp.

I put the truck into gear and eased it forward. As we passed, the corporal came to attention, grinning, and flashed me a salute.

He was still grinning after us as we climbed the bank on the other side. Now we were free. Free, and completely at Ti-Claude's mercy.

* * *

A vast grassy plain stretched in front of us, burned dusty-brown by the sun. The bumpy road ran straight through it toward the mountains shimmering in the distance, forty or fifty kilometers away to the southwest. There were fat dark rainclouds on the horizon, billowing up out of the mountain ranges inside Guinea, across the frontier.

We were driving straight into no-man's-land, the most rugged and isolated part of Senegal, nothing but bush and a few scattered Bassari villages hidden away up in the rocky foothills. There were no houses visible from the road. Only an occasional cleared field or the remains of a bushfire to show that people ever passed this way at all.

In fact, the only people we had seen had been hours ago, when we'd passed a peasant family trudging slowly toward Kédougou. They had scattered at the sound of the Land Rover, and as we roared past, they'd stood well away, watching us silently. Our dust cloud hung in the air for miles, a lonely marker to our passage. I wondered as I drove how long it would take before someone in Kédougou realized that we were gone.

Not nearly soon enough, I thought grimly. Not unless we were very lucky.

"You'll never make it across the border, you know," I said. Ti-Claude was sitting beside me now, pistol in his right hand. "The Guineans will pick us up before we've gone a mile inside their territory."

He shook his head. "I'm not going to Guinea. Neither are you." He gestured with the pistol at Demba, who was seated upright now, still gagged and bound. "And that *couillon* isn't going anywhere. So don't you worry, Chuck, about where we might or might not be going." He smiled. "You let me deal with that."

I shot a glance at Lindy in the rearview mirror. Her eyes showed the same sick despair that I felt in my heart. We drove past a dead cow, horribly bloated, its legs in the air. A clutch of vultures, gorging on the stinking meat, hopped sullenly aside to let us pass.

If I can't find a way out of this mess, I thought, we could all wind up like that.

The sun was beginning to dip toward the horizon. I checked my watch: four o'clock. We had been driving for hours, and now we were running out of daylight.

I glanced at the fuel gauge. Outside of Kédougou, we had stopped to refill the tank from the jerricans strapped to the bumpers, and now we had nearly a full tank. The Land Rover could probably go more than four hundred kilometers on a full tank, which could put us almost anywhere. The problem wasn't fuel, however.

The problem was water.

We had no water at all, and unless we were going to double back toward the Gambia River to our north, we probably wouldn't find much out here in the bush. Whatever plan Ti-Claude had in his head, it was going to happen soon. Otherwise, we'd all be dead of thirst.

Lindy and I are only alive because we're useful to him, I thought as I maneuvered the Land Rover along the bush track. But what about Demba? Why hadn't Ti-Claude killed him as he had all the others? If Demba was the 'Togolese' on his hit list, why wasn't he dead by now?

Because Ti-Claude needs him, I realized. Demba's got something he wants. I remembered the pineapples in Le Vieux's shop, sliced to pieces on the table and the ripped seats of the taxi. Ti-Claude's looking for something, and Demba's got it, whatever it is.

Diamonds? Perhaps the old priest was right. Diamonds would make sense, in a way. Something small enough to be smuggled, something valuable enough to kill for. Something that connected a chain of people all across Senegal, from a remote border town to a rich man's villa on the island of Gorée in Dakar harbor.

Links in a chain, with Demba the last link of all. And once he'd given Ti-Claude what he wanted, Demba, too, would be killed, ruthlessly cast aside.

Ti-Claude was a human killing machine, a man to whom other people's lives were worth less than pocket change. If I was going to prevent him from killing again, I would have to act, and act quickly. And now Ti-Claude was cornered, running for his own life. He hadn't counted on the police surveillance on the train down to Tambacounda, the chase through the bush, the roadblocks. He was running now, a rat in a closing trap, his plan gone wrong.

And that made him doubly dangerous.

The pistol rammed hard into my side, breaking off my train of thought. "Stop the truck," Ti-Claude said.

I braked and killed the engine. The road was now little more than a wide path over hard laterite pan. Just in front of us, the track dipped down and crossed a creek bed. There were a few puddles of water here and there among the boulders, but so far, the rains had only managed to create a thin, sluggish stream which wound like a tired snake between them.

This is it, I thought. This is where it happens.

"What are you going to do?" I said.

He smiled at me, a look that made my skin crawl. "Time for business." He raised the pistol. "Get out."

CHAPTER TWENTY

I clambered down from the driver's seat, wiping sweat off my face. The temperature had to be well over a hundred degrees, and I could feel the heat drawing moisture from my body.

Ti-Claude was staring at the creek bed, and now he turned to me, his eyes glowing. "She stays in the truck," he said. "Get Demba out on the ground here."

I opened the tailgate and tugged at Demba until I had him sitting on the ground. He was conscious now, his cheap shirt and trousers soaked with sweat and the stench of panic, his face grey with fear and shock. The buttons on his shirt had come undone, revealing dozens of leather-wrapped gris-gris charms, strung on rawhide cords around his waist and neck. Each of the small leather pouches would contain a magic charm. He would have bought them from one of the local magicians, hoping to ensure good luck, safety, and protection from evil spirits. I hoped they'd come with a money-back guarantee, because they didn't seem to be doing him much good at the moment.

Demba sat on the ground, his hands and feet bound with wire, his eyes darting from side to side. "Okay, get her out now. And take off her gag."

A moment later Lindy was on the ground beside Demba. I touched her cheek and looked into her eyes.

"You okay?" I whispered.

She gave me a small smile. It wasn't much, but it was all she had.

Ti-Claude came around the side of the truck, holding a map of the area. I recognized it as the one Lindy kept in her Land Rover.

"Keep your mouth shut," he said to me. "No talking unless I tell you, got that?"

I nodded.

Ti-Claude spread the map out in front of us and gestured at it with his pistol. "I need to know some things," he said to Lindy. "You tell me the truth, you and your boyfriend here both stay alive. If not" – he made a chopping motion with his gun – "I'll kill you both, right now. You understand that, lady?"

Lindy nodded, her eyes watching him carefully. "What do you want?" she said softly.

He smiled. "I want to get out of here," he said. "And you and your boyfriend there are going to help me. There's an airstrip in the game park, at a place called Simenti. I want you to drive me there."

Lindy's eyes widened in comprehension. She leaned forward to examine the map. Then she looked up to check the position of the sun, now a blood-red ball hanging low over the trees.

"Not easy," she said at last. "We're on the edge of Bassari country out here, about ten or twenty kilometers from the Guinean border. The road forks just ahead. If you turn left, you cross the border. The right fork goes back into the game park." She looked up at him. "It's not a good road, though; hardly ever used."

"Any cops or soldiers?"

She shook her head. "There's nothing out here at all, except for a few villages. Inside the park, there are a couple of rangers at the hotel; no one else." She paused. "Your problem isn't with the rangers. It's with the river."

"What the hell do you mean? What river?"

"The Gambia. It runs through the park and makes a big loop around Simenti, right where the airstrip is. We're on the other side of the river right now; to get to the airstrip, we've got to go back across it."

She pointed to a spot on the map. "There's only one place to cross. Here, at Malapa."

He leaned forward. "I see that, girl. So what's the problem?"

Lindy's eyes came up. "Don't call me a 'girl', you bastard," she said quietly.

Ti-Claude backhanded her across the mouth, snapping her head back and making a noise like a gunshot. I started forward.

He turned like a cat, grinning, his gun up. "Don't. Believe me, you don't want to mess this up right now. Behave yourself and you can stay alive. Give me any trouble and you die, got it?"

I nodded and drew back, lowering my hands.

He turned back to Lindy. "I'll call you anything I goddam well please, you bitch," he said softly. "Now, I asked you a question. I'm still waiting for an answer."

Lindy spat blood from her mouth and looked defiantly at him. "It's the river crossing at Malapa," she said. "I'm not sure you can make it."

Ti-Claude's smile was back. "We, *girl.*" He gave the word emphasis. "We. We're all going together." He peered at the map. "Why can't we make it? We got plenty of gas, after all."

"There's no bridge," she said. "It's just a sort of a causeway thing – made of rocks put there by the park guards in the dry season. They build it up every year, and then when the river rises in the rainy season, it gets washed away." She glanced at the sky. "It's rained a couple of times already in the past two weeks. The causeway's probably already under water. When the river gets high enough, the stones will simply be carried downstream. And when that happens, you – we – won't be able to get across."

Ti-Claude nodded, looking at the map and considering. His face was bright with sweat now, and his fingers tapped the map nervously.

Lindy cleared her throat. "Listen," she said.

Ti-Claude looked up. "You say something?"

"Yes." She was looking steadily at him. "Listen to me. I want you to understand something." She paused. "I know you're planning on killing Demba. You killed all the others, and now you're going to kill him, aren't you?"

Ti-Claude watched her, saying nothing.

"Well," she continued, holding him with her eyes. "I just want to tell you this. If you do – if you kill him, or anyone, anyone at all" – her eyes flicked to mine briefly – "you're dead, too."

"What the hell you talkin' about?"

"I know this area, and you don't," she said. "Kill Demba and you'll never get out of here alive. I won't drive you, I won't guide you. You can shoot me, too, but then you'll have nobody." She raised her chin and fixed Ti-Claude with her eyes. "Without a guide, you won't survive. You'll break down, run out of fuel, run out of water. And then you'll die. Slowly. I won't help you. You can kill me, but I won't help you. Do you understand that?"

Ti-Claude said nothing for several moments. Finally he looked up. "There's a shovel in the back," he said to me. "Get it."

I stood up. "What for?"

He pointed down into the creek bed. "You're gonna dig a hole for our friend here."

"A hole?"

Ti-Claude nodded. "I'm gonna bury the sonofabitch." He looked up at Lindy. "Alive, bitch. I'm gonna leave his head free, okay?"

Demba began to thrash on the ground, making choking noises against his gag. Ti-Claude chuckled.

"Go on, man, get the goddamn shovel like I told you. The sand oughta be soft down there. Dig it deep enough so's he can stand up – just his head sticking out." He stared at me, his eyelid twitching uncontrollably. His voice was steady, but madness danced just behind his pupils. "Do it now, Chuck."

I got the shovel and walked down into the shallow creek bed, stepping around the stagnant pools of greenish water, until I came to a soft, sandy patch in the shade. Keeping one eye on Ti-Claude, I began to dig.

He had taken the gag from Demba's mouth and was talking to him in a low, vicious voice. As I dug, I listened.

"Listen to me, motherfucker," he was saying. "Last chance. Tell me where they are and you live. Don't, and you die. See that white man down there? He's digging your grave, do you understand that?"

He grabbed Demba's ear and twisted it, causing the big man to cry out in pain. "You don't tell me what I need to hear, you're going down in the hole he's digging, and you stay there. Think about it." He turned to me. "Hurry up, goddamnit. It'll be dark soon."

I nodded, putting my back into it, mechanically throwing shovelfuls of dirt out of the hole. I was already three feet down, the sand soft and moist beneath me, but I was tiring fast. The heat was sucking me dry of water and energy, pulling the strength straight out of me. Whatever I was going to do, I decided, had to be done soon. Otherwise I was going to be too weak to do anything at all.

"You're the man, Demba," Ti-Claude was saying. "Everybody else is dead. Up to you now." He hauled Demba to his feet. "So here it is: you got thirty seconds to tell me where the goddamn diamonds are, otherwise you're going in the hole."

He spun Demba around and pushed him down the bank to the edge of the hole. Ti-Claude nodded in satisfaction. "Good work. Bigger than we need, but that's okay. Get on out now. Demba's coming down."

Demba's face was ashy-grey and glistening with sweat. "*Au nom de Dieu,*" he whispered hoarsely. "*Je t'ai dit la verité, je te le jure.* I've told you the truth, I swear it." His voice cracked with fear. "I never took a single diamond, not a one. Ever. Everything I got, I sent to the toubab in Tambacounda. Maybe he's been stealing from you, I don't know. But it's not me, not me, no, never." He began to cry. "In God's name, please don't do this."

Ti-Claude's voice was harsh. "The white man in Tambacounda is dead, Demba. So are all the others. You're the last one, the end of the line. It's you, and you're holding out." He sighed. "Okay. Down in the hole."

Demba gave a cry like a wounded animal and stood rigid, his eyes bulging. In one quick motion, Ti-Claude stepped behind him and struck him on the back of the head with the butt of the pistol. Demba dropped to the sand like a felled ox, giving a sigh like air escaping from a balloon.

Ti-Claude turned to me. "Get him in there. Fast."

"Jesus, man—"

"Do it. Before I shoot you."

I moved slowly, as if in a dream. My body took over from my mind, and I stopped thinking about what I was doing as I hauled Demba down into the hole and propped him upright. I was no more than a spectator, watching myself bury a man alive in slow motion, but at a great distance.

I was breathing hard as I finally hauled myself up out of the hole. This is it, I told myself. Now. You've got to do it now. There won't be any more chances.

I gulped air, flicking my eyes over to Ti-Claude, measuring the distance between us, and noting the angle at which he held the pistol. He needed to be closer.

I bent my knees and put my hands on the ground, like a sprinter on the blocks. I lowered my head and began to make gagging sounds, clutching at my throat and hunching over. I put all I had into it, making my body jerk as if I were retching.

"What the hell's the matter with you?" I heard him take two steps toward me and stop about six feet away.

Close enough, I decided; now or never. I launched myself at him.

I came up out of my crouch with every last ounce of my energy, and although I was moving fast, it seemed to take hours. I had the advantage of speed and surprise; he had the gun.

I saw the instinctive tightening of his facial muscles which signals the onset of the startle reflex, and then all I could see was the gun, its muzzle looking enormous, coming up fast. Then we hit.

Connect, chop, lift. I caught him cleanly at the knees and locked my arms around his legs, lifting with all my might. In slow motion, my thoughts were whirling. This was the part that had to work, I thought as I lifted him high, still moving forward. I had to get him to drop the gun, and the only way to do that was to slam him as hard as I could on the ground and hope that the weapon shook loose.

He hit the ground with a grunt and a whoosh as the air went out of him, and I knew then that I'd lost the bet. He still held the gun, and now it was coming up again, the black hole of the barrel flashing past my eyes, a glimpse of his bared teeth, finger tight on the trigger, Lindy's scream. Then an enormous flash and an explosion.

Blinding pain hit the left side of my head, and then there was nothing.

CHAPTER TWENTY-ONE

I struggled up out of unconsciousness slowly, so slowly that there was no real transition, as if waking from deep sleep in a totally dark room.

But eventually, I became aware that I was awake, that the night was not totally dark. That I was alive. With that thought came the first stirrings of fear, and the first wave of pain.

And then I realized that there were things crawling on my face.

That was when I really woke up. The events of the day came surging back, and with a gasp of despair, I discovered exactly where I was. I was buried up to my neck in a sandy creek bed, my hands and feet bound securely with wire, and there were insects crawling on my face.

Mosquitoes. Dozens of them. I could feel their tiny feet on my cheeks and forehead, hear the whine of their wings brushing past my ears as they homed in on fresh blood.

I began to hear the small night noises of the bush. The whisper of a passing breeze through the leaves above, the light wingbeats of a nightjar flitting by, the rustle of the insects in the trees and the grass. Now I could make out another dark shape a foot or two away from mine. Demba. Like me, he stood buried up to his neck in the sand.

I called to him in a hoarse voice, but he gave no answer. He wasn't moving, and I could see no sign that his eyes were open, no indication that he was alive. Lindy, Ti-Claude, and the Land Rover were nowhere to be seen.

I began to move slowly, experimentally, a little at a time. I tried again to move my arms and legs, stopping only when the pain from my head threatened to render me unconscious. My hands were tied with wire behind my back, and my feet were bound at the ankles, in just the same way as Ti-Claude had bound Demba. The sand was tightly packed, movement almost impossible. Exhausted after only a few seconds, I stopped trying to move, and began to try and think instead.

Lindy was gone, and so was Ti-Claude. He would have taken her with him, to show him the way through the bush to the airstrip at Simenti. I had no idea what time it was, but surely they were both deep inside the park's wilderness by now, perhaps even at the airstrip itself. And if they had already arrived at the airstrip, would Lindy still be alive?

My options were limited, to say the least. I wasn't gagged – I could always call for help. But who would hear, in this remote corner of the bush? And even if I got free, how long would it take me to find help?

Too long, I thought grimly. Far too long. For with every moment that passed, I was dying of thirst. Already my mouth hung open, my swollen tongue protruding out over my lower lip. I ran my tongue over cracked lips, brushing away insects in the process. Whatever else happened, I would die from lack of water before too long.

I remembered something I'd learned in a survival course many years ago. At an ambient temperature of 100 degrees, you lose about 10 pints of water per day, or even as much as a pint an hour when expending energy. Losing 20 pints can kill you.

I had had nothing to drink since yesterday afternoon, and I found myself wondering whether being buried in sand up to your neck counted as an energy expenditure or not. I decided I didn't really want to know the answer.

One way or the other, I was likely to be dead before another day had passed.

* * *

I awoke, hours later, to a blindingly bright light and the drone of flies.

I raised my eyes to the sun, already two diameters over the edge of the short bushes which provided the creek bed's only shade. The temperature was already oven-like, and getting hotter by the minute.

The mosquitoes that had come for my blood had drunk their fill and disappeared, to be replaced by flies. They buzzed around me in a cloud, drawn by the blood which crusted my head wound. They crawled slowly around my eyes, my lips, in and out of my nostrils and ears.

I craned my neck around and saw that Demba was awake. His eyes, red and puffy, gazed back at me. His face was covered with insect bites. I hoped I looked better than him, but doubted it. We stared at each other for a moment, and then he nodded at me, slowly and with great dignity.

"You – all right?" My words came out as a croak, past split lips and a swollen tongue which wouldn't move the way they were supposed to.

After a long moment, his reply. "*Vivant.*" It was a rasping whisper. "Alive. You?"

173

"My head hurts like hell."

Demba looked at my head. "He shot you, didn't he?"

I nodded, feeling ripples of pain spreading out behind my eyes. "Yes, I think so. Can you see my wound?"

He squinted against the harsh sunlight. "There is a lot of blood, but I think the bullet grazed you. How do you feel?"

"How do I feel?" I began to chuckle, and then to laugh. "How do I feel?" Pain rolled over me in waves. "I feel," I said at last, "like I'm going to die."

Then, mercifully, the pain washed me back into unconsciousness.

* * *

I came to again with a start, wakened by the rustle of heavy wings. I opened my eyes to see a vulture, grey and hideous, squatting two feet away from me. Its head was turned to the side, and it peered at me with one bright eye, bobbing its neck back and forth in a serpentlike movement. Its odor filled my nostrils, making me gag.

I looked up and saw more vultures above us, circling slowly. Bets were going up on the tote board, and the odds were dropping fast.

I ran my tongue over dry lips and shouted, panic and anger mixed together in my hoarse voice. "Demba, Wake up!" I yelled. "Wake up! Quick!"

He opened his eyes, blinking in surprise.

"Listen, Demba," I croaked. "We've got to stay awake. The vultures won't touch us as long as we're alive."

That last part was pure wishful thinking, but this was neither the time nor the place to say so.

"We've got to attract help," I continued. "We've got to make noise, to shout. Can you shout?"

He nodded weakly.

"Good. We'll take turns, every minute or so. First me, then you."

I shouted. It brought back the pain in my head, and produced a strange sound, rather like a wheeze, that bore no resemblance to my normal voice. The vulture was startled. It shrugged and hopped awkwardly back a few steps, pausing then to gaze at us calmly with bright beady eyes.

"Fuck you," I shouted.

It drew back a few more steps. Then I stopped, exhausted. A moment later, Demba raised his voice. When he grew tired, I began again.

I have no idea how long we kept it up. It seemed like hours. Eventually, everything took on a dreamlike quality, as my mind receded further and further away from the here and now. Our voices could be no more than loud whispers by now, and yet another part of me imagined that Demba and I were part of a huge choir, singing Handel's *Messiah* for Christmas on a brightly lit stage. It was toasty and warm inside the cathedral where we sang, but through the windows, I could see the fat, white snowflakes drifting slowly down, lining the windowsills and haloing the streetlamps.

Time passed, and then I found myself on an impossibly high mountaintop, yodeling down the steep crags to the valleys below. The air was cold and sweet, and the glaciers reflected their icy light in brilliant shafts which hurt my eyes.

After a while, it all began to seem wildly funny. I had another laughing fit, and then, my strength nearly gone, I subsided into giggles. I turned to Demba to share the joke, but saw that he was unconscious. A moment – or an hour – later, I, too, blacked out.

* * *

The second time, it was the dog that woke me. My eyes opened slowly, focusing on a dusty brown mutt standing on the creek bank, growling and snapping at the flock of vultures. As I watched, the dog lunged at one of the birds.

It hopped backwards, shook its long neck irritably, and then launched itself laboriously into the air. The other birds shifted nervously and stood blinking in the bright sunshine, their raw-looking necks craning in and out. The scene had a shimmering quality to it, receding and advancing to the throbbing pulse of the pain in my head.

This was very interesting, I decided, but I was having a little trouble keeping it all in focus. I was about to call it a day and go back to sleep when a small point of information swam up out of my subconscious and clamored for attention.

The dog. What was a dog doing here?

With a great effort, I raised my head and looked at the dog. It was hard to keep it in sight, because it pranced about, yapping at the birds, and I was having difficulty in keeping my head upright. The dog's image kept slipping sideways.

There shouldn't be a dog this far out in the bush.

I smiled to myself. If it shouldn't be here, I thought, then it's probably not a dog at all. It's a hyena. And that would explain why it's out here in the bush all alone. Right.

Thoughts rose again through the mist of pain. It doesn't have spots like a hyena, my subconscious insisted. And hyenas laugh.

Do you hear this animal laughing?

No, I admitted, gazing at the dog with dull eyes. Not laughing. Yapping. A high, irritating sound that was making my head ache all the more.

I was angry with the dog, I decided. For disturbing my sleep, for spoiling my siesta. I shouted at it to go away, but could only manage a whisper. The dog cocked its head at me, and began yapping even louder. Please, dog, I thought – go away and let me sleep.

For a moment, it looked as though my prayers would be answered. The dog suddenly stopped barking, pricked up its ears, and turned, its tail wagging. And a moment later, three people stood over me, gazing down from an altitude of many hundreds of feet.

They were naked, or nearly so, and they carried bows and arrows and large knives. They had ritual scars on their cheeks, teeth sharpened to points, and bones through their noses.

I looked across at Demba. He was awake. "Who the hell are these guys?" I croaked.

He stared up at them. "I think they're cannibals," he whispered. Then he passed out.

* * *

It didn't take long for them to dig us out. It just felt like forever.

They were Bassari hunters, two men and a boy. They murmured and exclaimed to each other as they scraped and dug at the sand, lifting us out gently and placing us in the shade of a baobab tree at the edge of the creek. In a few moments, the wire that bound us was off, and I began rubbing my wrists and ankles, trying to restore circulation. One of them offered a calabash of water, and I sipped it gratefully, glancing at them as I did so.

Okay, so maybe Demba overreacted a little. But dammit, they really did look like cannibals. They weren't entirely naked, however; each of them wore a triangular flap of what looked like monkey skin over their buttocks, and a long, thin pointed sheath woven of some vegetable fiber covering their genitals in front. And okay, those were porcupine quills through their noses, not bones. But they did carry bows and arrows, and sharp bushknives, and their teeth were indeed filed to sharp points.

They were the most beautiful people I had ever seen, I decided, as the warm, delicious water trickled slowly down my throat.

I looked at one of the men and tried to smile. God knows what I must have looked like. After a moment, I managed to make my lips work. "*Merci*," I said. "*Vous m'avez sauvé la vie.*" Seeing the lack of comprehension in his face, I asked, "*Vous ne parlez pas français?*"

The men spoke to each other in a series of low, liquid syllables. Then one of them called the boy. He rose from where he had been squatting and approached. "My uncle wishes to know," he said in perfect schoolbook French, "what you were doing buried in the ground."

"Tell him it wasn't my idea," I said. Slowly, I explained as best I could.

As I spoke, the boy translated. The older men shook their heads, clucking their tongues in disapproval.

"And where did you learn French?" I said when I had finished.

The boy grinned with pride. "I go to the mission school," he said. "Sister Dominique teaches me French, and many other things. But next year I will have to leave, because it will be time for my initiation." He smiled. "Then I will be a man. My name is Kali," he added.

Kali explained that he and his father and his uncle were on a hunting expedition. They had been out in the bush for two days, and now their goatskin bags were stuffed with fresh meat. They were hurrying to return to the village before the meat began to spoil. They had heard their dog barking and seen the vultures, and they had heard a voice, and come to see what the dog had caught.

One of the men advanced and squatted down close to me. Staring into my eyes, he brought his face inches from mine, holding my gaze for a long moment. Finally he grunted in satisfaction, leaned back on his heels, and began to rummage in his skin bag.

He brought out what looked like an antelope horn, plugged at the end and attached to a loop of rawhide. He spoke for several minutes to the boy, holding the horn in the palm of his hand. As he spoke, Kali's eyes grew wide, his expression serious.

Kali turned to me. "My uncle is a hunter. He is also a person who knows things. In our language, we call such people *anangarbeshan* – it means 'those who know about medicine.'"

"A bush doctor?"

"No, much more powerful than that. A kind of magician. The Catholic sisters tell us that magicians don't exist, but every Bassari knows that this is not true." He tapped his head. "The medicine we know is not just for the body, but for the mind as well."

Beside him, the older man nodded.

"My uncle uses this medicine to hunt. It helps bring the animals to him." He pointed to the antelope horn. "The medicine is inside, there."

"And this medicine brings animals to him?"

Kali grinned. "We Bassari do not hunt as others do. When we want to kill a koba, for example, we go into the forest to a place that kobas like. Then we wait. And while we wait, we think of the koba. We think of its beautiful color, of how long its horns are, of how strong and graceful it is. We think of it, and our mind calls to it. And if the medicine is working for us, the koba will come."

He looked at me with serious eyes. "My uncle thinks that you, too, are a hunter, and that you are in great danger. This medicine will protect you, and will bring that which you seek to you."

He nodded to the older man, who leaned forward and placed the horn around my neck. He picked up the horn, spit on it, and muttered a series of short phrases. Then he sat back, watching me with bright eyes, and said something to Kali.

"Now the gris-gris is yours. It will bring you what you seek. But if there is danger, it will bring that as well. So be careful."

I fingered the gris-gris. "Thank you," I said after a moment. "Your uncle is very kind. He didn't have to do this."

Kali shrugged. "My uncle says he is curious to know whether his medicine will work on a white man." He paused. "It is what Sister Dominique would call an 'experiment', I think. My uncle says that the gris-gris has always worked for him, but he is not sure about you."

He indicated Demba beside me, pointing to his strings of amulets. "These things are useless for some people, for example. The Muslim shaved-heads put prayers inside them sometimes, and they believe that they will protect their wearer. But look at how many he is wearing, and look what happened to him."

Demba glared at him, his eyes puffed into narrow slits, but said nothing.

Kali tapped the horn his uncle had given me. "This is a Bassari gris-gris, which is better than anything. My uncle hopes it will protect you and bring you what you want."

I nodded. "Thank you," I said gravely. "I think I will need all the luck I can get."

Just then, the dog began to bark. The hunters cocked their heads. A moment later, I heard it, too: a vehicle, laboring through the bush. We all got to our feet, and a moment later, a blue Gendarmerie Land Rover swung into view and stopped above us, on the bank of the creek. The doors were flung open, and Bari N'Dour and Père Daniel jumped down.

Kali crowed with delight. "You see?" he said. "It's working already!"

CHAPTER TWENTY-TWO

I sat quietly, listening to Bari interrogating Demba. Demba lay in the shade of the baobab, his shirt off in the blistering heat, fingering his gris-gris strings with a distracted air. Père Daniel had dressed our wounds, bandaging the side of my head where Ti-Claude's bullet had grazed me. I was starting to feel halfway human again.

The Bassari hunters sat on some large leaves a few meters away. They had found a nest of palm rats and were busy roasting two of them over a small fire. They turned the furry rodents on makeshift bamboo spits while they watched us with interest. From time to time, Kali would translate for the older men in a low voice.

In the Land Rover's mirror, my face looked like a Jackson Pollock original. I was covered with scratches, welts and insect bites. One side of my face was swollen so much that my eye was almost shut. I was badly sunburned and my lips were cracked and blistered. Père Daniel had looked worried at first when he saw my head, but after he had cleaned away the blood and dirt, he pronounced it no more than a graze. After careful inspection of my pupillary reflexes, he decided that I did not have a concussion. Although that was certainly good news, it didn't do much for my headache.

No one in Kédougou had missed me until the afternoon. The garde had not thought to inform Bari that I'd come through the checkpoint until well after lunchtime, and even then, it had been assumed that I'd simply gone for a drive around the area.

Eventually, they found Bari's Gendarmerie vehicle in Demba's deserted compound. And an hour later, a Bassari family arriving at the mission's dispensary had reported seeing a green and white Land Rover out along the road to the border. A white man had been driving, they said, and there were a white woman and a black man with him. By that time, night had fallen. At first light, Bari and the priest had set out.

I sat back against the tree, listening to Bari and Demba, chewing reflectively on a tiny drumstick that Kali had given me. The palm rat wasn't half bad, I decided. The Bassari had finished their rats, and now they were passing around a small bamboo tube. It contained a fine green powder, and every now and then, one of them would tap a little bit out onto the flat of his knife blade, hold it under his nose, and sniff hard.

Kali noticed my interest. "Tobacco," he said. "Special Bassari tobacco; very strong. Do you want to try?"

I grinned and shook my head. I was feeling better, but not yet adventurous. The green powder might be tobacco, and then again, it might be something a little different, and in my experience, once you open the doors of perception, it's sometimes hard to get them shut again.

I resumed listening to Bari and Demba. "You were telling me about the diamonds," Bari was saying.

"*Les diamants, oui.*" Demba thought for a moment. "I, ah, used to do small jobs for people coming through Kédougou." He spoke in a monotone, fingering his leather gris-gris. "Just every now and then, things they didn't want the customs agents to see, *comprenez?*"

Bari gave him a beady stare.

Demba shrugged. "All right, some of it was contraband, *bien sûr.* But nothing really important, just small *nyama-nyama.*" He stopped talking, looking at his magic charms as though for advice.

"*Continuez,*" said Bari.

"Well," said Demba, "about three years ago, a man came through town. A Lebanese, from Freetown. I've forgotten his name."

"You'll remember," said Bari matter-of-factly. "But it's not important now. Keep talking."

"The Lebanese stayed in town about a week, at the bar. I fed him and gave him the spare room, because he paid well and was *gentil.* On his last night, he made me a proposition. A business proposition."

He paused. "He told me that he travelled a lot. That he had a big family, many brothers and sisters, up and down the coast. He asked me if I'd ever been to Sierra Leone. I told him no. So he told me about it. In Sierra Leone, he said, there are diamond mines. And many of these diamonds, he said, find their way out of the country illegally. He said that one could sell uncut stones for a lot of money, but first one must get the stones out of the country. It is not worth selling stones in Freetown, he said; it costs too much money to bribe the police, and the diamond companies have their own investigators, too, who are not so easy to bribe."

"Get on with it," said Bari in an irritated voice. "This is going to take all day at this rate."

Demba sighed. "So, he explained, they take the diamonds out through other countries. Some go to Liberia, some go to Guinea. All this the man explained while he ate my chicken and drank my beer. I said nothing, just let him talk. He told me that his Lebanese friends in Sierra Leone were thinking of ways to send the diamonds out of the country, and they thought of Senegal. It's a better place than Liberia, he tells me; it's far away from Freetown, and people speak French, not English. And best of all, they're not thinking too much about diamonds, and the police won't be looking too hard. So he tells me he and his friends want someone to handle the diamonds in Kédougou – someone to take them from the carriers who come across the border, and send the diamonds on to Dakar. Somebody they can trust." He paused. "And then he asks me if I'm interested."

"And what did you tell him?" Bari's voice was a soft purr.

Demba closed his eyes, as if reliving the scene in his memory. "I told him to give me some time to think about it. And that night in bed, I did a lot of thinking."

He opened his eyes and looked at us, imploring. "Here's what I thought about: I'm a poor man. I'm from Togo, not from here, and these hopeless people don't treat me the way they should. I have no family here, no kinsmen, no one to help me. Who's going to care for me when I get old? When I get sick? All this I thought about in bed that night."

He spread his hands. "I try to make an honest living, but it's hard in a place like Kédougou, you've got no idea.

Aucune idée. I run a bar and restaurant for these hopeless people, they drink up everything, eat up everything, and then laugh when I say I want my money."

He leaned forward and spoke with quiet anger, the sweat shining on his face. "Back in Togo, we'd call these people the village idiots. Do you know what it's like to live in a whole town full of village idiots?"

He wiped his forehead with a meaty hand. "So in the morning I tell the Lebanese okay, what does he want me to do? And he tells me, and that's how it starts."

Bari nodded. "So tell me now. Tell me how it worked."

Demba took a deep breath. "Every couple of weeks, somebody comes to the bar, somebody from across the border. He gives me the diamonds. Then I put the diamonds in the pineapples. I grow nice pineapples, down by the river, send 'em to Monsieur Le Vieux in Tambacounda to sell for me. So every few weeks I make up a special crate of pineapples for Le Vieux. I cut a plug in one of the pineapples, put the diamonds inside, and seal it up."

"That explains the fruit in Le Vieux's kitchen being all hacked up," said Bari. "Okay, what happens next?"

"Le Vieux goes to Dakar about once a month, on business. He just puts the diamonds in his briefcase and goes, 'cause who's gonna search a French businessman, right? He takes the train, and Abdou Fall, the taxi driver, meets him. Le Vieux gives Abdou the diamonds; Abdou gives Le Vieux the money. When Le Vieux gets back to Tambacounda, he sends me my share with the Air Sénégal pilot, in an envelope."

I leaned forward. "And what happens to the diamonds then?" I asked.

Demba shrugged. "Who knows? Once Abdou gets the diamonds, they disappear."

"Do you know a woodcarver, a man named Thiam? He has – had – a small shop at Soumbedioune."

Demba shook his head. "Never heard of him."

Bari scowled. "You must have known who was running the operation in Dakar, who was putting up all the money. It wouldn't have been Le Vieux himself; he wasn't rich enough. So who was it?"

Demba hesitated. "The Lebanese was the *patron*. The one in Dakar."

"Khoury?" I asked. "Was his name Khoury?"

Demba looked confused. "Khoury? No, not Khoury. His name is Nassif. Samir Nassif. Big businessman, got a nice place in Dakar, out on the corniche. That's the boss."

This was the second time I'd heard Nassif's name. It didn't make sense, but I could figure out what it meant later. "So why did Ti-Claude come to see you, Demba?" I kept my voice neutral.

His eyes slid away from mine. "*Ce mec Ti-Claude, il est bien fou.* I mean, he's really crazy, I'm telling you. He showed up at the bar yesterday morning, him and the woman."

"And what happened then?"

"He came into the bar," Demba said, his voice low. "He had the woman with him, tied up. He woke me up from my siesta and he started to hit me. Trying to make me tell him where the diamonds were. I tried to explain to him, but he wouldn't believe anything I said." He paused. "He told me I was keeping back some of the stones. You know, trying to sell them myself."

"And were you?"

He looked at me with offended dignity. "Of course not. I'm a smuggler, not a thief."

Demba was lying, but I let it pass. "Keep talking," I said.

His voice rose an octave. "Do you know what he was going to do to me? He was going to scald me. Pour boiling water on my eyes. I'm telling you the truth. He tied me up, and put the teapot on the stove to get the water hot." Demba was breathing heavily, sweat running down his face. "He was just getting ready when he heard you drive up."

"And that's all he said to you? That he wanted the diamonds you'd been keeping back?"

"I told you." Demba's voice had a note of desperation now. "I wasn't keeping diamonds back. No, he didn't say anything else. Just that he was going to kill me."

He sat back and wiped the sweat off his face. "He's completely crazy," Demba said again after a moment. "*Carrément cinglé.*"

Bari and I were silent. There didn't seem to be much to add to that.

I got unsteadily to my feet. "Okay," I said, grasping the tree trunk for support. "We know where he's going, and we know why. Let's go." I glanced at the sun. "We should be there in–"

Bari grabbed my arm. "Don't be a fool," he said. "Sit back down. You're in no shape to do anything."

I slapped sand off my jeans. "Stuff it," I said. "We're the only ones who can stop him now." I set a course on rubbery legs toward the truck. "We've got a lot of ground to cover, and very little time left. If he's headed for the airstrip, that means he's found some way to get out."

"Wait," said Bari. "You've got to–"

I whirled to face him. "Don't you get it? He's setting up his escape. And once he does, he'll have no more use for Lindy."

Bari looked at me and nodded. "You're right," he said after a moment. "He'll kill her, won't he?"

"Yes, he will. And we're the only ones who can stop him."

CHAPTER TWENTY-THREE

We stopped the Land Rover on the bank and stared silently down at the mud-brown water of the Gambia, churning past below us. The river was high and fast, and I could see debris floating everywhere – tree branches, vines, palm fronds. On the far bank, I could see tire tracks in the mud, leading up and away from the water's edge, showing where Ti-Claude and Lindy had crossed. Further downstream, two fat crocodiles lay half-buried in the mud, sunning themselves.

"*Nom de Dieu*," Bari said softly. "We'll never get across that."

I looked at where the causeway should have been, my heart sinking. The rocks which had been used to build the causeway were completely under water. All that was visible was a humped swelling under the rushing brown water.

On the far bank, one of the crocodiles came alert with a grunt. It had spotted something moving in the water. Looking upstream, I saw a floating palm branch, and on it, a wet and frightened spider monkey. With a sucking sound, the crocodile heaved itself out of the mud. Short legs moving crabwise, it dragged itself to the water's edge and eased in. Moving like a slow torpedo, it set a course to intercept the branch, twitching its tail in anticipation.

The monkey began to scream softly as it saw the crocodile's snout rippling the water. There was a soft splash, a flick of tail, and both the monkey and the crocodile disappeared from view, swallowed by the river.

"I don't understand," I said quietly. "It hasn't rained for two days. The river shouldn't be this high, should it?"

"It rained last night, in the mountains," Père Daniel said. "Up in the Fouta-Djallon, across the border. This is the water from that storm. If the other two crossed last night, the water level would have been much lower then." He paused. "If no more rain falls tonight," he said, "the level of the river will fall again."

The crocodile crawled back out of the water and settled into the mud of the bank. The monkey was nowhere to be seen. I remembered that they stashed their prey underwater until it had decomposed just enough to be tasty. Like squirrels with winter nuts.

"We can't wait," I said finally. "We've got to get to the airstrip today. No matter what it takes. It'll be dark in a few hours, and then it will be too late."

I knelt, and began taking off my boots. My muscles were cramped and painful, and my head throbbed painfully under its bandage. I began to wade out into the current. We had no more time left. It was either cross now, or never.

The current was strong and bucked fiercely against my thighs. I forged ahead, feeling the way with my toes on the bed of stones that formed the causeway. As I edged forward, I kept one eye on the far bank, watching the crocodiles. They stared back, their yellow eyes unblinking. Come on in, they seemed to say, the water's fine.

The water deepened gradually until it came just below my crotch. Then it seemed to level off. I waded out a few more feet, bracing myself against the sideways pressure of the current. It didn't seem to be getting any deeper.

I stood in the water, thinking. The river was deep enough to come up to the wheel-wells of the Land Rover, well over the bottoms of the doors. It probably wouldn't swamp the carburetor or the electrical system, but that was hard to say for sure, because the current would force the water higher on the upstream side as we went across.

I stared across at the remaining two hundred yards of river. Provided it didn't get any deeper out there in the middle, we might just be able to make it. If we could keep our speed up, it might just be possible. We'd just have to try and see, I decided.

I trudged back up the bank. "Everybody inside, and sit on the upstream side, on the right. I'll take the wheel." I put the truck in four-wheel drive and shifted into low. "Hang on," I said.

Motor roaring, we churned down the bank towards the rushing water.

I had the accelerator flat on the floor as we hit the edge of the water. Keep it moving, I told myself. Steady forward motion was the only thing that would prevent us from being swept downstream. Even a few feet of lateral movement would be dangerous, if we fell off the causeway and into the deeper water.

The engine roared like a wounded buffalo, and we bucked and rolled as the truck fought its way into the middle of the river. I gripped the wheel with all my strength as the combined force of the water and the rough stones threatened to tear it from my hands.

The current was piling up against our right side, scant inches below the open windows. In another few seconds, I knew, water would begin leaking in through the doors, adding extra weight and slowing our forward momentum.

Two-thirds of the way across now, and I was praying that we would not stall. If the engine were to die, water would rush up the exhaust pipe, making it almost impossible to restart. Just a few more seconds, I told myself. Any moment now, we would come to the start of the up-grade, and begin to climb out of the river. The water level would drop, and the current would slacken. Any moment now, I thought triumphantly. We're going to make it.

Then we hit the hole.

The left front wheel of the Land Rover dropped, and the engine noise altered. I cursed as I realized what had happened. The swift current was pulling the causeway apart, and we had hit a place where the large rocks which formed the roadbed had been swept away. The hood was under water now, going down like a diving submarine, and I fought the wheel hard, praying that the four-wheel drive would be able to pull us up and out.

Then the engine died.

I ground the starter, knowing as I did so that it was hopeless. We were tipping over.

It was happening in slow motion, the right side coming up inch by inch as the rushing water bit into the exposed chassis. We were at a forty-five-degree angle now; in another few seconds we would tip completely over, falling off the causeway and into the river below.

I turned to Bari. "Abandon ship," I said calmly. "And hurry up, for God's sake. She's going over."

There was a scramble for the doors.

Water was pouring in now, and I could feel the heavy vehicle starting to move along the bottom. I fought down my rising panic until I was sure that everyone else had gotten clear. I know that the captain is expected to go down with his ship, but what the hell, I thought, this is a government vehicle. So I grabbed the top of the door casing and pulled myself out from behind the wheel.

The Land Rover was on its side now. I hoisted myself out the open window and stood up on the side of the truck. Bari, Père Daniel and Demba were hip-deep in the water, struggling toward the bank. All around me, the brown, evil-looking water rushed and swirled as it plucked greedily at the vehicle. I could feel the chassis move and lift slightly underneath me, and I knew that the current was working the truck off the raised causeway and down into the river. I got ready to jump.

I never got the chance. There was a grinding scrape and a jolt, and I lost my footing as the Land Rover disappeared beneath me. I fell backwards into the deep water below the causeway.

I broke the surface a moment later to see the truck, like a whale coming up for air, rolling over ponderously in the current and then nosing under again. All the while, it was being swept slowly and majestically downriver.

Just like me, I suddenly realized.

"*Les crocos! Attention aux crocos! Ils sont dans l'eau!*" Bari's shout froze my blood.

God's teeth, I'd forgotten the crocodiles. I turned and saw two bumpy-log snouts headed my way, barely visible against the rippling current.

I began to swim like a madman, knowing even as I did so that I'd never make it. I was thirty yards from shore, and the crocs were between me and the bank, on an interception course and picking up speed.

Bari stood on the bank, feet spread, holding his pistol in both hands. He started squeezing off rounds. I just kept swimming; I didn't have time to worry about what might happen if he hit me instead of one of the reptiles.

One of Bari's shots connected. The lead crocodile convulsed, leaping halfway out of the water, and began to thrash wildly, alternately sinking and rising. Bari had hit it in the spine, and it was crippled, no further threat to me. It drifted downstream, bright blood pouring from a wound behind its ugly head.

The other crocodile kept right on coming. It was ten yards away now, closing fast. I'd had to deal with hungry sharks before, but never a crocodile, and as I swam for my life, I tried to think of what to do.

Ahead of me, close to the bank, the branches of a large fromagier tree extended over the water. Liana vines hung from the branches, the lowest of them only inches from the rushing water. I redoubled my strokes, changing course to bring myself directly under the vines.

Reaching up, I pulled myself out of the water, scant inches ahead of the questing snout of the crocodile. And then, with horror, I realized that the vine was being pulled down with my weight. I was dropping back toward the river.

I scrambled frantically, hand-over-hand, raising myself another few feet. Below me, the crocodile waited.

"Shoot, dammit!" I shouted at Bari. "What the hell are you waiting for?"

"No more ammunition!" he yelled back.

Oh, great, I thought. Just then, the vine gave way partially, dropping me three or four feet. I realized that in a few seconds, it was going to break completely, and I'd be back in the water. With the crocodile.

They say your whole life passes before your eyes. Not in my case. What passed before my eyes at that moment was the day I was eight years old and my grandfather had taken me to a Florida gator farm. There, I had watched open-mouthed as an ageing good old boy showed a crowd of tourists how easy it was to hold a gator's mouth shut with one hand. Gators had strong muscles for closing their jaws, he'd explained; not for opening them. So he'd demonstrated, and we all applauded and shivered.

I'd never been much interested in trying it, personally. My acquaintance with alligators and crocodiles was limited to zoos. All I knew was that they were fast, aggressive, and hungry most of the time, and that about all they were good for was shoes, handbags and belts.

Belts. I felt the vine start to tear. That's it, belts and jaws. I let go of the vine with one hand and scrabbled for my belt, unbuckling it and ripping it from the loops on my trousers.

Then the vine broke.

I fell straight down, hitting the crocodile squarely on the head. The reptile thrashed underneath me as I slid off sideways and into the water. I got one arm around its neck and held tight as I went under, feeling the beast turning with me, its powerful tail lashing the water. Keep a grip, I told myself grimly. As long as you're holding on and away from the jaws, you've still got a chance.

Riding a croc like a rodeo cowboy wasn't my idea of a fun way to spend the afternoon, I decided, as I came up out of the water for the second time. I locked my legs around the croc's body in a wrestler's hold, leaned forward, and brought my belt up, holding it in both hands.

The belt was a wide strap of webbing with an airline-type quick release, and all I'd ever used it for so far was to keep my pants up. Now I was going to see if it would hold a crocodile's jaws shut. The beast was slippery and slimy, and it had breath that would strip paint. It was only a matter of seconds before I lost my hold. I had to get this right the very first time.

The croc was thrashing wildly, trying to shake me off, opening and closing its massive jaws in anger and frustration. I had to use both hands now, so I gripped the croc's body with my knees and legs in a desperate scissor hold as I put the strap of the belt through the buckle again to form a loop.

I leaned forward as the jaws snapped shut and quickly threw my belt around them, pulling the loop tight and pressing down on the buckle, locking it. The deadly jaws were now strapped shut, and if the man in Florida had been telling the truth all those many years ago, the croc wouldn't be able to open them.

I didn't intend to stick around to find out. Sliding off the beast's back, I kicked away from it, careful to avoid the tail and the legs. A moment later I staggered out of the water, holding my pants up with one hand. The crocodile moved slowly downstream, thrashing and tossing its head in the air.

"Are you all right?" Bari asked as he helped me up the bank.

I stretched and poked myself experimentally. "I think so," I said after a moment. "Thanks for taking care of the first one. Otherwise, I'd have had to borrow your belt as well."

We looked at each other for a moment, and then both of us burst into laughter.

We began to walk back to where Père Daniel and Demba stood waiting for us.

"You were lucky there," Bari said after a moment. He touched the Bassari gris-gris that the hunters had given me. "Maybe this had something to do with it."

"You never know," I said as I slipped the gris-gris from around my neck. Undoing the rawhide cord, I threaded it through my belt loops and retied it. "Anything that saves your life and doubles as a belt is damned useful."

We stood in the road and looked at one another. It was four o'clock in the afternoon, we were miles from the airstrip, and we'd lost our vehicle. We had no food, no shelter, and no weapons, and night was coming.

Nighttime would be a dangerous time to be near the river, I knew. There were plenty of other crocodiles where those two had come from, to say nothing of their smaller friends, the snakes and scorpions. The big predators drank at the river near sundown, and they, too, would be on their way here soon.

We had no chance of reaching the airstrip now. The best we could do, I realized with despair, was to get away from the river and find a large tree to sleep in for the night.

Then we heard the noise of a vehicle, just out of sight around a bend in the road, approaching fast.

Bari drew his pistol.

CHAPTER TWENTY-FOUR

I looked at his weapon. "It's not loaded," I said.

Bari nodded. "I know that," he said. "And you know that. But *they* don't."

An olive-drab jeep appeared around the corner. In it were two park guards wearing fatigue uniforms.

Bari stepped into the road, the pistol held down along his thigh. The jeep screeched to a halt.

The two guards stared at us; we were four strangers, soaking wet, on foot in the middle of nowhere. "*Putain, ce sont les braconniers*," the driver murmured. "Goddamn poachers." He reached behind him for the rifle strapped to the back of his seat.

"Freeze," snapped Bari, bringing up the pistol. "*Ne bougez pas*." He extracted his identity card from his pocket and held it up. "Brigadier N'Dour, Gendarmerie Nationale."

The driver put the rifle down. "A gendarme? What the hell are you doing here? We heard gunshots; we thought you were poachers. We've spent the last three days looking for a gang of Mauritanians who–"

"Never mind the Mauritanians," Bari said. "They're being taken care of." He gestured with the pistol. "Now get out. I'm requisitioning this vehicle."

The driver stared at him. "Our jeep? Absolutely not! This is national park territory. Unless you have a written authorization from the National Conservator of Forests, you are here in violation of the law. You–"

Bari put the muzzle of his pistol right up against the man's nose. "I've got your authorization right here," he said quietly. Taking the man by the collar, he pulled him out of the jeep. "There's no time for explanations. The keys, *couillon*, or I'll shoot you right here in the road."

I stepped up on the other side. "No false moves," I said to the second guard. "I don't have a gun, but I've just wrestled a crocodile, and I'm sure you can imagine how irritable that can make someone. You'll be no problem for me at all. I'll bite your damned ear off if you try anything, believe me."

The guard stared at me. "Oh, I believe you," he said.

* * *

An hour later, we turned off the dirt *piste* into the driveway of the hotel at Simenti, scattering a horde of grim-faced baboons. The hotel was a low structure built of cinder blocks and tile, with wide expanses roofed with grass thatch for a more authentically 'African' look. Everything was closed and shuttered. As we roared up the drive, I saw two small chimpanzees get up from where they had been sunning themselves on the wide veranda and race off into the bush.

"You the only ones here?" I asked the guard sitting beside me.

He nodded. "Just the two of us. We are supposed to be relieved next week, *insh'Allah*."

"Did you hear another vehicle yesterday?"

He looked puzzled. "Here? No. But we weren't here for most of the day. We were patrolling the western sector, looking for the poachers, checking that the ranger stations were locked. We wouldn't have heard anything."

I checked my watch. Nearly five o'clock; little more than an hour until sundown. "Get us some rifles and ammunition," I said. "And show us the way to the airstrip."

* * *

Bari and I lay side by side in the tall grass beside the airstrip and waited. We had two French Army 8 mm MAS rifles borrowed from the guards. I adjusted the web strap on mine and checked the angle of fire. The airstrip shimmered in the last of the day's heat, its edges running off in perfect perspective into the scrub. The rifles were old but serviceable, and I figured that I could make mine work well enough when the time came.

I ignored the insects and the aching of my muscles as I lay still, waiting, feeling the accumulated heat of the day rising up through the ground, fingering the Bassari gris-gris around my waist. Ti-Claude was out there somewhere, and soon he would be coming.

He's got to come. This is his only way out.

I wanted him to come very badly.

We had left Père Daniel and the guards back at the hotel. They had instructions to guard Demba, and on no account to approach the airstrip. It would be safer for everyone that way. Leaving the jeep where we had parked it, Bari and I had collected rifles and ammunition, and disappeared into the bush behind the hotel.

We moved silently through the forest, pausing every few minutes to listen and look. If Ti-Claude had arrived here last night, he'd be holed up somewhere not too far from the airstrip, and I didn't want to run into him unexpectedly. Once I thought I saw a chimpanzee moving in the branches overhead, but it might have been a baboon.

It had taken us forty-five minutes to reach the airstrip, a rough gravel *piste* cut through the scrub. We had found a stand of elephant grass on a small knoll and dug in.

Then we waited.

Now, the day was losing its harsh, washed-out quality, turning into the softer pastel colors of dusk. The temperature was dropping as the day died, and a light breeze had sprung up. I checked my watch, looking around warily. Beside me, Bari stirred uneasily and muttered a prayer.

This was twilight, the time of day the Senegalese called *timis*. *Timis* was the window to the spirit world, the time of fear and hurried steps through the forest toward home. *Timis* belonged to the night-creatures, the *djinn* and *dumm* – witches and strange half-human monsters who cast nets in the gathering darkness to trap unwary travelers. Soul-eaters also moved freely at dusk, turning men insane, eating them from the inside out, leaving nothing but the withered husk of a body on the dusty road to greet the hot morning sunrise.

The baobab and kapok trees looked sinister in the fading light, their branches reaching out hungrily for us. In the middle distance, the insects were beginning their eerie night songs, and further away in the forest, a leopard coughed.

"Why doesn't he come?" Bari whispered. "Where the hell is he?"

I shifted on the hard ground, brushing at a mosquito. "He's waiting," I said quietly. "Until it gets fully dark. Less chance of being seen, less chance of the aircraft being identified. It's what they call a drop-in extraction; the pilot won't even turn his motors off."

I settled back to wait some more. Every now and then I quietly worked the bolt on the rifle, moving the sights over the terrain, getting the feel of the heavy piece and imagining how I would fire it when the time came.

We're going to get only one chance at this. If we miss it, Lindy will be dead. And so, probably, will we.

The sky turned a deep red, the clouds shot with purple as the sun sank toward the horizon. A flight of snow-white herons flapped silently by on their way to the river to feed. Frogs were starting to peep from a nearby marigot. The night mosquitoes had discovered us, and clouds of them whined about our heads. The ground was hard and I was dusty and muddy, stinking of fear and sweat and anger.

Then I heard it.

An engine starting up, some distance away to the north.

Bari put his hand on my shoulder, listening. "Coming this way."

I nodded, working the bolt on my rifle and levering my elbow into the strap. "Come to poppa," I breathed as I snuggled down into the grass.

Visibility was down to only a few hundred yards when we saw Lindy's green and white Land Rover picking its way through the scrub bush on the far side of the airstrip, its yellow headlights shining like dragon's eyes as the vehicle crept closer.

"Two people inside," I whispered. "See them?"

Bari nodded, raising his rifle.

I put my hand on the barrel. "Not yet," I said. "We want the pilot too."

The Land Rover drove to the end of the runway and turned around, keeping its headlights on. A figure detached itself from the passenger's seat and jumped lightly to the ground. I drew my breath in sharply. It was Ti-Claude. Keeping his pistol trained on whoever was in the vehicle, he crouched on the airstrip, looking slowly in all directions, his head raised as if sniffing the wind.

I lay perfectly still, willing my hands to keep the rifle down.

Finally, he seemed satisfied. Walking around to the other side, he opened the door on the driver's side, and jerked Lindy to the ground.

It was too dark now to see her expression, but I heard her give a gasp of pain as Ti-Claude twisted her arm behind her and marched her forward. My hands tightened on the gun and my heart resumed its pounding, threatening to burst from my chest. Thank God, I thought, she's alive.

Prodding her with the pistol, Ti-Claude marched her around to the front of the Land Rover, positioning her so that she was clearly outlined in the headlamps. Leaving her blinking into the high beams, he climbed up on the hood and sat there, his legs dangling over the front of the grill, his gun pointed straight at her.

A moment later, we heard the unmistakable sound of an aircraft, coming in low across the savannah, straight toward us.

CHAPTER TWENTY-FIVE

It approached from the west, barely skimming the trees – a twin-engined Britten-Norman Islander with Senegalese civil identification numbers. Green and red navigation lights pulsing, it roared over the Land Rover's headlights. At the last possible minute, the engines feathered, the winglights blazed on, and the plane floated down to the gravel *piste* with a squeak and a bounce. Whoever the pilot is, I thought, he's good.

"*Allez*," whispered Bari. "Let's take them."

We stood up and raised our rifles. And then everything started to fall apart.

First came the chimpanzee. It came loping out of the bush, headed straight for Lindy, uttering sharp hoots of recognition as it came. In the fading light, Bobo's distinctive shock of white hair was clearly visible.

I pulled Bari back down into the grass. "Hold on," I said. "It's Bobo."

He stared at me. "It's who?"

"Bobo," I repeated. "One of the chimps from the research station."

"A chimpanzee? What the hell's he trying to do?"

I peered over the top of the grass. "I think he's trying to save Lindy."

Ti-Claude had seen the chimp now. He pulled Lindy around in front of him, his pistol at her head, and began backing up, moving toward the Land Rover. She yelled at Bobo to go back, but the chimp took no notice. He continued to advance, screaming now with fear and rage, swaying violently from side to side.

Lindy's words came flashing back to me: 'He flies into a rage if anyone points a gun in his direction ... Bobo is four or five times stronger than a human male, and a lot faster.'

Then the second thing happened. I heard a horn behind us, and turned to see the park guards' jeep careering up the road from the hotel, headlights flashing.

"Those damned fools!" Bari's voice was furious. "Why the hell didn't they stay where they were?"

As we watched, the jeep bounced out onto the airstrip, weaving crazily, heading toward the Land Rover. A park guard, his face frozen with terror, was at the wheel. Behind him, standing up in the open back, was Demba, clutching the guard's rifle and yelling something. I heard the word 'diamonds' once or twice, but could understand nothing more.

"Demba's gotten free," I breathed. "Oh, Christ."

Down at the other end of the runway, the Islander had turned around now and was revving its motors, straining against its brakes, its motors roaring.

The approaching jeep was spotlighted by the Land Rover's headlights on one side, and the Islander's wing beams on the other. Ti-Claude looked from side to side, first at the approaching jeep, then at the chimpanzee, and then back again. Then he planted his feet, raised his pistol, and began to fire at Demba's upright figure, now only thirty yards away and closing fast.

"*Nom de Dieu*," said Bari, and raised his rifle.

Just then, one of Ti-Claude's shots connected. The jeep's front tire blew and it flipped completely over. I saw Demba's body arc through the air, and then Bari and I were up and moving, snapping off shots as we ran.

Ti-Claude spotted us then. He spun around, dragging Lindy with him, causing her to cry out in pain. "*Arrêtez là!*" he screamed, bringing the muzzle of his pistol up against the side of Lindy's head. "Stop there, or I'll blow her brains out!"

And that, of course, was when Bobo attacked.

Teeth bared and shrieking with rage, Bobo flew across the gravel and launched himself at Ti-Claude. The Haitian got off one wild shot, kicked Bobo back, and leapt for the door of the Land Rover. Wrenching it open, he crawled inside.

Screaming at the top of his lungs, Bobo grasped the door of the Land Rover in both hands and tore it off its hinges. He pulled Ti-Claude out and sank his teeth into the man's shoulder.

Bari and I were running flat out now. We passed the guard's jeep, turned upside down, its tires still spinning. I caught the sharp stench of gasoline and saw a tongue of flame snaking out from under the chassis.

"Down," I said to Bari, and just then, the jeep's tank exploded.

There was a low thump and a billowing sheet of flame, and Bobo let go of Ti-Claude, screaming and retreating in terror.

Holding his injured shoulder, Ti-Claude set off at a dead run toward the waiting plane at the other end of the airstrip.

The puddled fuel formed deadly pools of fire around the wrecked jeep, lighting up the scene in nightmare fashion.

"Get the guard away from the fire!" I yelled to Bari.

Then I ran to Lindy where she lay sprawled on the gravel and picked her up, wrapping my arms around her. She looked up at me, her face streaked with dirt and tears in the flickering light of the flames, and then she turned and pointed down the runway.

"Look, Max. He's getting away!"

I turned. The cockpit door of the Islander was open now, and as I watched, Ti-Claude climbed in. Lights strobing, the plane's engines began to roar as it prepared for takeoff.

I turned to Lindy. "Where are the keys?"

"Keys? They're in the ignition. Why...?" Comprehension dawned. "Oh, no. No, Max, don't. You'll—"

"Shut up, please," I said. "And move back out of the way. This might be messy."

I flung myself behind the wheel, slammed the truck into gear, and shot forward.

The end of the runway looked very far away. The Islander was moving now, picking up speed with every passing second. I heard Bari shout a warning as I shot past, but I ignored him, shifting into second and pressing the accelerator to the floor.

He's not going to get away, I thought. Not now. Not after all this.

The plane was coming fast now, straight at me, its engines at full throttle. I shifted into third and held the wheel steady, aiming right at the cabin, between the deadly arcs of the twin props. I had never played chicken in high school, I reminded myself, and this is a hell of a way to make up for lost time.

I flicked my headlamps to high and saw Ti-Claude opening the cockpit window. He leaned out and fired twice, bright orange flashes in the darkness, and a split second later, my windshield starred and shattered. I struck out at the glass with my hand, clearing an open space.

The roar of the aircraft engines was deafening now. I was trying to calculate what our combined impact speeds would add up to when I suddenly saw that they had achieved rotation. The angle of the oncoming lights changed, and then the Islander left the ground, its lights swinging up and out of my face as the pilot hauled on the controls.

Sonofabitch.

That was my last clear thought. A split second later, the left wheel of the Islander came crashing through the Land Rover's broken windshield, inches from the top of my head. I pitched forward and felt myself skidding sideways, out of control.

There was a high-pitched, rending crash from somewhere behind me as several tons of metal hit the airstrip and stayed there.

I raised my head cautiously and looked around. My Land Rover was stalled dead in the middle of the runway, its windshield and top ripped away. Behind me, the Islander was broken-backed on the runway, its nose flattened and its propellers broken off.

Bari stood beside the plane, rifle at the ready, as Ti-Claude and the pilot extracted themselves from the wreckage. I recognized the pilot as Raoul Bigard, the young cowboy I'd seen at the Catholic mission in Kédougou the day before.

Lindy dragged me out of the wrecked Land Rover and threw her arms around me. Bobo grabbed my leg and pulled hard for attention, chattering and hooting. I hugged both of them.

I looked around the littered airstrip. Something was missing.

"Where's Demba?" I said to Bari. "Did he get away?"

Bari shook his head. "He's over there, Max." He pointed beyond the guard's jeep. "I think he's dead."

"Dead?" I untangled myself from Lindy and walked slowly across to where Demba's body lay, his neck at a strange angle.

Just then, something on the ground caught my eye.

I bent down. Pebbles, hundreds of them, gleaming dully in the flamelight, scattered all around Demba's lifeless body. I picked one up and stared at it. It was a diamond.

The pebbles were uncut diamonds. Big ones, little ones. Hundreds of thousands of dollars' worth of uncut diamonds, lying on the ground.

I turned Demba over. His shirt had ridden up his back, exposing the dozens of leather gris-gris charms he wore. Half a dozen of the little leather pouches had split open from the impact, and more diamonds spilled from them as I turned the body over.

I took my penknife from my pocket and cut open one of the intact charms, then another.

All of them were packed full of diamonds.

CHAPTER TWENTY-SIX

I checked my watch. "It's time," I said, extending my hand to Lindy.

She smiled and took it, jumping down lightly onto the deck of the *Blaise Diagne*. Darkness had fallen, and a cool breeze ruffled the water of the harbor. As the chaloupe prepared to cast off, we all moved forward to take seats on the open deck below the wheelhouse.

Lindy looked lovely. She wore a new dress for the occasion, a white fluffy thing which gave her a cool and formal look, while at the same time showing off her figure and her tan. The eyes of the other passengers followed her discreetly as she walked gracefully to the front of the boat.

Bari stood tall and handsome in his rented dinner jacket. The gun he carried in a shoulder holster was hardly noticeable.

I was the least presentable member of the trio. My rented dinner jacket was also stylish, but my face was covered with bites and scratches, and I still had a large white bandage behind my ear.

The chaloupe was nosing out of the harbor now. Most of our fellow passengers were native Goréeans, returning home after a day at work on the mainland. Now they began taking off their neckties and loosening their collars, unwrapping their parcels to show each other what they had bought, passing around the cigarettes and kola nuts.

"Are you sure Khoury's going to show up?" I said.

"He was due back today," Bari replied. "Your embassy had already invited him for this evening, as a matter of fact. Monsieur Khoury is quite the social butterfly, I understand. Yesterday, I persuaded the American chief of protocol to send across a personal note. Khoury will hardly want to miss the official Fourth of July reception. And besides" – Bari grinned – "he lives in the same neighborhood. He'll be there."

I looked back at the lights of the city. The Dakar skyline looked like a huge, brilliant Christmas display, with the yellow and white lights of the high-rise buildings offset by the red and green lights of the ships in the harbor. I was drinking in the scene when Lindy's hand tightened on my arm.

She pointed down into the water. "Look down there. Are those jellyfish?"

I glanced over the side. They were jellyfish, all right, big ones. There were hundreds of them, bobbing slowly up and down with the waves, each glowing faintly with the phosphorescence of thousands of tiny plankton trapped in their long trailing tentacles. They looked like dim underwater lanterns, and were all around the boat, moving up and down with the waves and pulsing with a slow internal rhythm.

"Portuguese men-o'-war," Bari said after a moment. "They're pretty, but it's a good thing we're not swimming. They come off the coast once or twice a year, with the changing currents. Their sting can paralyze you."

"Let's stay on the boat, then," I said. I looked up at Gorée Island, not far away now. "Is everything ready over there?"

Bari nodded. "All set. We finished interrogating Ti-Claude this afternoon. Bakary brought him out to the island earlier this evening. We'll still need Khoury to fill in some details, but we have the essentials. A surprising story, really."

"How so?"

Bari turned to me. "Remember what Demba said about the head of the smuggling network? It wasn't Rachid Khoury, but another Lebanese, a man named Samir Nassif."

"I remember that," I said. "It didn't make sense at the time."

"It does now," Bari said. "Nassif is another one of the big Lebanese businessmen. What we didn't know was that he's also an illegal diamond dealer." He paused. "Or was, to be more exact. We picked him up this afternoon."

"You mean the smuggling network was Nassif's, not Khoury's?"

"That's right. One of Nassif's men recruited Demba, years ago, down in Kédougou. Once he had Demba, he put together the rest of the network – Le Vieux, Fall, and Thiam. The diamonds came in over the border, to Demba. Demba passed them to Le Vieux, Le Vieux gave them to Fall, and Fall gave them to Thiam, the woodcarver. Thiam hid them in souvenir statues and passed them off to 'tourists' from Europe – people identified by Nassif."

I nodded. "Not a bad system," I said. "They did the work and took the risks, and Nassif made most of the money. Why'd it come apart?"

Bari smiled thinly. "Competition. What I believe you call a hostile takeover."

"By Khoury?"

"By Khoury's brother, actually. The one in New York. He was actually the one who hired Ti-Claude. Ti-Claude told us the whole story. A few months ago, Khoury's brother got badly overextended. He had to borrow a lot of money, fast. The people who loaned it to him weren't regular bankers."

"The mob?"

Bari shrugged. "I suppose so. Frankly, I've never understood organized crime in America. I think it must be hard for you to tell the crooks from the honest people, from what I've heard."

Lindy nodded. "Getting harder all the time."

"Well, Khoury's brother owed a great deal of money to some very powerful people," Bari continued. "And when he couldn't pay, his creditors suggested a trade."

I whistled. "Nassif's diamond business for the debt."

"Exactly. And here in Dakar, Rachid Khoury jumped at the chance; he knew Nassif, knew all his contacts. It would have been fairly easy for him to trace the members of the network."

"And when he had the names," I said, "the mob in New York supplied a professional killer, someone who would systematically eliminate Nassif's network."

"Thereby opening up the field for the New York people," Bari said, "who planned to operate through the

Khoury brothers, and send the diamonds to New York instead of Europe."

"But the killings," Lindy said, "why were they all so, so awful? I mean, look at how Ti-Claude killed them."

Bari nodded. "I think that was done on purpose," he said. *"Pour décourager les autres.* So that Nassif and anyone else would think twice before getting involved in the diamond business again."

"But what about Nassif himself?" I said. "Weren't they going to kill him?"

Bari shook his head. "According to Ti-Claude, they didn't think it was necessary. He might have been a business rival, but he was family, after all, and killing a rich Lebanese would have drawn unwelcome attention. Once the new network was in place, they figured Nassif's sense of self-preservation would keep him quiet. And if he got difficult, it would be easy to bring Ti-Claude back one last time."

I shivered. It all made a savage kind of sense. The Khoury brothers survive, the New York people acquire a new asset, and the diamonds keep flowing. Business is a game, after all, and the point of playing a game is to win it. When a lot of money is involved, the stakes are often a little too high for good sportsmanship. And the dead people are just a business expense.

I put my arm around Lindy's waist. "What about Bigard, the pilot? Why didn't Ti-Claude kill him, too?"

"We think he was going to," Bari said. "Bigard had filed a flight plan to Tenerife, in the Canaries. It's my guess he'd have been found dead just after landing there."

"So Bigard was part of it?" asked Lindy.

Bari nodded. "And he was skimming, just as Demba had been. They probably all were, in fact. Ti-Claude met him in some bar a few days after he arrived in the country–"

I snapped my fingers. "Of course," I said. "He must have been the third white man at Yaye Ganaar's that night. The one who left before I got there."

"That would make sense," Bari said. "Bigard's story is that they met for a beer one night. Ti-Claude told him he'd been sent to 'clean up' the network, but that he'd spare Bigard if he agreed to fly him out once everyone else had been taken care of. They worked out the signal through the Catholic mission in Kédougou, and Ti-Claude paid him some advance money."

"And Bigard went along with it."

Bari nodded. "Like Khoury, he didn't have much choice, as far as I can see. We think Bigard might have been thinking of trying to kill Ti-Claude, actually. We found a loaded pistol under his seat in the plane."

I shook my head, smiling. "Bigard wasn't even in the same league. You're right; he'd have died as soon as he landed at Tenerife. And then there wouldn't have been anyone left."

"Except us," said Lindy.

Bari looked at her. "You and Max weren't part of the plan," he said drily. "Ti-Claude thought he'd got rid of Max and Demba together when he buried them in the stream bed. He kept you alive only because you knew the bush roads. It's lucky that chimpanzee of yours arrived when it did."

Lindy smiled. "How are Ti-Claude's bites, by the way?"

"Dr. Renaudeau treated the infections and gave him some stitches. He says that chimpanzees must have teeth even filthier than humans. If you'll excuse the pun, Bobo made a big impression on Ti-Claude. During the interrogation, he kept talking about how Bobo ripped the door to the truck off to get at him."

I hugged Lindy. "I don't see what's so impressive about that," I said. "I was getting ready to do the same thing."

CHAPTER TWENTY-SEVEN

With a bump and a squeal of rubber fenders, the *Blaise Diagne* made contact with the dock. The motor burbled as the lines were snubbed, and then people began to pour across the side of the chaloupe and onto the concrete of the dock.

A uniformed gendarme approached. I recognized him as Bakary, the man who'd shadowed Ti-Claude to Tambacounda on the train. He nodded in greeting and then turned to Bari and saluted.

"Khoury arrived from France this afternoon, sir," he said. "He hasn't shown up at the party yet, but he's expected momentarily. We're watching his house and his seaplane. And we've got the Haitian under guard up at the DCM's residence. Everything's ready."

"Good," said Bari. "Then let's go up."

The deputy chief of mission's residence was on a side street off the Rue des Batteries, perched up against the cliffside which dropped steeply into the sea. There was an excellent view of the city and the harbor from the patio. The house itself was an old two-story mansion with a vaguely Arab-Portuguese style of architecture. Wide balconies protruded from the high upstairs windows, and as we entered the massive gates, I could hear music and the tinkle of conversation from the house.

The DCM met us at the gate. He was a thin, nervous man dressed in what I would call Italian Ivy League. Beside him stood Arnold Shacklady, the embassy security chief.

Shacklady got right to the point. "It's always nice to see local officials, Brigadier, but you could have saved yourself the trip. This is an embassy function, and what happens here is my responsibility." He looked at me, and then back at Bari. "You and your, ah, colleagues here would just be in the way, I'm afraid."

Bari ignored him and turned to the DCM. "Counsellor, is your residence American property, diplomatically speaking?"

The DCM frowned. "Well, no, actually. Only the embassy's really US property. This house is rented–"

"And therefore Senegalese territory," Bari said. "Under the jurisdiction of the forces of public order." He smiled thinly at Shacklady. "That's clear enough, I think. But let me state it directly, Mr. Shacklady. It's you who are a bystander tonight. I don't want you interfering with what's going to happen here, and if you get in my way, I'll see that you're deported. Got that?"

Shacklady turned red. His mouth opened and shut, and then opened again. "I–"

Bari looked at him. "Stay out of my face. Isn't that what you Americans say?"

I smiled at Shacklady. "Tough when you're not official, isn't it?" I said.

He looked at me for a long moment. Then he turned on his heel and walked off.

"Well," said the DCM finally. "We're, ah, so sorry about the unfortunate business which brings you all here tonight, and we'd certainly like to cooperate in any way we can." His face pinched into a worried frown, and he rubbed his hands together as if to warm them. "There won't be any violence, will there? We want to avoid trouble at all costs. At all costs," he repeated. "Most of the diplomatic community will be here, after all. This is our most important reception of the year, you know. I'd, ah, appreciate it if you'd all try to keep a bit in the background."

His concern was genuine, I was sure of that. Within the diplomatic community, the feeling was that nice people don't get mixed up in awkwardness. Diplomatic sensibilities being what they were, our very presence was awkward, to say the least. Especially me. With my scratches and bandages, I was about as conspicuous as a Franciscan nun at the Hooker's Ball. And about as welcome.

Bari nodded, his eyes sweeping the large reception hall, noting the entrances and exits, checking out the guests. "There won't be any violence," he said at last. "Once Khoury gets here, we'll need about ten minutes alone with him. We'll arrest him – quietly, of course – and take him back to the mainland."

The DCM's eyes were wide open. "Arrest him? In front of everyone?"

Bari shook his head. "No. Alone, if possible. Have you got a private room with a telephone?"

"Oh, yes. There's a guest suite on the second floor. It has a telephone and an intercom."

"Perfect. I'd like you to show me where it is, and then I'll instruct my men. Once Khoury arrives, we'll have someone call him to the phone. We'll take care of things from that point on. Your guests won't hear a thing."

The DCM looked relieved. "I'm certainly glad to hear that," he said. "Would you like to see the guest suite now?"

Bari nodded. He turned to me. "I'll call you when we're ready. You might as well go in and get a drink."

I took Lindy's arm and together we moved into the main reception area.

There were at least a hundred people already in the large room, and a lavish buffet supper had been set up on long tables against the wall. Waiters with heavily laden trays glided back and forth through the crowd. The music and laughter were picking up now, as the first few drinks started to hit the crowd.

It was a beautiful evening, and the beautiful people here tonight would be upset by any unpleasantness, any unforeseen intrusion of reality into their carefully crafted make-believe. A somewhat cynical member of the diplomatic corps once told me that most of his colleagues believed that because they negotiated the future of nations, they needed to be as insulated as possible from the everyday realities of life in those nations.

If you buy that premise, then it makes sense for diplomats to be the people who are put through the lines ahead of everyone else, who always fly first class, and who never pay full price for anything. They live a largely duty-free life, as my diplomat friend put it, and they meet frequently on occasions such as this to congratulate each other on their good fortune. And above all else, they don't like having their fun spoiled.

"Wow," Lindy said as she looked around.

"Our tax dollars at work," I murmured, snagging two drinks off a passing tray. "Let's mingle. I'll meet you over by the chocolate mousse in about ten minutes."

She smiled, gave me a fingertip wave, and moved off.

Off to one side, a small group of people stood listening intently to a tall, angular woman with bright red lipstick, upswept Dame Edna horn-rims and a voice like Jimmy Durante. She was holding court, complaining loudly and bitterly about the servant problem, all the while chain-smoking Chesterfield straights through a long ivory holder.

"They were stealing meat straight out of the fridge," she was saying. I stood behind her and listened with one ear. "Right from under our noses. Then someone mentioned that they have this religious thing about food, some silly Muslim version of kosher, I suppose, and they can only eat meat that's been properly killed or something.

"Well" – her voice rose in triumph – "what I finally did, was to start buying meat from one of those European export houses. It's frozen, of course, and it comes from Denmark or somewhere absurd like that, but it's not killed in traditional Muslim style. That's stopped the thieving buggers from helping themselves, I'll tell you. They don't touch it now that they know it's not pure."

A plump-faced cornfed woman nodded approvingly. "But isn't that rather expensive, Adele? I mean, it must cost ten times what meat from the market costs. To say nothing of the airfreight."

Adele shrugged. "Dakar's a hardship post, my dear. It's supposed to cost money to live well in places like this. And anyway, we don't pay; the embassy does. Charles gets a special allowance for it."

She turned and caught sight of me. Her gimlet eyes swept me up and down. "My, my. I don't recall seeing you here before. Are you newly posted?" She adjusted her horn-rims and peered forward. "And how did you get so banged up? Are you with the Peace Corps or something?"

I coughed, looking around for Lindy. "No, ma'm," I said with a shy smile. "Actually, I'm with the FDA – you know, the Food and Drug Administration? I'm an undercover special operative."

Everyone came just a bit closer.

"Really?" breathed Adele, her eyes glittering. "And what brings you to Dakar? Or is that classified information?"

"Oh, that's all right," I said. "It'll be in the papers next week, so I guess there's no harm in telling you." I paused. "I'm investigating a ring of Danish jackass bootleggers."

The plump woman wrinkled her brow. "Jackass bootleggers? I don't understand."

I smiled and spread my hands. "Well, not jackasses per se," I said. I liked the sound of that, so I said it again. "Not jackasses per se. Jackass meat." I paused. "Can you believe it, those sneaky Danes were actually selling frozen jackass meat to some of the diplomatic people, passing it off as Grade-A prime beef."

Adele's face froze. "Jackass meat?"

"Yes, indeed. Old jackass meat." I touched the bandage on my head. "They were a tough bunch of customers, all right, but I think we recovered most of the meat." I spotted Bari and the DCM coming back down the stairs at the end of the room. "Anyway, it wasn't all contaminated, so we'll just hope for the best."

Everyone was staring at me. Adele looked as if she'd just bitten into a dead rat. I smiled again. "Now if you'll excuse me, I think my beeper's about to go off."

I crossed the floor to Bari.

"All set," he said. "The guest suite fronts on the ocean, and it's got a communicating door. I've left the intercom switched on so that my men downstairs can hear what's happening."

He looked at me. "Do you and Lindy want to be in on this? There's really no reason for you two to be involved if you don't want to."

I looked steadily at him. "We wouldn't miss it for the world," I said.

He nodded. "I thought so. All right, go and find Lindy. Khoury will be here soon."

Lindy was over in a corner, listening intently to a woman who looked like an overweight version of Judy Garland. As I came up the woman was saying, "…twenty years in the Foreign Service, yes, that's right, dear, it is a long time. And it was just awful after Nixon resigned, you've no idea. Washington was just dead. Things didn't liven up again until the Bicentennial came along."

Her face grew thoughtful as she sipped her wine. "Of course," she said, "there was streaking just before that. That helped a bit, I suppose."

Lindy flashed me a brilliant smile. "Oh, there you are, darling. Mrs. Shacklady here was just telling me all about her fascinating life in the Foreign Service."

"I'm sure it's absolutely gripping," I said. "But the Ruritanian ambassador wants to meet you." I took her arm. "Excuse us, please," I murmured to Mrs. Shacklady.

"Here's a question for you," I said as we moved across the room. "How many Foreign Service Officers does it take to change a lightbulb?"

She looked at me. "I don't know; how many?"

"Two. One to call embassy maintenance, and one to mix the martinis."

She made a face. "That's dumb, Max. Really dumb."

"Khoury's on his way," said Bari as we came up alongside him. "Just entering the gates now. Stay close, all right?"

CHAPTER TWENTY-EIGHT

Khoury wasn't what I had been expecting. Somehow, I'd had the image of an overweight, balding businessman in a badly tailored suit, a Middle Eastern version of Sydney Greenstreet, wearing thick glasses and smelling of garlic and hair oil.

The man who came through the door was very different. Rachid Khoury was in his early fifties, and looked like a model out of *Gentleman's Quarterly*. He had the sleek build of the all-around athlete, someone who played tennis every day and worked out several times a week. His jet-black hair was full, glossy and expertly cut. He wore a midnight-blue tuxedo and a frilled shirt, and on his wrist, a thin gold Rolex peeped out from under his French cuffs.

He was tanned and attractive and vital, and I saw heads turning to look at him as the DCM greeted him and waltzed him down the receiving line. Khoury's eyes were sharp and alert as they scanned the faces around him. He glanced briefly at me, and then at Lindy. I heard her draw in her breath as his gaze locked with hers and stayed there for a moment. Then he turned, shaking hands with someone else, and was led into the main hall. He glanced back once more at Lindy just before he disappeared down the hallway.

I looked at her. "What the hell was that all about?"

She shivered. "I'm not sure. He– he makes quite an impression, doesn't he?"

Bari took a small walkie-talkie from underneath his dinner jacket and clicked it on. "Five minutes, on my mark," he murmured into it. He snapped off the radio and looked at me. "Let's go up."

We started toward the stairs.

* * *

The guest suite fronted on the sea, with wide French doors. I opened the doors and walked out onto the small balcony. The view was superb. I could see the ships in the harbor and, on the skyline, the lights of Dakar winking and blazing in multicolored confusion. Overhead, the moon had risen.

Below, the rocky cliff dropped straight down into the dark water, some thirty feet below. Looking out across the ribbon of moonlight which ran across the water like a shining road, I saw Khoury's seaplane, bobbing gently at anchor some hundred yards offshore.

My palms were moist, and there was a tightness in my chest. Any moment now. Any moment he will come, and then the last act would begin. My excitement was rising, and with it, a tiny taste of fear.

I came back into the room and went to the communicating door and opened it. Lindy was inside, together with Bari and Bakary.

And Ti-Claude. He stood between Bari and Bakary, his wrists handcuffed in front of him.

"Good of you to come," I said.

He glared at me. "*Fais chier*," he said.

I looked at Bari. "I hate a poor sport, don't you?"

Bari's radio bleeped. He listened to it for a moment, and then snapped it off. "He's on his way upstairs." He looked at Ti-Claude. "Behave yourself," he said. "Or I'll set Bobo on you again."

Thirty seconds later, people entered the room next door.

"The telephone's right here, sir," I heard a voice say. "I'll leave you alone to take the call."

A moment later, the door to the hallway shut.

"*Allô, allô.*" Khoury's voice was irritable. "*Allô?* What the hell is wrong with this thing?"

Bari drew his pistol and opened the door. "Police, Monsieur Khoury. Hands up, please; you're under arrest."

Lindy and I moved forward into the room, staying well back. Bakary stayed behind, with Ti-Claude.

Moving slowly, Khoury put the telephone down and moved away from it, his hands held in front of him at shoulder level, palms out and elbows bent. It might have been a gesture of surrender, but to me, it looked too much like an attack stance.

It looked that way to Bari, too. "Hands up, *monsieur*. On top of your head."

Khoury slowly raised his hands. "What do you think you're doing?" His voice was choked with anger. "Who the hell are you?"

Bari flashed his ID with one hand, keeping his pistol steady with the other. "Gendarmerie, Monsieur Khoury. You're under arrest for conspiracy to commit murder."

"Murder? What are you talking about?" His hand moved to the telephone. "I'm calling my lawyer."

"Don't move!" Bari's voice cracked like a whip. "Keep still, and keep your hands up. Bakary!"

Bakary appeared in the doorway, pushing Ti-Claude in front of him.

Khoury stood rigid as a statue, his eyes darting back and forth from Bari to Ti-Claude. "Who is this man?" he said at last. "I've never seen him in my life."

I stepped forward. "This is Claude Dieudonné, Mr. Khoury; Ti-Claude to his friends. The man your brother hired. He murdered four people, and he nearly murdered us."

"You're crazy." Khoury's voice was soft and silky, like a cat's purr.

"Ti-Claude has made a full confession," Bari said. "We know everything; about the diamonds, about your brother in New York, everything." To Bakary, he said, "Search him and put the cuffs on."

Bakary nodded and moved forward.

None of us had time to react to what happened next. With the speed of a striking snake, Khoury pulled Bakary around in front of him, plucking his gun from its holster.

Bari's pistol came up, but it was too late. Khoury had Bakary's arm in a tight hold, the gun against the back of his head.

"Don't move," said Khoury. "Drop your gun on the floor. Now! You have three seconds. I'll kill this man otherwise." He was speaking in a low voice, but his eyes were raging.

Static burst from Bari's radio, startling everyone. "What's going on up there?" The voice boomed into the room. "Are you all right?"

Bari held out the radio, keeping his pistol in the other. "Give it up, Khoury. All the exits are guarded; there's no way for you to escape. Don't make things worse for yourself."

"Drop it, I said!" Khoury hissed. "Now!"

He fired, hitting Bakary in the thigh. The gendarme screamed and sagged, but Khoury held him up, using him as a shield.

"Think I won't kill him? Don't be foolish. Drop your gun now. Otherwise, my next bullet goes into his head!"

"Do it," I whispered to Bari.

He nodded and dropped the pistol to the carpet.

Everything happened very fast then. Ti-Claude swung his arms out to the side, catching me right beside the ear. Pain exploded in my head and I dropped, falling on my arm. I heard a dry pop in my wrist as I hit the marble floor, and a jolt of pain shot up my arm. As I went down, I saw Ti-Claude dive for Bari's gun.

Beside me, Lindy sucked in her breath. She took one step forward, and, as Ti-Claude rose, gun in hand, her foot caught him squarely in the crotch, lifting him at least two inches off the floor. The gun popped out of his hand like a fumbled football, and skidded across the floor.

Bari started for it, but Khoury snapped off two fast shots, and everyone hit the floor as the slugs thudded into the wall. I looked up to see Khoury heading out the French doors, moving fast, pistol held high.

He sprang to the top of the balcony's low railing and stood there balanced for a second, his silhouette clearly outlined in the moonlight.

Then he dropped the pistol and dived over the side.

"Jesus," said Lindy.

We rushed to the edge of the balcony. The water below shone silver in the moonlight, and Khoury's head and shoulders were clearly visible. He had shrugged off his jacket, and now he was swimming away from the cliff face, toward the mooring buoy which held his seaplane.

Bari raised his pistol. "*Merde*," he said. "If he reaches the plane, we've lost him."

Khoury was halfway to the seaplane now, swimming strongly, closing the distance with each second. Bari braced himself against the railing, steadied the pistol with both hands, and began squeezing off shots.

He emptied his clip and threw the gun down. "He's too far away," he said, rising from his crouch. He turned away from the window. "*Putain*. The bastard's going to get away."

I walked back into the suite. Bakary sat on the floor in a small puddle of blood, a handkerchief tied around his leg wound. Ti-Claude lay in the fetal position, hands between his legs, moaning. I worked my wrist experimentally, hearing a grinding noise.

"I think we'd better call a doctor," I said finally. "Maybe a couple of doctors."

"Oh my God." Lindy spoke from the balcony. She stood at the railing, looking down at the water. "Max, come here!"

I looked at where she was pointing. Khoury was almost to the seaplane, but he had stopped swimming. Now he was flailing at the water, thrashing wildly with his arms. A scream came across the water, and then another. The water around him boiled and seemed to glow, pulsing with color and movement.

"It's the jellyfish," said Lindy. "He swam into a swarm of jellyfish."

Khoury's screaming grew louder. He was bobbing up and down in the water like a cork in a storm, going under and then thrashing desperately to the surface again, screaming to release the terrible pain from the hundreds of stings that the writhing mass of tentacles was inflicting on him. All around him in the water, we could see the ghostly illuminated shapes of the jellyfish, drifting slowly with the current. There seemed to be hundreds of them.

Lindy watched grimly, her head on my shoulder. Bari put down his walkie-talkie and stared horror-struck at the grisly scene in the water.

"*Mon Dieu, le pauvre,*" he whispered.

Khoury's cries were feebler now, his movements more subdued, as pain and paralysis overcame him. He would be dead from shock and toxicity long before help arrived.

I stepped back inside, bringing Lindy with me. "It's finished," I said quietly. "All finished now."

I opened the door to the corridor, where Arnold Shacklady and the DCM were standing, worried looks on their faces. "We heard noises," the DCM said. "It sounded like shots. Some of the guests are complaining; they thought the fireworks display had started early." He peered into the room. "Is everything all right?"

I looked at him. "All right?" I said. "Yeah, I think so. Just a little blood to clean up. Nothing that will spoil the party."

I took Lindy by the hand. "Come on," I said. "Let's get out of here."

We walked down the stairs and out the door and into the warm African night, far away from the lights and the crowd and the conversation.

CHAPTER TWENTY-NINE

North of Dakar, out along the peninsula, beyond the suburbs of Pikine and Cambérène, the beach is wide and flat and deserted. The sand is almost pure white, and except for small groups of nomadic Lebu fishermen, no one goes there.

Lindy and I lay on the warm sand with our arms around each other, watching the moon rise over the sea. It was my last evening in Dakar, and neither of us wanted it to end.

We had spent the afternoon paddling in the clear green water. I stayed in the shallows because of the plaster cast covering my broken wrist. At dusk, we built a fire and cooked fresh fish, eating it with our fingers and washing the bites down with chilled white wine from the small cooler.

Now we lay back, sipping the last of the wine and watching the stars come out. Out at sea, a trawler's lights came on, soft and fuzzy in the evening's glow. They would be fishing for tuna, out beyond the reef in the deep water. The tuna were abundant out there, and the nets always came up full. But every once in a while, they'd net a shark, a big one, and then the men on deck would have to stand ready with their clubs and rifles, watching anxiously as out of the mass of glistening scales came something large and fast, all jaws and teeth.

I shivered. Our encounter with Ti-Claude had been a little like that. Most of us fish our way through life – if you want to look at it that way – in a casual fashion, lines dropped off the transom as we drift slowly downstream. Every now and then we get a nibble, and once in a while, a good, solid strike on the line, a chance to really make it big. So we haul back, set the hook well, and pull. And once in a while, what comes snapping up over the end of the boat at us can be a big, dangerous surprise.

Demba had gotten badly surprised; so had Le Vieux and the others. When the fish are biting, good fortune starts to seem routine; people forget that the nice, fat fish they're hauling in are part of a more complex food chain, one with predators.

But it was over now, finally all over. Ti-Claude was in jail, Khoury was dead, and Lindy, Bari and I were alive. And Bobo was somewhere out in the limitless forest, running free. I smiled.

I felt a pull on my fingers, and looked across to see Lindy watching me with careful eyes.

"Penny for your thoughts," she whispered.

I turned. With my good arm, I pulled her close. "They're not worth that much," I said, biting her softly on the earlobe.

Far off across the water, two lights came on, and a moment later I heard the whine of engines rising above the quiet hissing of the waves on the shore.

"Look," she said. "It's a plane, coming in."

We lay back on the sand, watching. The engines grew louder as the pilot turned the big jet, inbound from Europe, into its final approach. We lay at the water's edge, our necks craned up as it screamed in directly over us. A wave of raw power coursed through our bodies for a split second as the huge aircraft passed overhead, and then it was gone, swallowed up by the darkness beyond the hills.

"Whole new set of people," murmured Lindy. She shifted in my arms. "New people, new problems. But not for us, right?" She sighed, rubbing her nose along the side of my cheek. "Once more, Max," she whispered. "Not for goodbye, not for anything. Just for the hell of it, okay?"

We made quiet love on the sand, in the warm darkness. We took our time, saying hello, not goodbye, celebrating life while we put death behind us.

* * *

She sat up, looking at her watch, pulling the towel around her. "It's almost midnight, Max," she whispered. "Doesn't the plane for New York leave in about an hour? We'd better go."

I pulled her back down on the sand. "There's been a change of plan," I said. "I'm not going to New York. And the flight to Brussels doesn't leave for another two hours."

"Brussels? Why on earth do you want to go to Brussels? I thought–"

"I don't want to go to Brussels, in fact. But that's how you get to Antwerp."

"Antwerp? Why Antwerp?"

"Because," I said, "that's where the diamond cutters are."

She looked at me for a long moment. "Max, you didn't."

"I'm afraid I did. But only a handful. I picked them up off the airstrip at Simenti. Everybody was sort of busy just then."

"Only a handful?"

I shrugged. "Okay, a large handful." I held up my cast. "Dr. Renaudeau agreed to wrap them into the cast, when he set my broken wrist."

She shook her head. "I don't believe this. Do you think they're worth a lot of money?"

"I hope so. Didn't you tell me you needed money to finish your project?"

She looked at me. "Yes, but–"

"So we'll split it. Half for the research station, half for us. How's that sound?"

"Are you serious?"

I nodded.

She grinned then, comprehension breaking like a wave over her face. "Then you mean you're coming back?"

"I'm definitely coming back. I stopped off in Dakar to relax, but never seemed to find the time, somehow. Now I've got this busted wrist, and Renaudeau said to give it a good rest for a month or two. Didn't you say that when the rains really get going you can't get in or out of your research station until November?"

She nodded. Her grin got wider.

"Well, then, if you can wait here for about a week, I'll be back with the money. And then you and I can go back to the forest together. I can't think of a better place to rest and recuperate, can you?"

She put her arms around my neck and hugged me hard. "Nowhere better in the world."

I drew back. "Good; then that's settled." Taking the Bassari gris-gris from around my neck, I put it gently around hers. "And no matter where you are, this will lead me to you. Even if I have to come in a helicopter."

"I'll be waiting," she said. "And now," she continued, starting to gently stroke my chest, "since we've got all this extra time before your flight, how would you like to help me practice some more long division?"

"I'd love to," I said, and kissed her.

THE END

If you enjoyed this book, please let others know by leaving a quick review on Amazon. Also, if you spot anything untoward in the paperback, get in touch. We strive for the best quality and appreciate reader feedback.

editor@thebookfolks.com

www.thebookfolks.com

Also in this series

ONE BEATS THE BUSH (Book 1)

Vietnam vet Max Donovan discovers his war-time buddy
has been accused of murder. Suspecting his friend has
been framed and unable to come up with the bail money,
he must solve the case himself. The feathers of a rare bird
were found near the crime scene, and Donovan heads into
the dangerous jungles of Papua New Guinea and the
shark-infested waters of the Coral Sea to discover the truth.

THE SERPENT'S LAIR (Book 3)

Max Donovan has survived a bomb explosion in
Colombo, Sri Lanka, but is handed a powder keg in the
form of a mission to protect the author of a manuscript
exposing insurrectionist plans. He's up against powerful
forces, not least the ocean and jungle, that he'll have to
strike at the heart to subdue.

All FREE with Kindle Unlimited and available in paperback!

More fiction by the author

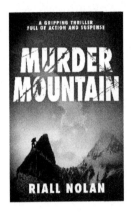

MURDER MOUNTAIN

A standalone action thriller

Wanted by the FBI and hiding out on a remote island in the Pacific, Peter Blake has an unwelcome visit. He's been rumbled by a man who "trades in information" and the price for not being handed over to the authorities is to use his mountaineering experience to lead a team on a dangerous mission to recover a fallen satellite. If he fails, it will cost him his life.

FREE with Kindle Unlimited and available in paperback!

Other titles of interest

BLUE HOLLOW
by Cheryl Rees-Price

The gripping standalone thriller

When a family friend is murdered, a journalist begins to probe into his past. What she finds there makes her question everything about her life. Should she bury his secrets with him, or become the next victim of Blue Hollow?

FREE with Kindle Unlimited and available in paperback!

DEAD SET ON MURDER
by Iain Henn

An exciting thriller full of action and suspense

Eighteen years after disappearing without a trace,
Jennifer's husband's body turns up, yards from her
home. Apparently without aging one bit. She knows
something is seriously amiss. Fortunately homicide
detective Neil Lachlan shares her concerns. But when
the case overlaps with a manhunt for a serial killer, it
will put Jennifer's life on the line.

FREE with Kindle Unlimited and available in paperback!

Sign up to our mailing list to find out about new releases and special offers!

www.thebookfolks.com

Printed in Great Britain
by Amazon